GETTING TO YES

TIM HUNNIECUTT

Copyright © 2023 by Tim Hunniecutt

All rights reserved. This book or any portion thereof may not be reproduced or used in any manner whatsoever without the express written permission of the publisher except for the use of brief quotations in a book review.

Published by Welling Up

Publisher's note: This is a work of fiction. Names, characters, places, and incidents either are the product of the author's imagination or are used fictitiously. Any resemblance to actual events, locales, or persons, living or dead, is entirely coincidental.

TimHunniecutt.com

Edited by Kristen Corrects, Inc.

Cover art design by Jessica Bell.

ISBN 979-8-9887420-0-5

First edition published 2023

Dedicated to Marie
My inspiration, my light, my love

Chapter 1

Dazzled by Chloe

On a hot and humid afternoon in mid-June 1978 in Brandon, Florida, I approached JB's pizza restaurant where I had worked the previous summer. I had just returned home from my first year at Florida State University. Nineteen years old, I stood a thin six feet. Skinny described me accurately. I had been a distance runner on the cross country and track team in high school and continued to run enough to keep myself thin. I had light hazel eyes and light brown hair, which I had cut in a short, feathered-back style popular in the age of disco.

Alas, I did not possess flawless skin. I had been plagued by freckles when I was young, and that had been replaced by bad acne in my teens. Most of it had retreated, but it had left some small permanent scars on my face, and my oily skin still contained a few pimples. I would call my looks neutral, neither ugly nor handsome. In my defense, some girls I dated in high school had described me as cute, so I accepted that I could be attractive.

Sonia, my shift supervisor, had encouraged me to come in this afternoon to find out my work schedule for next week and to meet some pretty, college-aged girls they had recently hired. An immigrant in her late thirties from Brazil, Sonia treated me like her own kid and always wanted to set me up.

I admit to wanting to meet new girls and would take any opportunity to seek the pleasure and intimacy they could bring. I could talk to them and was always dating someone new.

I hesitated, looked across the parking lot toward the door, and wondered about the girls working inside. Sonia thought one especially would interest me. She called her sweet.

The clouds in the sky had begun to build into the usual afternoon thunderstorms, and a distant rumble of thunder warned that they would be here soon. The damp heat already soaked me with sweat. I set off over the asphalt to the door.

I entered a new world by walking through that glass door and meeting her. She stood behind the counter where they made the pizzas in the center of three girls dressed in red aprons and bandanas. On her left stood Sarah, who had started last summer. I did not know the other girl on her right with black hair and a thin face. It didn't matter; I ignored the others and only looked at her.

The red bandana framed her round face, and I focused on it. She had shoulder-length brown hair and brown eyes—"Cow brown," she would describe them to me later. She had high, plump cheeks like a child that, combined with her radiant, flawless skin, gave her a look of innocence. She looked fifteen, not nineteen or twenty. I recognized a barely perceptible warm haze coming from her dewy skin, like a warm glow off the fluorescent lights on the room's ceiling. How could such a thing even be possible? I wanted to doubt what my eyes detected.

Astonished by what I saw, I could not tear my gaze away. She looked up at me, and it provoked my only possible response: I started smiling, and I could not stop.

I stood transfixed with only my smile speaking. It announced that she had dazzled me. She smiled in return and seemed to share the same inability to stop. We stood silently, smiling at each other. Our attraction became so evident that all the other girls and customers noticed, and the smiles spread.

The thunder boomed close, and the lights suddenly flickered, breaking our locked gaze. I awkwardly introduced myself, "I'm Chris. I'm sure you've heard about me from Sonia and Tammie." I heard a slight wobble in my voice.

She glanced at the other girl next to her, and her friend returned her look.

I steadied myself and glanced at the oven. "I cook the pizzas. I'm here to check the schedule to determine when I start." I nodded at Tammie, who stood at the register waiting to take customers' orders. I said, "I'm also here to order something." I looked back into her face, still smiling at me, and said, "I heard there were new girls hired, college age like me." I gestured at her with my hand. Her cheeks flushed red, but her smile continued. "What's your name?" I asked.

"I'm Chloe."

The dark-haired girl next to her spoke up. "I'm April. It's nice to meet the cook extraordinaire Sonia has been bragging about." April grinned at her joke.

Tammie interrupted, "Are you going to order?"

I ordered a small pizza and a beer and got my receipt with the number. I did not walk down to the bar to get my beer but stood to the right of the register, not blocking the line, and lingered. I looked again at Chloe, trying to find an excuse to chat while my smile continued to beam. I could not break my attention from her, and she smiled right back.

I asked, "How long have you been working here?"

"A little over a week. We just got back from school."

I heard a slight catch in her voice. "Where do you go?"

"The University of Kentucky. Where do you go?"

Tammie interrupted me and said, "You know we have to work up here, not socialize. I thought you came to look at the schedule. It's in the usual area in the back, and you're on it."

Chloe and April exchanged grins.

I broke my attention from Chloe and moved on. I walked into the back to check the schedule. I saw my name on it, but only on Thursday through Sunday. Then, I searched for Chloe's name and saw she worked several days during the start of the week, but we would not work together until Friday.

I stopped at the bar and got my beer. I positioned myself on the far edge where I could see the girls at the front counter and looked back at Chloe. She looked up in my direction. An embarrassed smile spread across her face.

I tried to stop staring but failed and continued stealing looks at her. She kept glancing my way and caught me looking several times. This continued throughout my meal until I finished and returned to the front.

I stopped at the counter on the way out and let my smile loose again. "I go to FSU. I got back a few days ago from our spring quarter. I checked the schedule, and I start next Friday."

Her eyes widened, and her mouth lit up into a bright smile.

I said, "I see you're on the schedule then too. I look forward to working with you."

She nodded. "It should be fun working together. I look forward to working with the cook extraordinaire." She lifted her eyebrows to emphasize her joke. Her voice sounded distinctly higher and a little strained.

I hesitated, trying to think of something else to say. She stood, waiting.

Tammie gave me a warning look, seeing me standing there again.

"I'll see you next Friday." I turned to head to the door. I looked back at her when I reached it.

She was still smiling.

I waved and walked out with my smile, still celebrating. I had seen nothing of Chloe but her face and that warm glow from her skin, and I chatted with her for less than a few minutes—but when I saw her, my entire world had stopped, narrowed, and focused.

The whole drive home I spent wondering about her. *Did I see her glow? What did that mean other than I'm crazy?* I had been enamored by beautiful girls before, but never had a girl attracted me with such force. As I thought about her, I kept smiling. Nothing came easy for me in love. My past experiences taught me that it only fails and hurts you. Despite that history, Chloe dazzled me so much that I resolved to ask her out as soon as an opportunity arose.

CHAPTER 2

Deb

I never had a goal of falling in love but sought only to enjoy myself. A bad experience taught me that love could only hurt you. Despite that, I kept falling hard for some girls. My inability to express my emotions always prevented me from succeeding with the girls, resulting in bitter disappointment and regular heartache. I felt too much and said too little.

I attracted a steady amount of female interest, attributed to my unusual maturity and ability to talk to girls. I never lacked opportunities with them. I always went out on dates, and at parties I would end up passionately making out with a girl in some quiet corner. I find myself astonished to count almost a dozen different girls I had some romantic interaction with that year. Yes, I did enjoy myself on multiple occasions, but I remember feeling lonely most of the time.

The theme of my year started not long after my eighteenth birthday in the spring while still in high school. The last romantic interaction I had with a high school girl occurred with Deb. The distance runners would often go out to party after meets at some secluded spot where we could park our cars, drink beer, and socialize without the supervision of adults. Our track season ended in May, the last time we partied that year. In 1977, eighteen-year-olds could legally buy alcohol, so some of us would purchase beer for our parties. The younger guys would roughly play and laugh, unable to handle the beer, but I focused on the girls, always drawn to them.

At this party, about a dozen cars parked along each side of the dirt road. Around twenty-five kids stood around drinking. After several beers, I somehow ended with Deb. Thinking back, I'm sure Deb placed herself deliberately next to me.

She leaned back against my car and looked at me. She was a tall, lanky girl with short wavy blond hair, pale skin, blue eyes, and long, smooth legs. Her hips thrust out from my car. Yes, I found her physically appealing. We talked aimlessly around about nothing.

She congratulated me. "I heard about the scholarship you won. That's amazing. I heard you're going to FSU. You will do well. I know how smart you are."

I grinned at this compliment and replied, "Where are you going to school?"

She shrugged. "I don't have any definite plans yet. Maybe HCC, but I'll probably work some first. I know you work at JB's Pizza. I've been there several times while you were working."

She smiled at me again, and I returned her smile. She fixed those pale blue eyes directly on me. Her interest turned my talking into flirting.

I said, "You should have stopped and talked to me when you came in. I could have gotten you a discount."

She replied, "You seemed so busy. You were working hard. I didn't want to bother you."

"It would have been a welcome interruption, seeing your friendly face."

She smiled at that and edged closer to me until we practically touched. She never stopped looking at me. I leaned toward her, and we kissed. We now faced each other very close, and I put my hands on her slender shoulders and pulled her toward me. I kissed her again, longer. She returned my kiss with eager intensity. I put my arms around her and pulled her tight against me. She helped by pressing her lanky, soft body against mine. We entangled so closely that her smooth bare legs touched mine. I could smell the scent on her skin as we kissed.

We barely came up for air. We kissed with open mouths, and I relished the taste of her. I did not want it ever to end. Deb agreed, pressing herself against me throughout. At each break for air, I looked into that face. She stared at me with her blue eyes always on mine. She kissed me with such hunger as if she craved me. No one had ever wanted me like that, and it exhilarated me. She filled me with herself with her mouth on mine.

Taking a break for air, we looked around. Most kids had already left. The few still there piled into cars and prepared to leave. She realized her ride had departed. Only we stood alone outside a vehicle.

"I need to get home. Would you give me a ride?" she requested with those earnest eyes on mine.

"Yes!" I would have done anything she asked.

We got into my car. She sat close in the middle and gave me directions to her house. She lived on the edge of Brandon in an old wooden house in an orange grove.

In those days, orange groves still grew everywhere in Brandon, and in the spring, the air hung heavy with the beautiful scent of their blossoms. When we arrived, the house was shabby and run down, and she told me her father had a job taking care of the groves. The job included housing. I did not qualify as a rich kid—we lived in a modest house—but our house looked palatial compared to this place.

Before she got out, she leaned over and kissed me goodbye. I sank into that lingering kiss. When we parted, I pleaded, "Don't leave. We can go somewhere else."

She shook her head no. "I need to go on inside."

I asked, "Can we meet tomorrow after practice?"

She said, "Yes, I'll see you tomorrow."

She got out and walked into her house, and I admired how good she looked.

Somehow, I had not noticed her before that evening. Still, I realized she had been hanging around me after practices. She had been talking to me a lot. I thought about her all the way home. The impression she left enveloped me as I lay in bed. I embraced how her warm lanky body felt pressed against mine. Sleep drifted over me in the haze of my tasting her kisses.

I awakened the following day filled with her. All morning in class, I wondered which classroom she occupied. I pondered where to take her on a date and made a list of things we could do. I could not stop thinking about her, but it went beyond that into a hunger, a yearning for her.

I could not keep my eyes off her during practice, admiring that body of hers with her long legs and firm bottom. Damn, she looked incredible. She caught me looking and smiled at me from a distance.

After practice, I tried to brush off anyone who wanted to talk so I could focus on her. It took a while, but I finally got to speak to her alone. She gave me a cautious smile.

"Hard practice?" I asked.

She smiled. "Your practice must not have been too hard. I noticed you kept looking over at us."

I replied, "I couldn't help but look at you. I had an amazing time last night."

She gazed into my eyes with that same intensity as last night.

I felt an overwhelming urge to kiss her. I did not care that sweat had soaked us from running in the heat. I composed myself and asked her, "Do you want to go to a movie with me on Friday?"

Her smile disappeared, and she broke her gaze from me and looked at the ground. She raised her head and said, "No."

I did not expect this answer. That could not be correct. I asked again, "What about Saturday? We could do something else if you don't want to see a movie?"

She shook her head. "No, I can't." She kept looking at the ground instead of me.

This girl had been all in with me last night, nothing but yes. She made out with me for hours. I was sure this girl liked me. I said outright, "I like you, Deb. I enjoyed being with you last night. I want to go out. When can you go out?" She had moved me in a way I could not comprehend.

She pleaded, "I cannot go out with you. Please understand. We need to leave it at staying friends."

Stung, I dropped my head.

She said, "Last night was incredible for me too. You are amazing. Can we leave it at last night? It would mean a lot to me to stay friends." I could hear the strain in her voice. Her face had tightened, and her eyes glistened.

I nodded and choked out, "Yes."

She turned and hurried off with me still standing there.

Bewildered, I watched her. When she got in her friend's car, I turned and went to mine.

It made no sense to me. I had dated many girls and made out with others in the last couple of months alone. Of course, I had been refused dates before by other girls. None of them provoked this kind of emotion. I had only spent one evening embracing her, but Deb had awakened some longing

I could not satisfy. She had knocked me askew. Nothing I tried allowed me to suppress my thoughts about her, but it was worse than that. I felt this unbearable longing.

My track and field season had ended. As a senior, I had no reason to continue going to practice, but I did. I made the excuse that I went to support the other guys, although only two guys on our team still competed at this level. In reality, I came to see her. She had no reason to go either, but I had hope.

She did come and greeted me with a smile. I did not talk to her until after practice but kept looking at her. She smiled again at me. After practice, I hung around until finally, we had a chance to talk to each other. I tried not to be awkward, but I smiled too often. "I see you came to practice even though you're a senior," I said.

She grinned in return. "Just wanted to support my team since they still have a chance. Is that why you're here?"

I could have told her the truth that I came for her. Instead, I nodded and said, "Yes, I wanted to support them. It's just a couple of weeks until the end of season anyway."

She agreed. "Are you ready for finals? You're taking all those hard classes. I don't know how you do so well while working and running." She hesitated, still smiling at me. "You are so good at everything."

I beamed at her compliment and basked in the warm smile that came from her. "Thanks. It does get hard sometimes, especially if I work late. I would rather not work, but I must save for school."

She nodded. "I understand. I need to get a job and start working. Not sure where to start."

I responded, "They're always hiring at JB's Pizza. I would put in a good word for you. We could work together this summer."

She blushed at that and mumbled, "Maybe I'll try them. Transportation is a problem for me as well. I don't have a car, but I can see what I can do." She changed the subject, and we spent the next ten minutes discussing the chances of the runners still competing.

When she left, I felt more bewildered than before. I'm not clueless. I know when a girl likes me, and she did. I needed to accept that nothing more would happen, but I could not stop feeling an intense urge to kiss her every time we got near each other.

The following week went like that. I kept looking at her during practice and found any excuse to talk to her. She seemed to like my attention and always readily spoke to me, even eagerly talked to me, but underlining all her interactions with me ran a line of sadness.

The Wednesday of the last week, I felt particularly desperate. I could not stop myself from going to practice. I felt compelled to be near her, look at her, and hear her. When we talked after practice ended, I used all my willpower to appear normal. I felt my need had been thwarted, a need I never knew I had until she summoned it. I grinned and asked Deb, "Are you attending the state meet on Saturday?"

She did not look at me and said softly, "I don't have any way to get there."

"I can give you a ride. Several of us are going together in my car."

She paused and stood looking at me as if considering whether to accept. She had this sadness in her eyes, but I thought she wanted to accept it. Finally, she lowered her head and shook it no. "I can't. I just can't." We went back to talking about nothing, and she soon left.

I then cornered her best friend, Michelle, to intercede for me.

Michelle frowned at my request. "Chris, she already told you she couldn't date you. I'm not going to pester her."

"But I really like her, and she seems to like me."

"Of course she likes you. She's had a terrible crush on you all year, and you finally notice her when the year ends."

"What does that matter?"

She sighed. "You're leaving for school."

"Not until September," I protested.

Michelle shook her head. "Deb is moving this summer too. That night after you made out, her father told her he had gotten a better job in Sebring starting in early July, and they would relocate. She won't be here either. It's too late. You should have noticed her earlier."

"Why can't we date until then?"

Michelle shook her head. "Guys are so weird. You ignore her all year and then suddenly fall like a ton of bricks? She can see you fell for her. She's also upset. She doesn't want to make it worse. Chris, it's hopeless. You need to let it go." She walked off.

After my conversation with Michelle, Deb stopped coming to practice. The end of the school year soon ushered out any final opportunity. I never saw Deb again and never got a chance even to say goodbye, but I kept thinking about her. I spent the next few weeks moping around.

I often wondered about Deb. Should I have told her what I felt? Would it have made a difference? The emotional response she provoked caused me to open the door to something more, but we had inadequate time to go through it.

I accepted that dating would have made it worse. I would have fallen even harder. The time to part would have inevitably come, and there would have been a lot more pain. She had decided to stop it at the beginning. Deb liked me but was smarter than me about it. Girls were always wiser than I was. But despite that, I still wanted her, and I still felt pain. I doubted she made the right decision. We had real chemistry.

She had changed me and opened my eyes to something I needed, something more I wanted. Before her, I had only focused on kissing girls and having fun with them. She moved me to seek something more intense. I could not articulate this or even describe what drove me, but in hindsight, this underlying desire, this overwhelming hunger, this unfulfilled need she had awakened now animated all my subsequent interactions with girls.

Chapter 3

Cathy

After graduating from high school, I survived the boredom of my summer by working full time to save for college. The incident with Deb had disturbed me, and I wanted to forget it. I did not want to develop feelings for girls. I wanted only to enjoy myself. Work gave me an excuse to be busy and avoid thinking about her. A full-time job at JB's Pizza provided a way to save for school, but it helped fill my summer.

I headed to college in September with one significant advantage compared to most other students: I had a car. I had saved my money diligently and purchased a pale cream-colored 1968 Chevrolet Impala. This enormous old car had no air conditioning, but the size allowed me to fit six people comfortably in it.

This car made me popular with other students. I always gave someone in the dorm a ride somewhere. Anytime I went off campus with friends, I drove. This started before I had even gotten to school, as Gregory, a teammate from the high school cross-country team, asked me to give him a ride up to FSU for the start of the fall quarter. This gave me a guide since Gregory had already attended FSU for a year. Also, he lived in the same dormitory as me and could help me navigate.

Gregory first suggested we go on Sunday evening before classes started on Monday. I thought this would not work as I needed to move into the dorm and get my books and bearings, so we compromised on Friday evening. The dorms had opened on Monday, a whole week ahead of classes. I should have gone up then. When you start as a college freshman, you need time to meet your dorm mates and roommates, sort things out, and begin making friends. Coming up so late, I missed most of that.

The day came to depart for college. We piled our belongings into my Impala until we filled the back seat to the roof and crammed the trunk so full it became almost impossible to shut. We set out on the tedious five-hour drive to FSU. The environment only turned interesting when we entered Tallahassee. I admired the towering skyscraper capitol building sitting atop a large hill that Highway 27 pointed at like some long, paved arrow. The university lay only a short distance from it. Gregory gave me directions to the location of our dorm.

Magnolia Hall had been built into a hill. The second floor came out at ground level on one side facing Landis Green, and at the other end, you had to take a flight of stairs down to the ground.

Residents jokingly referred to the first floor on one end as "the dungeon," as it sat below ground level with the room windows only at the top. The school had painted this concrete block building a dull green. This ugly building stood out among the beautiful old brick buildings nearby. Still, it had a perfect location, directly on Landis Green in the center of the campus. It had been built in the post-WWII building boom to accommodate the rising number of students due to the GI Bill. I lived there for one reason and one reason only. The dorm cost less than any other dorm on the entire campus.

This all-male dorm housed approximately three hundred guys. Every room had two people in it. If you did not indicate a roommate, they assigned you one. Each floor had large basic bathrooms in the middle that the entire floor shared. The dorm had one television in the lounge and one phone by the entry office. If you wanted to make a long-distance call, you had to find a phone booth and feed it coins. Also, they enforced a strict ten-minute time limit on calls to keep anyone from occupying the only phone. Each room had bare concrete block walls, a hard floor, two single beds, old dressers, wooden desks and chairs, and small closets. The dorm had no air conditioning. If you wanted to cool down, you had to bring a fan and keep your windows and doors open. Under these conditions, with such a small space and shared bathrooms, you quickly got to know your dorm mates. You had absolutely no privacy and no secrets. Everyone knew everything and everyone else. The dorm's characteristics encouraged everyone to socialize.

Most of the new students lived with an assigned roommate, so naturally, most of us disliked our roommates. I did not get along with mine. I found him just plain weird. This tall skinny guy acted beyond awkward. He rarely socially interacted with anyone, including me. I doubt I had more than a dozen conversations with this guy despite living with him for two quarters. He had this bizarre belief that you did not need to sleep, and he was determined to prove it by trying to stay up all the time. He could often be found asleep in the lounge early in the mornings after succumbing to reality. Most of us followed a typical college student schedule. We stayed up most nights well past midnight and slept till noon.

A few weeks passed in the quarter, and I still had not made many new friends. The lack of a normal roommate also set me back. I still leaned on Gregory for advice and social interaction. I asked Gregory, "Can you recommend a good place to take a date?"

He suggested the on-campus theater. One or two nights a week, it showed artistic films associated with a class. Most of the time, it featured recent popular movies. It had the advantage of being free and close. He also suggested we each take a date to the upcoming home football game and bring our respective dates together.

I appreciated this advice. It motivated me to find a date.

I don't remember how I met Cathy. I did not meet her at a party or in a class. I must have met her somewhere where students milled around. A cute and perky girl, she was short with dark brown wavy hair, blue eyes, a round face, and a curvy figure. I don't remember any of our conversations other than I asked her out, and she said yes. We made plans to go to the campus theater on Thursday evening. Cathy gave me her dorm's name and location so I could meet her there.

Our date occurred only two days after I met her. I arrived at the dorm and requested a blonde girl walking in to please notify Cathy. Some of the girl's dorms did not allow any male visitors. We had no cell phones, Internet, or phones in the rooms. Most dorms, including the girls' dorm, had a single phone in a common area. If you wanted to retrieve someone for a date, you had to find someone walking in and ask them to bring back whomever you wanted to meet.

Cathy soon arrived wearing a tan cotton dress with some pink on it. She greeted me with a "Hi." She smiled with her lips pursed, making her grin appear flirtatious.

I returned her smile and said, "Hi."

She rocked in her tennis shoes, lifting on her toes and then back down. She appeared to be bouncing, which I found oddly attractive.

Pleased with my new date, I set off with her to the theater, holding hands on the way. We arrived at the theater, showed our student IDs for entry, and found a place to sit.

I don't remember the movie. During high school, movie dates typically turned into making out in the back of the theater. Early in the film, I put my arm around her. She moved around, uncomfortable with this arrangement. After a while, I removed my arm.

We just watched the movie. On the way back to the dorm, she acted as friendly, flirty, and perky as before. She held my hand and grinned when I reached for it.

She said, "I really enjoyed going to the movie with *you*. I had a great *time*." She talked with the same peppiness that animated her walk and ended many sentences by strongly emphasizing the last word as if it bounced.

It commanded my attention, and I took the opportunity to ask her for another date. "Would you like to go to the football game with me next weekend? I'm going with a friend who is also bringing a date."

She beamed and said, "Yes, that sounds like a lot of *fun*. I would love to *go*. Can I ask you something? Would you go to church with me on Sunday?"

This request surprised me. I had visited a Catholic church several times with my first girlfriend, a dark brown, voluptuous girl of Cuban heritage. I did not find church experiences pleasant but could not describe them as horrendous either, and there were things you did to please the girl you were with, so I replied, "Sure, I'll go with you."

She explained, "The church is too far to walk. We'll need a ride over there."

"I have a car. I can pick you up and take you."

She smiled and replied, "Awesome. You do have to dress respectably in a collared shirt and nice dress slacks."

"Okay."

My agreement with her church request charged her perkiness. This compact girl started bouncing around much faster. I took this as a good sign. We arrived at her dorm, and I leaned in to kiss her.

To my shock, she leaned away and stopped me. "I can't kiss you," she said. "My religion does not let me kiss a boy until we are committed."

I stood with my mouth agape. I had never been on a date when a girl did not kiss me. I had dated a religious girl; at least, she appeared religious, attending church every week. It did not stop her from making out with me across Brandon at every opportunity. But this girl would not kiss me. Maybe it was a first-date thing?

She smiled encouragingly at me. "So, I will see you on Sunday?"

"Yes, at eight thirty a.m.," I confirmed.

Now, I began to dread Sunday morning. I had to dress up (I only had one pair of decent pants, one shirt, and one pair of dress shoes), but I had to do this and arrive at a church by nine on a Sunday. What type of church was this? Despite my second thoughts, I had already agreed to take her and committed to a football date. I could not back out.

Sunday arrived, and I picked her up wearing my best clothes. She dressed nicely in an attractive but modest dark blue dress.

She greeted me with a sweet, warm smile. "You look so nice all dressed up!" she said. She continued with that perky bouncing way she had that I thought the girl had springs on her feet.

It worked on me, and I found myself forgiving the kiss and feeling attracted to her again. "Thanks, you look nice in your dress as well."

She beamed at this compliment and talked to me nonstop on the drive to the church. She kept smiling and would twirl her hair with her finger. I found it hard to focus on the drive and not her.

I had decided to get this over at the church, sit in the back with her, contribute some of the cash I had, and make my getaway when the service finished. An usher greeted us at the door and identified me as a guest. He gripped me on the arm, escorted us to the first pew, and placed us in front of the pulpit.

I attended no ordinary church but one filled with hellfire and brimstone. The chorus sang in full-throated passion. The minister thundered, roared, and manipulated the crowd like the most experienced concert artist. They erupted, parishioners leaping in religious ecstasy, shouting their faith. He made it the most uncomfortable experience I had to date. He directed the entire madness at me. He stood a few feet away, looking at me, talking to me, exhorting me, and doing everything possible to convert me. I could not escape, and this man was good. He shook me, frightened me and my urge to stand rose again and again despite myself. It took everything I had to suppress that urge, to resist this man. We spent what seemed like hours wrestling for my soul. He worked to convert it and collect it, and I hung on to keep it. Finally, the whole thing ended, and I filed out of that place.

Drained and shaken, I shuffled forward. Cathy bounced with an extra giddiness. She reached for my hand as we exited the church and grinned at me.

She spoke again in that same bubbly way, "Thank you so much for going to church with me. I really appreciate you coming. I've been unable to get anyone else to go with me. Thank *you*!"

I looked at her after that emphasized you at the end. She smiled at me with her lips pursed again. I managed a slight smile and replied, "You're welcome."

She said, "We can get some snacks in the community center."

I mumbled, "No, I'm not hungry."

I stumbled to the car, holding hands with her, drove to her dorm, escorted her to the door, and did not attempt to kiss her.

Cathy just beamed at me when I turned to say goodbye. "I'll see you at the football game. I'm really looking forward to going with you. Thank you again for taking me to church." While she said this, she bounced on her feet.

I mumbled my goodbye and headed back to my dorm. I collapsed on my bed, exhausted, and fell asleep, wanting to forget the entire surreal experience.

When I awoke, I thought of only one thing. I had to take this girl to the football game next Saturday. I had already asked her and told Gregory, so I couldn't back out. Despite this, I got excited about going to the game. I had not been to a college football game before, and the dorm had this buzz about the entire thing, this budding excitement. I found myself also getting caught up in it. Gregory assured me it was also a great place to take a date.

Have you ever attended a college football game and sat in the student section? It is one of the most extraordinary college life experiences filled with excitement, exhilaration, and partying. We walked into one giant party with everyone either already drunk or on their way to getting there. Uninhibited, drunken students partied with exuberance. I wanted to get drunk and drink beer, but I could not. I went with a religious girl on a date. It was the worst place to take a religious girl.

Behind us, an endless stream of obscenities came from a group of drunk guys. Still, Cathy ignored it all and enjoyed herself. When our team proved successful, she cheered with the rest of us, as caught up in the excitement as everyone else.

We held hands while walking to the stadium, and she kept smiling at me in the stands. She certainly acted like she genuinely liked me. She mystified me.

Gregory had brought a girl named Colleen to the game. She had thick dark brown hair with a luxuriance that looked almost black. She had dark brown eyes and such pale skin that she appeared nearly a luminous white. I found her dark hair against her pale skin quite striking. She stylishly dressed up for a date with an outfit highlighting her full figure. She sat next to me, with Gregory on her other side and Cathy on my other side.

A tall, gangly guy, Gregory faithfully attended church. Gregory did not drink, he did not party, and I am confident he did not kiss his dates when he took them home.

Gregory asked her if she wanted a Coke to drink. She nodded yes, and he offered to get ones for Cathy and me. I gave him some money to cover our costs. After he left, Colleen asked me, "He doesn't drink, does he?"

"No, he doesn't."

"Oh well, having a beer would have been nice." She gestured around. "Everyone else is drinking."

"Yes, it would have been good on a warm afternoon."

"Cathy doesn't drink either?" she asked.

"No." I glanced at Cathy. She chatted with someone on her other side and seemed oblivious to me.

Yes, Colleen attracted me. I smiled at her. "Is this your first football game?"

"Yes! How about you?"

"Mine as well. I did not realize how much partying went on in the stands." I gestured at the guys drinking heavily below us. One of them even had a bottle of Southern Comfort whiskey.

Collen laughed. "They do seem to be enjoying themselves."

Our running back broke through their lines and dashed to the goal line, scoring a touchdown. The whole crowd erupted into a roar, with everyone standing and cheering. Cathy even hugged me in celebration. Gregory took the opportunity to squeeze back in.

You don't go out on a double date and spend all your time talking to the other guy's date, so I tried to control myself. Colleen did not seem interested in Gregory and kept talking to me. I found her so attractive that I couldn't stop responding to her. I didn't think she made a suitable date for Gregory. I tried to play it cool, but we kept talking, and our mutual attraction became increasingly apparent. Gregory got irritated. My date still appeared oblivious.

The game ended, and we separated to walk our respective dates to their dorms.

We had won that football game, and everyone celebrated while distributing that giant party to every dorm on campus.

Cathy bounced around as we walked to her dorm and flirted with me again. I did not know what to think of this girl, but she seemed to like me. When we arrived at her dorm, people were milling around everywhere.

I squared myself before her to see if she would permit a kiss.

She stepped back. Despite her flirting, she clarified that there would be no parting kiss.

I said my goodbyes and departed. It was a big no from me, and there would certainly be no more dates. Her face drooped with disappointment when I did not ask her out again.

As I walked back to my dorm, I realized it takes more than attraction to be compatible. I needed the physical aspect of a relationship. She lived in a world without it that I did not want to enter.

It seemed like a sour ending to a bad week, but when I entered the dorm, my dorm mates were in full party mode with a keg procured, tapped, and available in the common room. Todd, a shorter, thin guy, invited me to join their party, and I did so with gusto. I spent the rest of the evening drinking beer and getting drunk. I made a new set of friends, drinking buddies, party friends, and other guys more like me. My college experience began that evening.

I met several former high school runners. Todd had been a runner, and he introduced me to other runners in the dorm—Larry, a guy about my height with dirty blond hair and bad acne, and Scottie, another short guy who barely talked. I also met several of my party buddies for the first time that night, including Nelson, another short guy with black hair and dark skin, Mike, a laid-back art student who had transferred in as a sophomore, and Lawrence, a nerdy Canadian student who wanted to be a meteorologist.

Word soon got out that I had a car, a big car. Most of the kids in that dorm did not drive. It makes sense when you realize the poorest collection of kids on the campus lived in the dorm. Having a car made me popular. Several guys soon regaled me with stories about a glorious nickel beer night on Wednesdays at a nearby bar. We made plans to attend.

That evening, Gregory wandered past and saw me drunk and partying with the rest. We did little together for the rest of the quarter. He stayed clear of drinking, and I joined the party crowd.

Ed, another older student, wandered by us later in the evening after we had become quite drunk. He stopped to instruct us, "You guys need to swim in the fountain out front. No one becomes a true Magnolia resident until he has made a drunken dip in the Landis Green fountain."

We all started laughing, finding this tradition hilarious. Todd shakily stood up and shouted, "To the fountain!"

We all stood up and dutifully filed outside to join the practice. We surrounded the large white fountain big enough for a half dozen guys. It stood on the green in front of our dorm. It had a tall ornate centerpiece surrounded by a low circular white wall. The water circulated between the wall and the centerpiece. The fountain was ice cold, but I climbed in and dunked my head, baptizing myself into my college life.

We ended the night drunkenly splashing each other and any onlooker foolish enough to stray too close. They surrounded us, laughing, cheering, and applauding. Some of them took snapshots for future blackmail purposes. Embarrassing pictures of me drunkenly playing around in the fountain with several of my freshman friends do exist. It was a great ending to the night.

Chapter 4

Anna Lina

Nickel beer night lived up to its reputation. Guys crammed every table, drinking aluminum cans of PBR and getting extremely drunk. I don't remember a single girl. The tables competed to create pyramids from the empty cans, stacking them ever higher, boasting of their table's drinking exploits.

Guys in the dorm focused on drinking and girls, not necessarily in that order. My priorities centered on girls and drinking. Oh yes, I went to class, studied, and received excellent grades, but my focus remained on dating and partying.

Word had circulated to the dorm about a disco place filled with gorgeous girls wanting to dance. Several of us from the dorm made plans to attend. I liked disco music. I liked to dance. I especially liked the girls. I even went out and bought myself a silky disco shirt. This qualified as quite a luxury purchase for me though it was a cheap knockoff of a Nik Nik shirt. My experience attending that church and having to dress up made me realize I needed some better clothes. I remembered how Colleen dressed stylishly at that football game. Everywhere you looked, the girls dressed well.

As the date to go dancing drew near, one guy had to drop out due to a conflict, so we were down to five.

Todd asked if he could bring a girl he was dating.

I said, "Sure, why not."

The six of us crammed into my car. Todd's date, Anna Lina, sat next to me in the front seat in the middle. Todd sat on the other side of her. Anna Lina had kinky black hair and dark brown skin. Todd introduced her as a girl of Cuban descent from Miami. I did not pay much attention to her even though she sat beside me. When we arrived and got out, she stood next to Todd. The girl was considerably bigger than him. They seemed a bit of the odd couple, this husky dark girl and this short, thin, pale guy.

The disco turned out to be everything advertised. College students jammed the place. The girls outnumbered the guys. The girls dressed up, wearing fancy dresses, heels, and full makeup. Amid the loud, pulsating music, couples danced closely packed on the dance floor. They even had cocktails! The alcohol did release my inhibitions, and I asked girl after girl to dance. I did not dance with skill but with enthusiasm. As the evening drew on, I became soaked in sweat from so much fast dancing with so many girls. I must have danced with a dozen girls. The crowds began to dwindle as it got late, and fewer and fewer girls remained as closing time approached.

The cocktails hammered the other guys, especially Todd. He did not normally drink hard liquor and got so drunk that he became incapacitated and could not even stand to dance with his date.

I walked past Anna Lina, returning from a dance, and she sat alone. I looked for Todd only to spot him slumped over at a table. I approached her and asked, "Would you like to dance?"

The forlorn look on her face vanished, and she nodded yes with a smile for me.

We walked out to the floor. We started dancing, and I studied her. A curvaceous girl whose dress hugged her figure. She had a big head of hair that bounced around as she moved. Anna Lina danced well. I found myself drawn to her as she enthusiastically wiggled about in rhythm.

I leaned forward and complimented her, "Wow! You can dance well."

She smiled at this and continued to smile at me as we did a second fast dance and then a third.

As it got near closing, the bar mainly played music for slow dances. One came on, and I pulled her close to me. Anna Lina pressed close and kept looking at me. We danced another slow dance. She again pressed her warm body against mine. She met my eyes with that dark gaze and that wide smile. The combination of her soft full body and vivacious smile aroused me. At the song's end, I kissed her on the dance floor, long and slow.

The place closed, and we headed out to my car. Several other guys carried Todd and dumped him into the back seat. Anna Lina walked out with me on my arm. She sat next to me in the front seat. Close, her bare legs against mine, and she rested her hand on my leg.

When we arrived at the campus, the other guys carried Todd toward the dorm. We lingered, hanging by the car, not talking. We stood waiting until the other guys disappeared.

I opened the car door, and we got into the back seat. We turned to each other and began to kiss, long, deep, and full of desire. I had my hands all over her. I got my hands under her dress and got her bra off. I pulled her dress down, kissed her large, dark brown breasts, and tasted her saltiness. I had my shirt off. I tried to remove her panties, but she stopped me. We stayed in the car for a long time. I kept kissing her, touching her, and grinding against her.

She stopped me again and said, "It's late. I need to go in."

We got dressed, and I walked her to the back door of her dorm, holding hands with her. No lights illuminated the back entrance, and as we stood in the dark, we pressed against each other again and hungrily kissed some more. She broke away and went inside.

The next day, I awoke in the early afternoon with a terrible headache. I had my first hangover.

Nelson stopped by my room and asked, "How did last night go?" He smirked at me. "I heard you ended up with Todd's date."

I grimaced and nodded. "Todd drank himself into a stupor."

He laughed. "Looks like you have a hangover as well."

"Yes, my head hurts like hell."

He wandered back out, and I felt guilty about Anna Lina. Larry stopped by, saying, "Todd has been sick as hell, throwing up last night. He's pissed at Anna Lina. No way he's going out with her again."

I glanced at Larry feeling apprehensive about Todd. "Did Todd say anything else?"

Larry recognized my unease and replied, "Todd blames Anna Lina. Everyone told him she fell all over you. He had just dated her a couple of times. No big deal."

I nodded in relief as Larry left. I still felt guilty as I had crossed a line, and it didn't matter that Anna Lina helped me. I still crossed it.

That night the dorm hosted our first fall party. I wondered if she would attend and what would happen. I then thought of something incredible. Did I even remember what she looked like? Everything did occur in the dark, and I did drink a lot. Of course, I remembered! But I felt guilty, this time toward the girl. I slumped around that afternoon, trying to recover from my hangover.

The evening came, and I drank very little beer. My heart did not feel like partying. Apprehensive, I looked around after walking into the room. Todd acted calm but kept his distance. Anna Lina arrived, and I did recognize her. She wore a white dress and white sandals. It looked pretty on her with her dark brown skin and big head of hair bouncing around.

She searched around, spotted me, and headed straight toward me. She greeted me with a big smile.

I looked at her and confirmed she was cute as I remembered. I liked full girls, and I did find her attractive. I still felt guilty, though, about last night. I sensed others were watching me and realized I could not be with this girl tonight. It would have been social suicide. I nervously shifted from one foot to the other and kept looking around as she tried talking to me. I replied to her curtly. When she paused, I made an excuse about needing a beer and moved away.

This upset her. She soon left in distress.

Typical of guys in a male dorm, everyone blamed the girl, not me. But I know I shared the guilt, and treating her cruelly added to it. While she made her own mistakes, she did not deserve this treatment. Ashamed at my behavior, I vowed not to repeat my actions regardless of intoxication. A drunken, one-night stand is a poor way to start a relationship. I tried to push her and that evening out of my head as soon as possible.

The following weekend when I went out, I did so on my own, seeking out a fraternity party I could crash.

Chapter 5

Colleen

Attending a fraternity party as a freshman resembles a timeshare sales pitch with beer. The fraternity brothers ply you with beer until intoxicated, followed by a high-pressure sales pitch. They apply constant pressure to pledge to join their fraternity.

I did not want that, so I headed to the fraternity I had discovered that summer during orientation. Those guys had been relaxed—no one pressured me. Everyone sat around drinking beer. Only a bunch of guys partying.

Once inside, I was getting a beer when I spotted the same Dave I had previously met on the other side of the room, talking to a girl. I realized he was speaking to the same girl Gregory had brought to the football game as a date—Colleen, the same girl I had found so attractive. She dressed impeccably in a dark green outfit that showed off her figure and cleavage. She was of average height with that luminous pale skin and long, gorgeous dark hair. I made an instant beeline for them.

She recognized me. "Hi. How are you?" she asked me as I approached. She smiled at me.

I smiled back. "Great."

We spoke only to each other, and she ignored Dave, which irritated him. Looking to escape him, I asked, "Do you want to dance?"

She nodded. "Yes!"

We headed to the dance floor. We danced a slow dance, embraced, still excitedly talking. I asked her, "So you aren't dating Gregory anymore?"

"No," she responded with a smile.

I asked, "You're not here with a date, are you?" I nodded toward Dave.

Her smile widened, and she replied, "He's just a friend. I'm not here with anyone. What about that girl you took to the football game?"

"That didn't last long. She wasn't the right girl for me." I matched Colleen's smile with my own. Our embrace tightened as we continued dancing. We both felt the attraction and chemistry between us when we first met. Circumstances had given us a second chance to act upon it. I liked this girl. As the dance ended, I asked her, "Would you like to leave? We can talk more outside."

She smiled at me and said, "Yes, let's go outside."

We exited the front door holding hands. I doubt I had been at that party for ten minutes, and here I walked out of the front door hand in hand with Colleen.

We strolled close together, talking. "It's kind of cool out here," she said.

I put my arm around her to help warm her. "Does that help?" I asked.

She grinned at me. We stopped, turned to each other, and began kissing.

I loved kissing Colleen. Something in her kisses tasted so tender, warm, and sweet. She kissed well. I liked the scent of her pale, luminous skin and her thick, long hair. I don't think I've seen another woman with more beautiful hair. I enjoyed her body pressed against mine. In short, I found her irresistible, and we spent the evening slowly making our way to the campus and her dorm. We walked a few feet at a time, stopping to kiss every few moments. Walking that short mile from the fraternity to her dorm took us over three hours. Good kissing can take a lot of time.

She lived in Reynolds Hall, a girls' dorm that did not allow male visitors. By the time we arrived, we had set up a date to eat at a restaurant by campus the following week.

I arrived at Colleen's dorm at the scheduled time, met her, and we set out, walking to the restaurant. We held hands on the way. Colleen again dressed impeccably. Did I mention the beautiful hair? She talked in an excited and rushed manner, and that excited me even more.

We got seated at the restaurant and opened our menus. Colleen kept turning the menu around when she ordered, squinting at it.

Finding this behavior strange, I asked her, "Why do you keep turning the menu around like that?"

She replied, "I'm legally blind. My vision is like 20/800. I can't even drive a car legally. I do wear contact lenses, but I still have trouble seeing."

I asked incredulously, "You have to get someone to take you everywhere?"

She replied, "Yes, it's a real problem sometimes, but usually, I can find someone helpful."

I offered, "I can give you a ride anywhere if you need it."

She smiled at me, pleased. "So you have a car?"

"Yes, I have this Chevrolet Impala. I use it to go off campus about once a week."

She nodded. "I know. You can walk everywhere on campus. Most of the time, I don't need a car. It is nice to have access to one, however."

I said again, "Anytime you need to get somewhere, let me know. I'll take you." I found her lack of independence horrifying. More than anything, I valued my car. It gave me freedom.

This admission of her vulnerability made her even more attractive to me. I acted on my desire to help her and reached my hand across the table and took hers.

She smiled at me over this gesture. Then, she remembered something, stared straight at me, and said, "I have a boyfriend back home."

Wait, what did she say? This couldn't be true. A boyfriend? My smile disappeared. I withdrew my hand and looked down at the table.

She quickly continued talking. "We agreed that we could date other people while at school. We wanted to experience college fully. It's too hard to make long distance work."

I looked up at her. "Okay, you can date, but he's still your boyfriend?"

She started talking faster, trying to explain it. "Yes, yes, but it doesn't affect us. We can still date." She changed the subject. "What are you studying? What do you want to be?"

I responded to her, and we were off. We talked excitedly as if the previous comment about a boyfriend had never been made. But that fact lay on the table like an inert object between us, significant but now ignored. I let it lie undisturbed. I liked her too much. I wanted to talk to her, to be with her.

I replied, "I'm studying psychology but want to be a writer. I like to write poetry."

She grinned at me. "I would love to hear some."

"I can read you some another time," I said. "I haven't shared it with many people."

She said, "I'm a music major. I want to be a singer. I love performing."

I grinned and replied, "I would love to hear you sing."

Colleen burst into singing a short demonstration. The short bit she sang sounded operatic.

My mouth flew open in wonder. "Wow! You're amazing!"

Smiling widely, she said, "Now you must read me some of your poetry!"

I nodded at her, still smiling.

She replied, "We're both artists!"

I nodded. "Something we have in common."

She reacted to this by talking faster as she told me about plays the theater group would perform during the quarter.

I had never been to a play. Colleen convinced me to try one, and we made plans to attend the play *Equus* in a couple of weeks. We talked about movies at the campus theater. I had been to one of the art movies, and she found that interesting. We made plans to attend one of those on a future evening. We kept bringing up things we could do together. We made plans for the next date to see a movie together in a couple of days. She invited me to a concert recital she had to perform at for a month in the future. We had at least four dates scheduled by that conversation's end.

We sat talking long past consuming the pizza, having some beer, and paying the bill. We kept at it until the exasperated waitress finally told us we needed to vacate the table.

We left holding hands, walked away from the building and the lights, stopped in the darkness, turned to each other, and started kissing. I forgot about the boyfriend. It didn't seem to matter. She held nothing back, and it no longer seemed pertinent. We slowly made our way across campus, stopping to kiss every few feet.

When we reached her dorm, she said, "You are really good at kissing." She gave me one last lingering kiss before heading up. She kept looking back at me as she walked up to the door, then she tossed her hair, waved, and went inside.

I floated across the green, barely touching the ground until I stopped at the fountain. I watched the bubbling water and recognized as something welled up in me for her. It came despite the nagging presence of a slight, persistent undertow of worry around one word: boyfriend.

We went to the movies on campus for our next date. We held hands. I put my arm around Colleen, and she snuggled against me. We kissed during the slow parts. After the movie, I asked her if she wanted to go to my room. She agreed, and we headed over. My roommate was absent, but he had left the lights on. Sitting on my bed, we talked in a low tone for a while.

She began telling me about her "defects." She had an entire catalog of them and seemed to think she needed to give me full disclosure.

I found the whole thing inexplicable. How could this beautiful girl think she had so many issues?

She started with her hair. "My hair is too dark and straight. It's not very attractive."

I corrected her, "Your hair looks great. It has this sheen about it."

She said, "I'm not very pretty. I'm plain."

I corrected that: "No, you are pretty. I find you very attractive."

She smiled but continued, "I'm plump, and my skin is too pale. I look washed out."

I shook my head. "You have a great figure. I think you look perfect. I like your pale skin. Your pale skin and your dark hair together can look quite striking."

She smiled shyly at me over this compliment. "Well, my pinky toe can stick straight out. It's weird and defective." She took her shoes off and demonstrated.

I laughed, and she also started laughing.

I pulled her in close and hugged her. She tightly returned my hug, and I reassured her, almost whispering in her ear, "I find you incredibly desirable. I want you. I want you so badly." I released her and stared at her, still sitting close.

Her eyes crinkled, and they had become a little moist. She had a slight smile and nodded yes. No one said a word about the boyfriend. We both completely forgot him.

She lay down on my bed, pulling me on top of her. We began to kiss, and I could sense a tenderness in her. She always kissed so sensually, but now I detected something more. I soon chased her tenderness with my hunger. I wanted her. I wanted all of her. Her top came off, and my shirt came off. I struggled to remove her bra. I kept working on it. Finally, laughing, she helped me. This young woman had large, firm pale breasts with dark pink nipples.

My heart beating furiously, I said, "Damn."

She gave me a rueful smile.

I placed my hands on her breasts and explored them.

I marveled at how soft and sensual they felt under my fingers. I put my mouth on her and tasted her breast while my hand cupped and caressed the other one. I moved between them. As I did this, I pressed myself into her and pulsated against her. I paused, put my hands on her dress, and pulled it off. She removed her panties and lay naked on my bed. I stared at her dark bush against her pale lustrous skin. I stood up to remove my jeans and underwear, and my erection, pulsating as I pressed it against her, suddenly dropped. She had watched me as I removed my briefs, and I saw a flicker of concern in her eyes.

I was still a virgin. I lacked the experience of knowing it was not uncommon to rise and fall. I panicked and started to worry. I tried to ignite it by kissing her more, touching her, but my mind now thrashed and buzzed with this bitter worry. It had killed all my relaxation and crowded out everything else. I grew frustrated.

She displayed concern in her eyes, her brows furrowed. We flipped around with me lying down, and she tried kissing, touching, and pulling me. I did not respond. Unsuccessful, she sat back, naked, with her large full breasts hanging in front of me, and looked at me with frustration.

At that moment, the door swung open, and in walked my roommate. He stopped short, staring at her with his mouth open.

She shrieked and grabbed a blanket to cover herself.

He hastily retreated, closing the door behind him. We said nothing to each other but got up and got dressed.

I started walking her home. We strolled quietly across the green, holding hands.

She stopped and began to cry. "It's me! It's all my fault! Something is wrong with me! I warned you about my defects!"

I faced her and told her the truth. "It's not you. It's me! You are desirable. You are pretty. There's nothing wrong with you." I confessed, "I'm a virgin. I just got nervous."

She stopped crying and stood studying me. It was the right thing to say. She understood. She smiled at me, pulled me close, and hugged me. As we hugged, she whispered in my ear, "There's nothing to be nervous about. We'll fix this." She looked at me after this quiet promise, and I kissed her.

We shared a new goal. Holding hands on the way back to her dorm, we made plans for the next date. We kissed again when we arrived at her dorm. She hugged and reassured me again, smiling at me as she went up. She stopped again at the top of the stairs and looked back at me still watching her. She smiled and tossed her hair before she entered.

I spent the next couple of days in hell. How could I let this happen? I berated and attacked myself. *What is wrong with you? She looked so unbelievable. You wanted her so much, and then!* As I pondered what caused my problem, the image of my mother with another man popped into my head. Maybe that had damaged me? I did have an opportunity to lose my virginity in my senior year but had anxiously stopped short. Was I damaged? I shuddered and pushed that horrible thought away. Better to accept an embarrassing truth. I was a virgin who just got nervous. If I focused only on her, everything would be fine. I needed only to relax to fix this.

On our next date, I picked her up in my car and drove off campus to eat out. After we finished our meal, she indicated she did not want to return to my room unless I knew my roommate would be gone. I had not cleared it, so I suggested that I knew an excellent place to park, and she nodded in agreement.

I steered my car to the school's golf course. The setting turned out perfect, with only one light shining by the building, leaving the parking lot in darkness. I could not see the street or any sign of anyone else being around. I pulled in and parked in a corner.

We kissed slowly and steadily, pressing against each other. Colleen touched me and verified my excitement and my readiness. We removed our clothes. She felt me again, and I stood up excited and ready.

We moved around clumsily, trying to find a suitable position. We jostled each other. The steering wheel kept getting in the way, and no arrangement worked, and I dropped. I did not panic. I kept kissing her, but worry began to creep in again. She stayed patient.

I suggested, "Let me do something for you. Let me please you."

She nodded, and I lay down on the seat. She mounted me, adjusting up to my face.

I licked her slowly. I had never tasted anything like her before. I admit I liked it. I started to rise in excitement. I kept at it and looked up at her. The dark obscured her face, but I could see her large breasts moving and lifting with her breath. She rocked back and forth on me gently. I kept patiently at it. She tensed and gasped and suddenly lifted. I asked with concern, "Is it okay? Did I do something wrong?"

She responded breathlessly, "No." She moved off.

I asked her again, "Was it okay?"

This time she smiled and nodded. "Yes."

I sat up, and we moved close to each other and hugged. She glanced at my erection and placed her hand on me. Neither of us talked.

She removed her hand, and we embraced and got dressed. I headed the car back to her dorm, and we maintained our silence. Everything felt different.

After I parked, she offered, "It was good." She smiled, leaned over, and we kissed.

We made plans for the next date, and I told her, "I'll talk to my roommate and make sure he won't come in for that entire evening."

She nodded at me. The car had not worked well, but something else, something intimate, had happened between us. Something successful.

Our next date occurred on campus. We went to see *Equus*. We sat close, leaning against each other, often holding hands. We talked about the show afterward. I had never seen a play before and found it extremely interesting. This play had some shocking parts with full nudity and some graphic violence. Still, I loved seeing it in person. I thanked her for exposing me to this type of experience. She smiled, pleased that I enjoyed it.

I suggested we go to my room and confirmed that my roommate would be out all evening. She agreed, and we headed straight to my dorm. We did not linger this time. We had a destination. When we arrived, the dorm room was empty. My roommate had vacated the room as promised.

We kissed and touched. I never satiated long my desire for Colleen. I kept kissing her, touching her. Soon, we took our clothes off and pressed against each other.

She reached down and touched me, and I stood rigid, ready without a doubt. She adjusted on the bed, and I got on top of her. She held me and guided me into her. I pressed myself entirely inside her. How wet and warm she felt surprised me. It sounds funny, but I had not expected that. I moved up and down on her.

She told me, "Make sure to pull out when you come."

I had not planned on birth control. I had no condoms. Her solution was the pullout method. I nodded and kept moving, more intensely now. She kept kissing me. I breathed heavily, and everything sped up and slowed simultaneously. I could not believe how perfect she felt beneath me. I gasped, moaned, and it happened.

She looked at me suddenly. "Pull out."

I complied and pulled out. She quickly sat up. I had gotten it all over her.

"What are you doing?" I asked.

She appeared agitated. "Did you come inside me?"

I hesitated, not sure what to say. "Yes, once or twice," I truthfully responded.

Her look told me that I had provided the wrong answer. She replied, "If you sit up, getting pregnant is harder."

"I'm not really in complete control," I said, then I emphasized, "It was my first time." I kept stupidly talking.

Her reaction had utterly rattled me. I blurted out, "It's not official unless I come inside you."
Beyond stupid and wrong! I thought.
She began to cry. "I don't want to get pregnant."
Aghast, I would have done anything to stop her from crying. Her tears had a furious stimulating effect on me. I could have lifted cars and torn down doors. I would do anything to stop it. I put my hands on her shoulders and said something else: "Thank you."
She stopped crying.
"I'm so sorry I messed up. I didn't mean to do it on purpose," I offered again. "Thank you." I meant it, and she understood that. We cleaned ourselves up and got dressed quietly.
We held hands as we walked to her dorm. The night air felt cool and crisp. Twinkling stars and a glowing full moon filled the sky.
Colleen scolded, "Next time, you need a condom."
She had not forgiven me yet. I nodded yes, and we resumed walking.
Just before the door, she stopped abruptly as if realizing something. She smiled ruefully. "Well, I now have your virginity." I returned her smile, and we kissed long and full before parting.
I strolled back, savoring the coolness of the night air. I wanted to remember this night, the clearness of the sky and the brightness of the moon and stars. I wanted to remember what she looked like, the softness and scent of her skin, and

the feel of her against me. I wanted to remember every detail of my first time with a woman. The first time I was with her.

We had set up a meeting time after one of her afternoon classes a couple of days of the week on the green. Most of the time, we sat on a bench, talking and holding hands. It provided another regular opportunity to be with each other. Inevitably, this bench sitting would end with us kissing. We would be embraced in each other's arms, passionately making out. No amount ever seemed to be enough.

That following week when I met her on the green, I brought a poem I had written. I told her she inspired it.

Her eyes widened, and she responded, "No one has ever written me a poem."

I read it to her slowly.

<u>Fulfillment</u>
I cling close to your frame,
a bed of pale white blossoms
burst from black earth.
I cusp my hands on a handful of petals,
bouquets of your breasts
and caress my lips across—
a gardener's kiss.

You emerge from your form
into insistent beauty beneath me.
We press together,
skin sliding across skin.

*I gasp in the grip of my promise,
and we release into life fulfilled.*

She grabbed me and passionately kissed me. "Wow! That was intense. I loved it. Thank you!" she exclaimed. She kissed me even more fervently. We sat for a long time that afternoon making out.

She went with me to the next home football game, where we sat with the Magnolia section and cheered and yelled with everyone else. She drank beer with us at the after-game party, and everyone treated her like my girlfriend. I noticed my roommate preparing to exit, caught his attention, and nodded toward her. He understood. I took Colleen's hand, and we headed back to my room.

We took our clothes off, and she lay naked on my bed. I put my hands and mouth on her. I wanted her so intensely. I stood up to put on the condom, admiring her pale luminous skin, dark hair, and that dark bush. I gestured at her, standing naked next to her, fully erect. "You are so sexy. You look so good." I handed her the condom.

She put it on me, smiling at the intimate contact.

I climbed on top of her and slid inside her. I moved against her soft, silky skin. I made love to her, kissing her, caressing her, and rubbing against her. I had never enjoyed anything this good. I let myself sink into her yielding softness while I thrust against her. I soon dissolved inside her.

We lay together, with me still inside, both of us not wanting to break the intimacy. We kept kissing and touching for a long time.

I went to pull out. The condom broke. I got it all over Colleen, including some inside her. "What the hell!" I exclaimed.

She sat up, looking upset. She did not cry this time, but she appeared distressed. "Maybe I put it on wrong," she said. I shrugged. I did not know. We then did something we should have been doing all along. We were adults having adult sex, but we had never really discussed birth control except in an oblique, childish way. We launched into it and agreed that condoms did not work well. After some discussion, she decided on the pill. She mentioned she could obtain a prescription at the school's clinic during the week, and we agreed this settled it.

I attended her recital on our next date. I walked into the fine arts auditorium to discover a formal affair. She wore a long formal dress, and the guys wore tuxedos. Everyone had dressed up but me. I was the only one wearing a T-shirt and jeans and looked out of place in this formal and stuffy atmosphere. When I first spotted her in that dress on stage, I thought, *Wow, she looks amazing.*

The performance began, and she had a solo. Her voice rang out, and she sang with passion and life. Her voice sounded full, round, deeply feminine. She sounded wonderful. I had never heard her sing in a performance before, and she impressed me.

The performance ended, and performers filed off stage to meet their friends and families in the audience. She spotted me and greeted me warmly.

I smiled widely at her.

"What did you think? Did you like it?" she asked.

I gestured at her dress. "You look amazing."

She smiled sweetly and asked me again, "Did you like it?"

"Yes! You sounded amazing. Your voice sounded so good!" I raved. "I'm now a fan! I am in awe!"

Pleased, she took my hand. "I want you to meet some of my friends." We moved around the auditorium and stopped to talk to another young woman in the same formal dress. She introduced us.

This woman asked her with a smile directed at me, teasing her, "Colleen, this is your boyfriend, Chris, that you are always talking about?"

Colleen flashed a big smile. "Yes, of course."

I know I lit up after that comment. Colleen kept laughing and smiling as she pulled me around the auditorium and introduced me to several more of her friends. I could not take my eyes off her. Everyone we met greeted us with smiles. Laughter rang out in the background. I spent the rest of the afternoon in a haze. It only ended when she had to go backstage to change and attend another event for the performers.

We said goodbye and made plans for our next date that weekend. Thanksgiving was the following week.

We became a couple. We did so many things together that fall. We went out to movies, plays, and concerts and partied at football games together. I spent most of my time with her.

We held hands, walking to our date to get pizza. We sat across, fixed on each other, smiling and talking. We leaned across the table and kissed affectionately. When we exited, we held hands again, walking across the green. I headed to my dorm, and she stopped me.

She told me about her birth control. She had a prescription for the pill and had started taking it. She hesitated. She acted a little diffident, not her usual enthusiastic self. She had something to tell me. "It doesn't work for a month. You must wait a month to have sex."

I reacted to this bad news by suggesting, "We can just keep using condoms."

She shook her head and said, "I can't trust them. I don't want to take any more chances."

I could not argue. The holidays were upon us, and we would be apart back home. I asked, "So that means what date can we resume?"

She replied, "With the holidays coming up, I guess that means January."

"January?!" I exclaimed, startling her.

She smiled sheepishly at me. "January, after the holidays," she confirmed.

With Thanksgiving the following week, we planned to meet Tuesday afternoon after classes on the green by her dorm before we left for the holiday.

She greeted me warmly that Tuesday afternoon. She dressed up. She always dressed up. I remember she wore the same dark green outfit that she had on when we had first gotten together at that party. I remember everything she wore. She had such style. We talked for a while and kissed together on the bench.

When we paused, I said, "I'm going to miss you over the holiday."

She tilted her head, leaned toward me, and whispered, "Me too."

We kissed. When we parted, she tilted her head again as if she needed to focus. I always found it endearing.

I asked, "I have my car. Can I see you after Thanksgiving? We don't have to wait until we both return."

She hesitated and shook her head.

"Saturday, Sunday, tell me which day or time will work?"

She responded painfully, "I'm going out with my boyfriend this weekend."

I stood up, looking at her, my face tight and my fists clenched. I refuted her, "I am your boyfriend."

She shook her head no. That word now stood between us, blocking us. I could find no way past it and could not think of anything else to say. She stood too. We stood looking at each other, and tears moistened her eyes. I could not handle making her cry again. I bid her goodbye, and I wandered off.

I did not schedule the next date.

My feet dragged as I stomped across the green. Her boyfriend walked with me in my mind, shadowing me, even mocking me. I could not shake him.

My temper raged. *Was she just dating me? Having fun with me? Was that all I meant?* Those questions stung me. I had never told her how I felt about her, and we had never discussed our feelings. They were out there. We both experienced the pull toward each other. We never reached the destination. I realized then that the knowledge of the boyfriend had blocked this. It stood like a dam stopping the stream from reaching the sea. I halted my march at the fountain to calm myself. It had been turned off, and the water sat stagnant.

I spent all Thanksgiving weekend stewing, imagining her with him. Dating, kissing, doing all kinds of intimate, terrible things. *Stop thinking about her!* I told myself. But I could not block the boyfriend. He kept gnawing at me like a small dog locked on your ankle that you could not shake off.

Since I had not scheduled another date with her, I remembered she had a class on Wednesday afternoons, and we had met after it several times on the green near her dorm. I resolved to catch her the following Wednesday. I needed to talk to her.

When I saw her that Wednesday, she greeted me with a big smile, as warm and sweet as if nothing had occurred. Colleen dressed impeccably with that long beautiful hair. I had things I wanted to discuss with her, but I'd forgot them. I'd forgotten all of them in the warmth of her smile. The way she tilted her head when she looked at me. The way she tossed her hair. Her affection and warmth toward me swept everything away. We held hands and stopped by a tree, and started kissing. We moved to a bench. We hugged each other tightly and kissed. I wore blue jeans and a long-sleeved red flannel shirt on the cool December afternoon.

She made affectionate fun of my shirt, calling me her redneck. She told me, still in high spirits, "You know I have a terrible reputation on the floor of our dorm because of you."

I asked quizzically, "What do you mean?"

"I am always on the green making out with my redneck boyfriend!" She laughed.

Her comment lifted a weight off me, and I gratefully kissed her. I tried to convince her to come back to my room.

On that, she held firm. Instead, she asked me something else. "I'm having a Christmas party at my house back in Tampa. I want you to come. I want you to meet my friends."

I responded, "Yes!" She wanted to see me over the holidays! She gave me details about her address and how to get there.

We spent the rest of the afternoon together. She sat on the bench, and I laid my head on her lap. I looked into her face as she leaned over to kiss me. I settled down into her softness and surrendered to the bliss she brought me.

Back home in Brandon for the Christmas holidays, I looked forward to her party. When the time arrived, I dressed up. I wanted to impress her friends. I thought I might even meet her parents, which made me a little nervous about the whole thing. I assumed we would be together.

Finding it took me a long time, with many streets branching everywhere in her neighborhood. The Carrollwood subdivision sprawled endlessly. I had to locate her house manually in this age before mapping software. I used a paper map and written instructions on how to locate it.

I found her street and saw the shiny new cars parked in the drive and up and down the road. My shoddy old vehicle did not fit on this street. I found her enormous home and stood looking at it looming over me. A girl I had never met before answered the door. I told her my name, and she introduced herself as Michelle.

"Oh," she said, "You're Colleen's friend from FSU. I'll take you to her."

Colleen stood next to someone in the kitchen. She wore a fancy black dress with some sheen on it. She had a pearl necklace on. Everything on her looked new and expensive, including her black shoes. She greeted me not in the usual way but cautiously.

Glad to see her, I gave her a big smile. I then noticed some guy standing next to her—a big, tall, husky guy who rested his hand on her waist. It must have been her boyfriend. He glanced at me, and I stared straight at him.

Colleen anxiously moved toward me. She took my arm. "I want you to meet somebody," she said as she guided me away.

I let her lead me, not saying anything.

She took me into another room. We found this small, thin girl with cropped hair dressed casually, even sloppily. I thought she looked unattractive. Colleen introduced us and talked with nervous energy. "Linda likes soccer players," she babbled. "She likes those thin, athletic guys. You guys should hit it off. I really think you will get along well."

The girl smiled at me, a little embarrassed at those comments. Colleen scurried away.

Wait! I screamed internally, startled. Was she pawning me off on this girl? *This can't be.*

The girl tried to talk to me. I glared at her, feeling my temper fire with rage. She made small talk. I barely responded to her. She got the hint and walked off, leaving me alone. I looked around. I didn't know anybody. *Maybe I should find her boyfriend and punch him.* I didn't care that he was much bigger than me, but I knew this would upset Colleen. It would ruin her party, so I stalked out instead. I said nothing to anybody. I doubt I stayed even ten minutes.

I raged while driving, telling myself, *We're done! This is it. There is no just dating. Colleen's out. You're either all in or all out.*

My anger lasted for the rest of the holidays. In disbelief, I kept asking myself why she did that. It was beyond intolerable. She had deeply wounded my pride. I could not stand to see her with that guy. I thought she had become my girl. It made me sick when I thought of him standing with his hand on her.

Seeing her with another guy caused me to remember another terrible image from several years ago—the one of my mother with another man. I came home early one day from school. A strange car I had not seen before sat in the driveway. Our house had been robbed the previous year, so I carefully entered the house from the side, making no noise. As I got inside, I heard my mother laughing. The sound was coming from the back, from her bedroom.

I kept quiet and crept down the hall toward her room. The door was open, and I glanced inside. My mother stood naked in the arms of another man. They were passionately kissing.

I turned around and headed out. I said nothing and never told anyone what I had witnessed. I did everything I could to suppress the memory of that horrible day, but seeing my girl with someone else brought it back.

I went to a party a couple of days before the end of the year. I drank heavily. When we ran out of beer, I entered their parents' liquor cabinet and started drinking small bottles of vodka and whiskey.

The bright sunlight woke me up the following day, where I lay sprawled in the back seat of my car. I sat up, investigated the front, and saw my keys in the ignition. I had no idea how I got into the back seat. I did not remember anything about the previous night. My stomach was nauseous, and my head hurt. I stumbled into the house, entered my room, and fell asleep.

When I woke up that afternoon, the failure to remember any details about the previous night alarmed me. I called a friend who had attended with me and asked what had happened.

He laughed at me. "You were so drunk you couldn't even stand. I drove you home. You spent the entire way screaming out the window about Colleen and her boyfriend. Who the hell is that?"

I said nothing and realized I had blacked out. This frightened me. I resolved never to drink like that again.

Later, I decided to go to this kid's party who did not drink. I had known him since high school, and he had invited me to his New Year's party. I knew his party would have no liquor.

When I arrived, he reacted with surprise. I looked around and recognized that most kids had been in my high school's smart-student clique. A cute, curvy girl I knew from high school sat down next to me. She had been one of the smartest kids in school.

She had dirty blond curly hair and was dressed casually in a blouse, jeans, and sandals. She started talking to me, flirting. She worked hard to interest me. I understood that this girl liked me, and I tried to be friendly to her. I did not want to spread the hurt, but I was not attracted to her. Colleen still occupied my mind. Soon after, I left, leaving her looking disappointed.

A couple of days later, I returned to FSU. I had no plans, and I did not want to party. As I walked across the green in a grumpy mood on the first day of classes, I met Colleen. I had not expected this. She greeted me more warmly than ever before, beaming at me. Her smile spread across her face, and her eyes twinkled.

I can't. I just can't, I thought. I grunted a "Hello" at her and kept walking.

I heard her say, "Chris? Chris? Chris!"

I kept walking away. I had my revenge. Now she knew what it felt like to be treated like no one special.

I stalked down the dorm hall to my room. I did not feel triumphant but terrible. I plopped onto my bed and hid my face. This dark cloud in me flowed out everywhere. It even affected the weather. The sky clouded, and it grew cold and began to rain. Not hard rain, but a slow dripping rain. Drip, drip, drip. I could not escape this dull dampness.

It rained daily, and it seemed like the sun would never rise. The skies had become only overcast. An endless, gray fog cloaked everything and drained all color from my world. I clung to my room, leaving only for classes and to eat.

I compounded my misery with something a stupid freshman would do. I signed up for a humanities class on existentialism. I fancied myself an artistic intellectual, but this class was the worst possible subject for a depressed kid. The course focused on our hopeless and meaningless existence.

A word from the class stuck in my head, *inadequate*. We were inadequate for the challenges of our world. I certainly felt inadequate. The word hung around me like someone had tattooed it on my hand. It followed me around and made suggestions in my ear, filling me with anxiety. I even started to shake with nervousness when talking to others. I went to parties to drink, to kill this feeling.

I got so drunk one evening that I fell down the stairs, and the following day, I awoke to find my ankle so swollen that I could not walk. Two friends from the dorm semi-carried me to the medical clinic. They x-rayed me and confirmed I had not broken it, just severely sprained it.

The clinic fitted me with crutches so I could stay mobile. Now, I had broken myself. I hobbled around, crippled by my own emotions. Nothing lifted my spirits. I sank into my loneliness. I went to my classes and kept to myself. I did not socialize.

Each weekend I drank heavily until smashed and stumbled to my room to pass out. I did not want to think or feel. I only wanted to escape this feeling that clung to me. I tried not to, but I kept thinking about Colleen. I missed her. I had spent most of the fall quarter with her. We did things together all the time. And now, I had not given her a chance to explain. Why didn't I talk to her? It was not her fault. It was mine. I broke it deliberately in my stupid angry pride. I found myself upset that I had hurt her. It did not matter what she had done to me. This feeling that I failed her bothered me more than anything else.

I limped along, trying to make it through the winter, unable to process my feelings. Later I realized I had ignored and denied what caused my problems. I had suppressed that I suffered from breaking up with Colleen.

After almost two months, I finally asked myself, *Did I love her?* I never told her. I never said it to myself. She always evoked intense emotions in me, but this boyfriend stopped their progression and prevented them from making any destination. I demanded to myself again, *Did I love her?* I found no way to answer. I knew she filled my depression, but I did not think I had made it to love. Then I remembered that last afternoon in December with Colleen. She had made me happy, and I broke it.

Toward the end of the quarter, I bumped into Colleen on the way to the library. She acted surprised, but she greeted me warmly. Happy to meet her, I returned her warm greeting. She dressed well as usual. I would not describe Colleen as beautiful, but something about her always deeply attracted me. We stood for a while talking. She circled, talking about anything other than what she wanted to know. I knew what she wanted to ask me.

It came out in a rush of questions. "What happened in January? Why didn't you stop and talk to me? Why didn't you ever come by? Why did we stop dating?"

I looked straight at her. Relieved to talk to her, I told her the truth: "I felt upset about your party. You were there with your boyfriend. I thought I was your boyfriend, and seeing you with him humiliated me. I just felt so angry. I couldn't keep doing this, dating someone who had a boyfriend. I couldn't keep sharing"—I paused—"you."

She rushed her words out. "I knew that party had been a mistake. I wanted to talk to you there and tell you what was happening, but I could not find you. I was going to break up with him. I broke up with him afterward." She hesitated then said, "I wanted to date you. I thought we would be a couple. You would be my boyfriend."

We stood looking at each other after we had confessed. We started laughing and agreed together, "How stupid were we? Why didn't we talk?"

"I missed you," she said. "We had so many good times together in the fall."

I looked into her face shining with happiness. Whenever I spent time with her, she exerted this incredible pull on me. I wanted to say yes to it.

She tilted her head to focus on me in the way I always found so endearing. She stepped forward, placed her hand on my arm, and leaned in to kiss me. I returned her kiss. She put her arms around me, and I responded with my arms around her. All the emotion she evoked rose again, and I remembered the happiness she had brought me. *Yes, we could just start again.* I kissed her back with hunger.

The image of her with that other guy popped into my head, and I stopped cold. I pulled back from kissing her. I could not say yes to that. She had broken my trust. We were still hugging, and she stared into my eyes. I lowered them, pulled out of her embrace, and stepped back.

Her expression fell, and she asked, "It's too late?"

I nodded and lied, "I'm sorry. I started dating someone else." I had started dating other girls, but none moved me like Colleen.

She did not hide her disappointment. She responded, "I'm sorry too. If things don't work out, I want to try again." She managed to smile.

I nodded, and she turned and hurried off.

Colleen always affected me in person. Something about her melted me. I could not say no to her, but I had hurt too much over the winter and could not endure that again. She had lost my trust, and it was too late.

Chapter 6

Brenda

The rains lifted at the start of March, and we had a sunny day on the first Saturday. The dorm had scheduled a party. My ankle had healed, and that evil word *inadequate* faded until forgotten. The sting of missing Colleen was beginning to lift. I decided to go to the party. I drank some beer and talked to some girls. I danced. I circulated, talking to more girls. I flirted and drank more beer. I then wandered by her. I had not met or seen this girl before, so I introduced myself.

She introduced herself as Brenda. A short girl, around five feet tall, with light brown shoulder-length hair, hazel eyes, and a pale oval face. She had a nice figure, not too thin or too full. I concluded she looked pretty, not beautiful, just pretty. She seemed happy to engage with me. She did not know many people at the party. She lived in Jennie Murphree Hall. I hadn't previously met any girls who lived there, as most of the girls at our parties came from our sister dorm, Reynolds Hall.

We discussed our majors, the lousy weather, and the hope it had lifted.

She told me she came from Fort Lauderdale. She had been a volleyball player in high school.

I told her about Brandon and cross country.

We finished our beers, and I got us both another one. We kept talking to each other. I asked Brenda to dance, and she joined me in a slow dance. She stood so small in my arms, but I enjoyed her warm body against mine. I had missed girls, and I found myself wanting her.

I picked up my flirting and steered us to a quiet, darker section of the room. I leaned in to kiss her. She met me, and we kissed. Brenda kissed differently, soft and sweet, but she included something I had not experienced before. She delivered her kiss like an invitation. I received it and opened it. It excited me, and something stirred in me. We kissed long and hard, focused on each other, ignoring the rest of the party.

Someone noisy and loud came by, interrupting us. We paused.

Brenda looked at me. "Let's go someplace quieter. We can go to my room at Jennie Murphree. My roommate went home for the weekend." She took my hand and led me out.

No girl had invited me to her room before. I entered and looked around with curiosity. The décor surprised me. The guys in Magnolia did not decorate their rooms much, leaving the stark concrete block walls exposed. She and her roommate had filled the walls of this room with posters and pictures. They had blankets with designs on the beds and rugs on the floor. Curtains covered the windows, making everything neat, tidy, and clean. I saw no garbage anywhere.

"You have such a nice room," I said. "Very comfortable and even homey."

She beckoned me to sit on the bed next to her. I sat close to her, and we talked in low tones. We kissed again. She lay back on her bed with me on top of her, and we kissed with fervor now. I put my hands on her. She put her hands on me. All the rest of the girls had lain still, reacting to my initiative. She had her hands all over me and delivered the full force of her invitation. I wanted to take it—and her—now.

Yet as I moved my hand to her pants, my doubt returned. It flung itself upon me, gripped me, and whispered an evil word in my ear: *inadequate*. My recovery now seemed like a trick, and I trembled.

Concern showed on her face, and she asked, "What's the matter? Are you cold? Why are you shaking?"

I sat up and spilled the truth. "I'm sorry. I'm just feeling nervous, anxious."

She studied me. Her body language changed from invitation to concern, but she said nothing.

Then she told me, "We don't need to do anything but hug and cuddle. It will make you feel better. Come." She gestured to me and lay back down.

I lay next to her. She enveloped me in her arms, hugging me. I dug into it, embracing her warmth, my arms around her. We lay like that for a long time.

"See," she said. "You do feel better."

I had stopped trembling, and the word disappeared. I did feel better. I looked at her and found her more attractive than she had been all evening. This girl radiated warmth. I blurted out, "Do you want to go out? We could go see a movie or something."

She studied me for a while. She smiled slightly and shook her head. "I don't think it's a good idea. I don't have time…" She trailed off.

I knew what she meant. She did not have time for someone hurting like me. I deserved that answer. I had earned it. She had offered me all of herself, and I had rejected her. Now, she rejected me. Soon, she asked me to leave her room with no final kiss, her disappointment in me obvious.

I strolled back to the dorm. I looked up into the clear sky, filled with stars and a bright moon. Despite the ending rejection, she treated me well. I remembered her hugs. This girl had done something warm and generous for me and had unselfishly lifted me.

CHAPTER 7

Amanda

Nelson greeted me inside the dorm, where he smirked at me with a knowing smile. "Have a good time?" he asked.

I stopped and responded, "What?"

"Come on, man. Everybody saw you making out with that girl and leaving with her."

I stared at him. "Brenda is her name." It was none of his business. He was drunk, and he had disturbed us earlier. He had done it on purpose!

He added, "Another party, another conquest. You'll be as legendary as Ed at this rate."

Anyone who's lived in a guy's dorm knows the social hierarchy. At the top stands the guys who get the girls. At the top of our dorm stood Ed, a junior, now in his third year of living in the dungeon of Magnolia. Ed had become famous for the constant progression of girls through his room.

Tall girls, short girls, blonde girls, dark girls, freshmen, seniors, an endless progression of girls circulated through his room. Rumors circulated that he even dated grad assistants in their late twenties.

His reputation exceeded just numbers. Other guys had seen beautiful girls like beauty contest winners, cheerleaders, and models go to his room.

Everyone gossiped about Ed. Many guys insulted him and called him a "slut," but throughout all of it, we were envious. At parties, girls would even be seen seeking him out. He was a normal-looking guy. How did he do it?

I responded to Nelson, "Seriously, dude, get a grip on yourself. You're making fun of me. I mean, come on, comparing me to Ed? That's way too much." I started to walk off. I felt like a failure right then, not some ladies' man.

He said, "We all know you had a naked girl in your room. It was all over the dorm. Guys saw your used condoms in the garbage."

What? My roommate had told that story. He talked to nobody! Did they look in my garbage? I could not believe the lack of privacy. Did everyone know everything? "Get yourself a girl, dude, and leave me alone." I walked off.

But they did not leave me alone. Other guys started to ask me for advice.

"What did you say to them?"

"How did you ask them out?"

"How did you always get them to make out with you?"

I also became the target of slurs and scurrilous hints of bad behavior.

"Who was your favorite girl?" *Wink, wink.*
"Did you get a blow job?" *Wink, wink.*
Those kinds of questions made me angry. "Come on, man. I'm not going to tell you that. I'm not going to talk about the girls!" I would retort. I thought about the girls. I thought about Colleen. We had not been about that. I did not mind the questions about advice. I found it flattering, and I understood. Most of the guys were in their first year of college.

I had met guys who had never been on a date, never even kissed a girl. I found their behavior incomprehensible. I had my first girlfriend after I turned fourteen. I dated girls throughout high school. I always had some girl in my life. Yes, I wanted them. I constantly desired them, but I never had a goal of just sex. I always wanted something else, even though I still could not articulate what that something else meant. I knew I needed more from the girls.

The weather continued to stay good. Winter had lifted, and bright sunshine filled the days, resulting in warm afternoons. All around campus and all around Tallahassee, flowers bloomed. Azaleas with their brilliant pink blossoms, camellias with their dark red flowers, white dogwood flowers that seem to fall from the sky, and redbuds opened up in the trees across campus. Spring filled everything with color and light.

The dorm had no party scheduled that Saturday night, so we started our own. We hung around in the halls drinking beer. Some girls from Reynolds Hall joined us, including Amanda, a short girl with dark brown hair and glasses. I would describe her as cute. She was a smart girl who had entered the honors program and made straight As.

I had done well in school but earned a B in my first quarter. She always acted friendly to me and implied that we intelligent people needed to stick together. She always attended our dorm parties.

Despite this, I found her awkward, and she always acted uncomfortable. She came from a tiny rural community in northern Colorado. A group, including her and me, sat in the hall, drinking beer and talking. She sat opposite me against the other wall. I spoke to multiple people, not only her. She seemed to be focused on talking to me. I then realized something. Amanda had started to flirt with me. Sitting in the hall made it noisy and hard to hear. She gestured for me to move across the aisle and sit beside her to hear each other better.

I got her clear signal and moved next to her. I started to flirt back with her, focusing on her now. I had too much beer to resist and had become drunk. She flirted, but "tried to flirt" would be a better description.

I asked her a leading question to encourage her to talk. "What's your favorite class? What do you like about it?"

She responded, "Philosophy." She looked at me and said nothing else.

I asked her another question, and she responded yes or no. I told her a funny story, and she laughed before I reached the punchline. She kept smiling at me the whole time and only stared at me.

Then, I recognized she had this expectation. Others in the hall seemed to be watching me, anticipating something. I wondered if they thought I would live up to my reputation. I did not find Amanda that attractive, but now intoxicated, I gave into it and moved closer to her. She opened her eyes wider and nervously laughed but kept looking at me.

I leaned toward her to kiss her, and she moved her head to meet mine and caused me not entirely to land my lips on hers. I tried to adjust, but she was too clumsy in returning her kiss. The whole thing was awkward. I knew the fault lay with her. I mean, did she not know how to kiss?

During the entire kiss, I looked through her glasses. Her eyes were open wide.

When I pulled back, a huge smile broke out on her face. She glanced around and saw people in the hall looking at us. Her cheeks flushed, and her smile dropped. She stood up and kept looking around at the others in the hall and then at me. I stood up too, and she stepped back out of my range. She fiddled with her glasses and touched her hair to move it out of the way. Her hand trembled a little. She kept looking at me but did not smile.

Had she rejected me? She kept looking at me but at a safe distance. I could not decide what she wanted. Irritated, I accepted her rejection.

I stalked off. I thought I had cleared off my winter funk and endless depression, but as I climbed the stairs, the darkness rose and gathered around me. It whispered "inadequate" in my ear and clung to my legs as if to pull me down into a fall. I tried to shake it off, but it went to my room with me. Too much beer had made me drunk and defenseless.

I could not hold it off, and this rejection renewed its strength. I slumped into it. The doubts piled on me, filling me with terrible thoughts. If even this girl rejected me, my situation would seem hopeless. I was unlovable.

I then thought of Colleen and our breakup. All the pain from losing her finally came out. The alcohol had removed all checks on my behavior, and I cried.

As my tears fell, another terrible memory came back to me. I remember my father talking to me and crying. He had pulled me out of the house and into an empty lot across the street.

"I just need someone to talk to. I don't have anyone else I can tell." His voice quivered as he talked. I had never seen my father upset like this.

"Your mother told me she no longer loves me. She wants to get divorced." He began to weep openly.

I did not say anything. I stood frozen, but I remembered my mother with that other man. It had just happened the previous week.

"I know I've become boring, but I can change. I don't want to get divorced. I still love her."

I tried to comfort my father, but the emotion choked out any response. I was only fifteen. I had no idea what to say or do.

He must have seen the horror on my face. He put his arm around me, and we returned to the house. We said nothing else, and I never discussed it with him again.

That horrible memory added to my despair, and I sobbed out loud. It did not last long, and I soon passed out.

In the morning, embarrassed and exasperated, I went to do my laundry. The ghosts had departed. *How did I let them in again? How stupid of me.* Still, I felt strangely relieved.

The RA lived in the room next to me. He entered his room as I exited mine. He stopped and expressed his concern. "Are you okay? You seemed upset last night."

Embarrassed, I dismissed it. "I had way too much beer. I was being stupid."

He smiled at this and let me go. Being stupid with alcohol was a common problem for freshmen.

After I started my laundry and returned to my room, I had only sat down when someone knocked at the door. Now what? Did the RA come back again? I opened the door, and there stood Amanda.

She asked, "Are you okay? I stopped by your room last night, and you were upset."

I thought, *Come on, can I do nothing in private? Do I have to do this with this girl?*

I dismissed her concern. "I'm okay. I had too much to drink last night. It made me sick."

She accepted this but kept looking at me. Again, she stared into my eyes and managed a half smile. She had come by herself, and it occurred to me as she looked into my room that she wanted me to invite her inside.

I stood looking at her. I misread last night. This girl lacked experience—she didn't know how to act to communicate what she wanted.

She looked past me into my room, looked up at me, and smiled. She waited for her invitation to enter.

No, I thought. *I'm not going to do this with her.* I stepped into the doorway, blocking her way.

She appeared uneasy, and she tried to make small talk.

I cut her off. "I really need to study this afternoon." I moved to put my hand on the doorknob and stopped at her reaction.

Her smile had dropped, and her face contorted a little. This alarmed me as I did not want her to cry. I dropped my hand from the door.

Her voice dropped to almost a whisper as she asked, "You left so quickly last night. Did I mess the kiss up? Did I do it wrong?" She tried to control herself, but her eyes cried, *Help me.*

I forcefully said, "No." I stepped toward her and put my hands on her shoulders. I leaned in to kiss her. This time I made sure my lips landed on hers and gave her a long, tender kiss.

Her eyes opened wide. When I pulled back, a huge smile spread on her face.

"See," I said. "Nothing wrong with the kiss." I smiled at her.

She looked into my room again and at me with that huge grin.

I said, "My roommate will be back shortly. He just went downstairs to start his laundry."

Her smile dropped, but she kept looking at me.

"Another time?" I smiled.

She beamed and nodded.

"I'll see you later, Amanda."

After she left, I thought that she required too much work. I did not like her enough, and despite her interest, she did not like me enough to commit to being with me. She wanted an experience, nothing more. I needed a girl who wanted me.

Soon after, Bill knocked on my door. It seemed as if a damn parade marched to my room. He excitedly said, "Dude, I heard you kissed Amanda last night! Do you know how many guys have tried to do something with her and came up empty?"

I wanted to slam the door. These idiots thought that kiss had been a success. I did not know how to answer, so I tried to change the subject.

I talked to Amanda several times over the next few weeks. She always hung around our dorm. I ensured that she understood I wasn't interested, but I always could feel an interest from her.

At our next party, I saw her with Todd. He complained to me afterward that she didn't know how to kiss. I did not bump into her again that quarter.

Toward the end of the quarter, as I passed the common room one day, I overheard Ed talking to some of his friends from the dungeon. I stopped because I heard him say, "Amanda."

"Yeah, I added to my cherry collection last night. This nerdy girl, Amanda. She was not too attractive and lay there like a deer in headlights, but man, what a tight ride."

His audience laughed.

I grimaced at his bragging and resumed walking. I wanted to avoid hearing any more.

CHAPTER 8

Rosemary

We entered the last weekend before the winter finals in March. It was time for a dorm party. Our parties had gotten a reputation—we had become the party dorm. At the last two parties, many more girls attended. They outnumbered us. Of course, we loved that.

We needed a way to escape the pressure before finals. We decided on a Hawaiian party. This would allow us to wear funny shirts and straw hats and make a fruit punch to drink. The girls did not always like beer, but they liked punch. Of course, we would spike the punch. We were, after all, a guys' dorm.

All clouds had lifted from me, and I felt normal. I no longer became nervous. I had hung in there as I had with that minister. That same part of me had won this.

I purchased a Hawaiian shirt. I helped make the punch, and I helped procure the beer. This party had a completely different feel from the beginning. Everywhere I looked, girls outnumbered us. Their numbers made us giddy with excitement. We drank and celebrated.

Something else strange also occurred. Girls kept coming up to me. Usually, I had to initiate the contact. Now, I stood in the same place. They kept rotating to me. They did not only talk to me. They actively flirted. They stayed around. Most would not even take a hint when I showed no interest. I danced with three different girls on slow dances in quick succession. Each of them pressed themselves against me.

I moved away from the last one to retrieve my drink when she approached me and introduced herself as Rosemary. She had straight blond hair that fell over her bare shoulders, pale skin, and blue eyes, and she wore full makeup with pink lipstick. She was average height and wore a tropical-themed white dress with straps. Her dress showed her cleavage, and I admired her shapely figure. She wore matching white sandals showing her pink nails. I stopped hard and stood gawking at her. She looked stunning from head to toe. I thought she was among the most beautiful girls I had ever seen. We talked, and I made sure to show my interest.

"Where are you from?" I asked.

"A small town outside Montgomery, Alabama," she replied in a soft Southern drawl. It added to her appeal. We talked about our hometowns and discussed our classes. We discussed the dorms we lived in and the friends we knew. I found out she lived in Reynolds. I had not seen her before at any party.

I asked her, "Have you been to our parties?"

"No, I've avoided the parties. I'm not a party type of person. I focus on school and my classes." She hesitated then said, "I needed a break. I'm ready for finals. Sometimes you need to talk to others. It can get lonely."

I understood that and responded, "It's strange with all these people around all the time and the lack of privacy, but it's easy to be lonely here."

She looked at me when I confessed that. We now talked closer with more urgency. We had something in common to solve. We dispelled our loneliness in each other's company. She told me she studied English and focused on writing. "I want to be a writer," she said.

I replied, "I want to be a writer also. I write poetry."

We grew excited about this common interest and moved to a quieter place to sit together.

We only talked to each other. We talked about writers we liked. We discussed what we were writing and offered to read the other's writing to provide feedback. I told her I had one short poem I had recently created that I could quote her.

Excitement lit up her face. She said, "No one has ever shared a poem they wrote with me."

I quoted it to her talking low and soft.

I am the stem of the rose,
the root of the tree,
with enough intensity of passion
to press bud into blossom.

She stared hard at me. I sensed something intense in her gaze, her eyes. "Repeat it slowly," she asked.

I recited it to her again.

When I finished, her whole face lit up. "Wow, that's good!" She leaned toward me.

I leaned in and kissed her, and she returned it with soft and gentle tenderness. She kissed as beautifully as she looked. She opened her eyes wide at me. I knew mine widened as well. I leaned in, and we kissed again, this time much longer. We both abandoned ourselves to it.

Together, we kissed away our loneliness. We kissed away the distance between us. We kissed ourselves close and intimate. When we paused for air, I accepted the yes from her. I had delivered her mine already. I kissed her again, longer, fuller. My arms went around her, pulling her warm body against mine. She surrendered completely to my kissing, to me, to us. She put her arms around me, pulling me tightly against her. We clasped together, hungrily making out. I smelled the scent on her skin and gave myself entirely to her. I met her surrender with my own.

I wanted to take her back to my room, but I could not—my roommate made it clear that afternoon that he would be there. She lived in Reynolds, where no male visitors were allowed. We had nowhere to go, so we sat together. We ignored everyone else. The party and the noise around us disappeared. We sat together, only us two, hugging and kissing.

The party wound down, and the RA chased visitors out of the common area. It was time to go.

I walked out of my dorm with her, hand in hand, to escort her home. We laughed at some other freshmen, thoroughly drunk, who played in the fountain.

Spring had warmed the days, but the night stayed cool, and she shivered from the cold. I put my arm around her, and we strolled to her dorm. We stopped in front and kissed again. We paused, looked at each other, then resumed kissing. Neither of us wanted to stop. I looked down at her face in her vivid blue eyes.

"Can I see you tomorrow? Can we do something together? Anything together?"

She nodded yes. "I have to do something most of the day, but I can meet you here on the green at ten thirty. Will that work?"

"Yes."

She walked in, and I thought, *She is stunning*. I had never before kissed such a beautiful girl, and that evening with her had left me utterly enamored.

I thought about her until I fell asleep, and I woke up early thinking of her again. I did nothing but think about her until it was time to meet.

I arrived fifteen minutes early. I had a list in my head of dates we could go on.

When she came out, I saw she had dressed up again, wearing a fancy dress and full makeup. In the bright light of the morning sun, I admired how she looked truly stunning.

I did not hide my thrill at seeing her. She greeted me with a diffident smile and did not display the same enthusiasm. I complimented her, "Your outfit looks amazing."

She nodded.

I asked her, "Can we go out? What would you like to do?"

She hesitated, then said, "I can't today."

I asked, "What about next week? Even lunch is fine."

She replied, "I don't have time next week because of finals."

I paused and studied her. She seemed sad, even a little distressed. She appeared to be preparing herself for something. I started again, "What about the weekend after spring break?"

This time, she said, "I just can't. I can't go out with you."

I tried to comprehend this. This girl who had been so giving last night now refused to go out with me? I responded, "I want to see you again. When can I see you again?"

She replied, "I can't," and said, "I have a boyfriend back home."

This stunned me, and I stared at her. I couldn't think or speak.

She looked at me with her eyes moist. She said, "I'm sorry. I didn't mean for anything to happen. I felt so lonely, and you were easy to talk to, and then you read me that poem. I'm sorry." She turned and walked off.

I stood there watching her, not saying anything else. I dropped my head and shuffled back to the dorm. *How do I keep finding these girls with boyfriends? Why do I fall for them? What is wrong with me?*

It seemed like all it took was the right girl to puncture my surface, letting my emotion pour out. I was like a volcano swollen with lava ready to burst. Nothing could control me when I erupted.

It did not occur to me to ask Rosemary the night before if she had a boyfriend. She had been all in without restraint. *In the future, I'm going to ask that question.*

Despite her behavior, I did not blame her. I could not because I still wanted her. I concocted a plan. I knew several girls who lived in her dorm, and I would ask them to intercede. They could convince her I cared for her. Several of them tried, but the answer always came back as no.

I changed my route to class to pass her dorm, hoping to run into her, but I never met her again. She avoided coming to any of our future parties.

I kept thinking about her, still hoping until long into the next quarter. I could not stop. I spent only one evening with Rosemary, but it was enough.

Chapter 9

Quentin

The weather continued to warm as we headed into late April until it became hot. In our non-air-conditioned dorm, the heat sapped any initiative.

My desire for women never rested, but I decided only to date safe girls who did not tempt me. Shelly was the first in that group. She was a tall, voluptuous blond who attracted my attention in the cafeteria one day. We flirted, and I asked her out. She invited me to her room to cook for me.

The meal she prepared tasted delicious. I enjoyed it and her that evening. I did not feel anything for her other than desire and moved on.

After two weekends of not doing much, I was ready to party again. My college Republican club hosted an event scheduled for statewide clubs that weekend in May, including free barbecue and beer Friday evening, followed by meetings and seminars on Saturday. I know, I know. College Republicans? Most of our membership consisted of stuffy older guys studying at the law school, but after our meetings, we would drink beer, and they would pay for it. Our president also told me the Florida club had several cute girls who would be attending. Our club would provide free food and beer. Who can argue with free food, beer, and pretty girls?

The party lived up to my expectations. Beer flowed freely, and I ate all I wanted. The University of Florida members had arrived, and we were slowly circulating and introducing ourselves. I met this tall, gangly girl with pale skin and dark hair that curled under. She dressed casually in shorts, a top, and flip-flops. Her elbows, knees, hands, and feet looked thin and bony. Despite her bony thinness, I did find her attractive. She had a pretty face with nice skin.

"Quentin? What kind of name is that?" I asked her.

"It's my grandmother's last name," she responded.

"What? You have your grandmother's last name as your first name?"

"It's a Southern thing to give girls a family name as their first name. I'm from Mississippi," she elaborated.

"I guess it's distinctive. No one else has that name," I offered.

She smiled at me. "True. I am the only Quentin I know."

We were supposed to move on and keep meeting everyone, but she had stopped at me, and we now talked to each other. As she stood in front of me, I kept finding things appealing about her. She had a strong Southern accent and nice skin. She seemed content to stand and talk to me as well. Already a sophomore, a year older than me, she did not seem to think the age difference mattered. I flirted with her, and she reciprocated.

After a while, this older guy in his late twenties intruded on our conversation. He was already working in the capitol building for some politicians. He showed his interest in her, but she ignored him. His interruption reminded me that I had drained my beer mug and needed to refill it. When I got back, he was still there. I kept talking to her, but he would not quit.

What an aggressive guy, I thought. I got another beer and then another until I became drunk.

Quentin looked askance at me when I went for the fourth. "You can't do much if you're too drunk."

I did not understand that comment. What did she mean? I had not come for a woman. I had come to drink free beer and intended to keep imbibing until drunk, so I brushed her comment off.

Some activity had started, so we split up, and I did not see her for a while. Some more beers and completing the tasks left me wandering around aimlessly. I decided to head home before becoming too drunk to return.

As I got ready to go, I bumped into Quentin again. That guy stood close to her, talking to her. She seemed resigned to being with him. She gave me a look of disapproval and even disappointment as I left.

Saturday's activities included several workshops and some meetings. When I sat down at the first one, Quentin surprised me by sitting beside me. We talked amiably. I saw no sign of the pushy guy from the previous night. She sat beside me at the next session, and I understood she signaled me out. I paid close attention to her and thought, *I do find her attractive! She lives in Gainesville, so she would be safe.*

During the next break, I asked her, "Do you want to go out this evening? We can do something together."

I barely finished my pitch when she already said, "Yes." She added, "Not all beer, right?"

I laughed and responded, "Sorry, but I did get it all out of my system last night, so tonight will not be a beer night."

She smiled widely at me, a friendly smile. Our day wrapped up, and we walked off together, heading to a local pizza place next to campus. We walked off hand in hand. Our club president, David, saw me and flashed me a strange grin.

I ordered a beer, and she gave me a reproving glance. "Just a couple," I said. "I'm not going to get drunk."

She nodded and ordered herself a wine. We ate and talked, covering basic stuff such as what we studied and our hometowns, and then she said something odd to me: "This is different for me. I never go out on a Saturday night."

"Why not?" I asked.

She replied, "I stay in my room and watch *Love Boat* and *Fantasy Island*."

"You have a TV? A TV in your room?" I didn't know a single student with this luxury.

"Yes, there are four of us in our suite. I have a TV."

I had not watched a single moment of television my entire first year. I leaned forward to make fun of her. "Really?

On Saturday, when everyone else is out partying or on dates, you stay home and watch TV. Really?"

She leaned toward me and said, "Yes. I watch TV on Saturday nights. I can go out any other night, but my shows are only on that night."

I leaned back and studied her. A conservative college Republican, perhaps she did not date a lot. It did not go with her behavior toward me. She sat relaxed, confident, and even experienced. She smiled back.

After we ate and I paid, we headed out with no particular destination, strolling back into the campus. I stopped after a while, and we kissed. Quentin kissed me sensually. She kissed exceptionally well, and I kissed her again longer.

Standing close, still holding each other, she smiled at me and said softly, "You are really good at kissing."

I responded, "We can go to my dorm, my room, and talk some more if you like."

She nodded yes, smiling more. We headed over. My roommate sat on his bed, but he saw I had a girl, and he prepared to exit.

We managed to have a quick conversation outside the door after I seated her in the room on my bed. My roommate had to go somewhere early in the morning, so I could not be late—two hours we agreed on.

The rooms only had two old hard wooden chairs for the desks. If you wanted to sit and talk, you had to sit on the bed. As we chatted, she scooted close to me, expecting something.

I began kissing her again. Her kisses were beyond sensual, so inviting. I had never kissed anyone who kissed this well. She pressed her lips against mine, so soft and sensual. I put my hands under her blouse, seeking her breasts.

She said, "Just a moment."

She took off her top and removed her bra herself. I pulled my shirt off in response. She had small, pale, pointy breasts, with small pink nipples forming softly rounded points. I tasted her and put my hands all over her. She put her hands on me. I moved my hands toward her shorts.

Again, she said, "Just a moment."

She removed her shorts and panties. She put her hands on my jeans to unbuckle them herself. We pulled them and my underwear off. Standing, she wrapped her hand around me and pulled me toward her.

I said, "Condom?"

She responded so softly, "I'm on the pill. We don't need it." She lay down with her legs apart and guided me into her warm wetness. I kissed her hungrily as I moved, wanting to taste her soft skin. She behaved so differently than Colleen, who had only lay there. She had one hand on my back, the other on my rear, and she moved with me, pulsating against me. She began orchestrating my movement, directing me on how she wanted me to move.

I gave her control, and she said, "Let me be on top."

We managed to flip around with me still inside. She moved gracefully against my clumsy movements. She rocked hard and fast on me. She pulled my hands onto her breasts.

"Pull them, suck them," she commanded.

I leaned forward and did what she said. I began to groan, to feel it coming.

"Not yet," Quentin gasped. "Hold it. Hold it a little more."

I tried to think of anything else to hold off my orgasm. She moved fast and hard, her eyes always on mine, fixing me in place. I moaned as I got ready to release.

"Wait," she gasped, those eyes commanding me to hold. She rocked until her eyelids flickered, and she gasped, "Okay."

I let go and exploded in her, gasping with joy. She slowed but kept deliberately moving on me, kept moving even after I had finished. She kept rocking for a long time, her eyes always on mine, holding me firm until she wanted to stop. She pressed her hands on me, stilling me, and leaned forward, putting her lips on mine.

I had never been kissed like that, so full of the reward of what just happened.

Quentin sat back and pulled off. She turned toward me and lay against me, resting her hands gently on me. I lay quietly next to her. I would do anything she asked, anything she wanted. I had never met anyone like her.

After a while, I turned my head to her and whispered, "You are amazing, absolutely amazing."

She half smiled and asked, "How much time till your roommate returns?"

I glanced at the clock. "Soon," I responded.

She said, "Do you have a towel we can clean up with?"

I walked to the closet, retrieved one, and handed it to her. She cleaned herself up and gestured for me to stand close. She cleaned me up as well, relaxed and familiar. We got up, dressed, and headed out of the room. She took my hand, and we held hands as we exited the dorm.

My roommate sat in the lounge with other friends. They all looked at us. It was late, after midnight. The air had cooled, and twinkling stars and a bright moon filled the night sky. We walked with no purpose.

She stopped and asked, "Where's your car? It's a bit of a drive to the girl I'm staying with."

I took the lead and headed to my car. We got in, and she sat in the middle next to me. She told me which sorority house. I knew the exact location and headed us over. We found a place to park on the street, turned to each other, and began kissing again.

I wanted more, always more. I moved my hand under her blouse.

She stopped me. "Not here on the street. We can only kiss here."

I remained in her embrace. She had the lead, had the initiative on even how we kissed. After a long time, she stopped. "I need to go in. My ride is heading back early tomorrow."

As I walked her to the door, I asked, "Can I write to you? Can we get together again? I can find a way to visit you in Gainesville."

She smiled softly at me and wrote her address on a scrap of paper from her purse. She handed it to me. "That would be nice. I'll write back. We'll figure it out." She walked in, and she was gone.

The next day, our club had a short wrap-up meeting. David approached me with a grin. "I saw you leaving with Quentin last night. She has quite the reputation."

I gave him a sharp look and retorted, "She's a nice girl."

He understood and backed away. "I'm sure she is a *very* nice girl." His grin said otherwise.

I walked away. I refused to have this conversation about Quentin with him.

I worked on that letter to her for a long time, carefully editing and parsing what I said. I did not want to be too obvious or fill it with too much desire. I liked her, but it differed from the pull toward Colleen or the intense emotion Rosemary evoked. Still, I did have feelings for Quentin. I wrestled the letter to completion and ended it with that emotion. *I like you, really like you. I would like to see you again. I want to come and see you again.*

I got a response within a week of my posting it.

Her letter back read sweet, even tender. *I enjoyed being with you. I greatly enjoyed my time in Tallahassee with you. I would like you to come and visit. I want to see you also. Let me know when you are coming.*

I did not respond to that letter. The quarter was ending, and I had no money left. I became so short of cash that I was reduced to eating peanut butter and jelly sandwiches and going to the cafeteria once a day. I would gorge myself on the buffet to make it to the next day. I could not afford to travel and stay in Gainesville. I had to save what I had left to make it home for the summer.

She lived too far away. How could I hope to make something like that work? I also realized that seeing her again would not be safe. It had only been one night, but I remembered my experience with Rosemary and how a single great night ended the next day badly. I could not take another heartbreak. Those doubts and the lack of money kept me from responding.

Events would soon sweep away any other opportunity, and I never saw this extraordinary young woman, Quentin, again.

Chapter 10

Hannah

I first met Hannah at one of those survey classes on Western Civilization, a required course that continued across all three quarters of the first year. The university held the class in a large auditorium in the center of campus near my dorm. The auditorium probably seated three hundred kids. I don't know why I did not walk in, but I hung back.

Then I saw her. She stood tall, with long straight blond hair down the middle of her back. She had a pale round face with blue eyes and wore a white sleeveless top with a tropical flower print and matching hemmed shorts. She had these long, gorgeous tanned legs and pretty feet in white sandals showing her pink nails. She walked with physical grace, confidence, and even prowess. She dressed stylishly, not the usual college bum comfort but stylish. Everything about her was put together well, and I stood gawking at her. I knew I had witnessed the most beautiful girl I had ever seen walking past me.

She headed down the aisle for a seat, and I followed her. I sat next to her. She gave me a greeting with a slight smile. I am sure she was aware of my interest. We began to talk. I introduced myself and asked for her name.

"I'm Hannah," she said.

I asked, "Where are you from?"

"Kansas." She told me where in Kansas, but I don't remember.

I kept talking to her. "I ran cross country and track in high school and still run on my own. Not quite good enough to make the college team, though."

She proudly responded, "I'm on the FSU women's golf team. I have a full scholarship and live in the athletes' dorm. We even get to have all our meals there."

She displayed her pride in her accomplishment, which impressed me. I had spent my entire high school career distance running to earn a scholarship to pay for college. I poured my heart and soul into running ten miles daily for years. At that age, I still believed that if you tried hard enough, you could make anything happen, but I did not have the talent to go with my determination and never got anywhere close to earning a sports scholarship.

I said, "That's amazing. You must be extremely talented to have earned a scholarship." I began to flirt more aggressively. "I could tell watching you come in that you were athletic." I decided I would ask her out after class.

I must have conveyed this interest as she said, "I have a boyfriend."

Her comment deflated me though I tried to pretend it did not matter.

She kept talking to me. Hannah showed kindness to me in a way I had not experienced before with a beautiful girl. I had known beautiful girls in high school who were "stuck up." They treated your interest with disdain as if you stood beneath them.

Hannah kept talking to me. "I do play golf daily with a lot of walking, so I guess that keeps me in shape." She smiled at me. "I can tell you run. You look in shape also."

I am sure Hannah kept talking to me to make me feel better. She radiated warmth and sweetness to go with her beauty. She also had this inexplicable grace, a graciousness I have not seen since in any woman. It kept my attention riveted. Still, it had the opposite effect of her declaration that she had a boyfriend. It fired my attraction into an infatuated crush.

Class after class, I sat next to Hannah, and we talked before, during breaks, and after class. I excelled at talking to girls. College, in the beginning, could be a lonely time. We became friends. That constant daily talking became my most persistent relationship with any girl that year.

Hannah talked about golf. She encouraged me to try it out and check out the FSU golf course near campus, where students played for free. Despite the boyfriend, I had hope, and one day I drove out to the golf course.

Hannah told me when the golf team practiced, and I hoped to talk to her outside class. I pulled into the parking lot. Before I got out, I spotted Hannah. Her height and those long legs, even at a distance, made it easy to pick her out. She stood next to a tall boy, holding hands. He was tall, handsome, and with Hannah. Embarrassed, I stayed in the car. I sat for a while, staring at her before I pulled out. I found it hard not to look. Even at a distance, I could see her beauty.

Four or five weeks after class began, my relationship with Hannah moved in a new direction. We had just taken our first exam, and the student assistants handed out our graded tests. Written on the first page of mine in red ink were a -2 and a 96. These had been crossed out; next to them, someone had written a 100 and an A+.

The professor discussing the test results said to the entire class, "We had the only one hundred I have given out this quarter in this class. This was remarkable because my graduate student assistants had incorrectly marked two correct answers. Here was a freshman student doing better than my grad students. I am impressed by this performance. Please stand up and let us recognize you."

He looked around the auditorium. I had a sheepish grin, but I did not stand up. I had not sought this public recognition, and public exposure never appealed to me, so I stayed seated.

Hannah stared at me with amazement. She had seen my grade and my reaction. "That was you? How is that even possible? How did you do that?"

My accomplishment impressed her. After that, she treated me with honest respect. She would ask me questions about the class and even seek a little help. It became another way we interacted. She treated me as someone she found attractive. She still had a boyfriend, so she kept this discreetly low, but I sensed it.

Her interest in me flattered me and kept my crush alive. My inexperience kept me from knowing that for some women, intelligence in a man makes him attractive and counts as an essential trait. Despite feeling this attraction, with her having a boyfriend, I had no hope, and I remained hopelessly stuck as a friend. My crush did not diminish, and the regular interaction with her kept it alive.

Hannah sat waiting for me at the start of the spring quarter in early April. I usually reached class first as my dorm sat close to the auditorium, and she had to walk from the other side of campus. This morning, she had already arrived. Hannah smiled at me. I smiled back and noted how good she looked in her blouse, shorts, and sandals with those legs, painted nails, and makeup. She always put herself together so well. I could not help myself in her presence.

Despite my sense of hopelessness that I could date a girl this beautiful, I still wanted her. I smiled too much at her.

She inquired, "How was your spring break? Did you do anything exciting?"

I thought, *I spent it moping over Rosemary, who broke my heart.* Of course, I did not tell her the truth! I responded, "No, I didn't do anything interesting. I went home, but I lay around doing nothing. Well, I guess I did one thing."

She looked at me expectantly.

"I managed to set up a summer job. I will be home for the summer and work full time at the pizza place I used to work at in high school. I will do my summer session at the local commuter school, USF, so that I can work all summer." Florida universities required every student to attend one summer session full time to graduate. Most of my dorm friends planned on staying at FSU for the summer, but I needed to work and save money.

"You're not one of those guys who throws pizza dough up in the air, spinning it, are you?" she asked, smiling at this image.

I laughed. "No, I cook the pizzas, cut them with a big knife, call out the customer's number, and wash a lot of dishes, but nothing interesting. Did you go home to Kansas for spring break?"

"No, I couldn't. Too much golf, and it's too far and expensive to go for anything that short. I stayed here. Our season is in full swing," she responded, gesturing with her hands, imitating a golf swing.

I smiled at her pun. "How is your season coming?"

Disappointment displayed on her face, she said, "Well, not that great. I had hoped to do better, but I still have time left."

"I'm sure you're going to be great," I responded.

She smiled at me. She paused and looked straight at me as if considering something. "I broke up with my boyfriend," she finally said. She stared at me, waiting for a response.

I thought, *Why is she telling me that?* Yes, I know. How stupid can you be? But in my defense, I already felt whipsawed between my feelings and rejection from Rosemary and a little upset still about Colleen. I did not want another girl. Also, I lacked the confidence that a girl like Hannah would find me attractive.

"Why did you break up?" I asked.

Full of disdain, she said, "He treated me very poorly and cheated on me. He was not interested in me at all except… I'm not going to be treated that way. I'm a real person, not his…whatever."

I responded, "I would never treat a girl I cared for like you that way."

She gave me a half-embarrassed smile, and I realized, *What did I just blurt out to her?!*

The professor rescued me by walking in and asking for our attention, ending any opportunity to stumble or talk.

She leaned over and whispered, "Can we talk more after class?"

Despite myself, I know I blushed.

After class, she stood and faced me with that long, graceful, athletic figure and said, "I changed my schedule this quarter. I have an hour after class, so I have time to talk."

I grimaced and responded, "Unfortunately, I have a required class that is only available right now, so I can't talk. It's on the other side of campus. Can we chat some more on Wednesday?"

She nodded, looking disappointed, and I walked off.

What the hell was that about? I wondered as I hurried across the campus. Despite what I wanted, I lacked the confidence to believe a girl this beautiful could be interested in me.

Hannah greeted me warmly at the next class, the one after, and the one after that, and I found myself warming to her, even daring to flirt. This went on for several weeks, forcing me to recognize what she had hinted at and daring to think I could ask her out. I tried to force my courage up, look for an opportunity, and do what I wanted. But always, the time available dwindled before me, and an audience sat around us in that class setting. Three weeks into the quarter, I had an opening as my following class had been canceled.

I smiled too much at her and tried not to be too nervous, but I failed and croaked, "Do you have time after this class? I have time today, so maybe we can have some time to talk."

She responded with disappointment. "Ohh, I can't talk today. I have to leave right after this class for a golf tournament. Sorry, maybe we can another time?"

Defeated by this comment, I sunk into my seat.

She added, "I want to have some time to chat. It's just that I'm swamped right now with golf."

This aborted request did not retreat but sat between us, waiting for action. I searched for another chance but continued to shrink from my public audience.

In May, I thought, *Enough. Ask her out!* I would ask her for a moment to talk after the next class.

I got my conversation request out, and with a smile, she said, "Sure!" The class ended, and we stood face to face in the courtyard outside the class.

I danced nervously around it, making small talk as Hannah patiently waited. I got ready to ask when a female friend of Hannah's walked into our small circle and interrupted us. She and Hannah greeted each other happily and even hugged. I stood flatfooted, defeated. Hannah kept looking at me frequently with an expression like a question mark. Her friend stopped and looked at me as well. Hannah asked, "What did you want to talk about?"

I shrank from this addition of an audience. What if Hannah said no? I could not take public humiliation. I punted and said, "It's nothing, just something about the class. I'll tell you about it during our next class. See you." I walked away.

Puzzled, she said, "Okay, see you."

Dejected by this failure, I stumbled back to my dorm. Why did I have such bad luck?

We were down to a few weeks left in the quarter in late May when Hannah came in one morning looking distressed.

"What's wrong?" I asked her with alarm.

"I lost it!" she responded. "I lost all of it!"

"Lost what?" I asked.

"My scholarship! They are going in a 'new direction' and won't renew my scholarship next year. I won't get room and board, tuition, and books. I'll get nothing! I can play as a walk-on, but I must pay for everything myself! Even out-of-state tuition! I can't afford it. No way I can afford it! I don't know what I'm going to do!" She acted like she might cry.

I leaned toward her and put my hand on hers to comfort her.

She paused and looked at my hand on hers. She slowly smiled. "Thanks," she said softly.

I realized what I had done and withdrew my hand when the professor called us to attention. I found myself feeling upset as I walked to my next class. *Why are you upset? What is it with you and Hannah?* I asked myself in exasperation.

In the next class, she sat looking resigned. "What are you going to do?" I repeated.

"I have no choice. I'm going to withdraw and go to school back home," she sadly responded.

"You're leaving?" I asked incredulously.

"No choice," she replied with a sad smile. "I'm leaving." She paused, looked at me as if considering something else, and asked, "Do you want to study together for our final test? We have a study hall at my dorm, and we can help quiz each other and prepare for the exam."

I looked at her, but my mind kept saying, *She's LEAVING!*

I shook my head. "I study by myself. I don't need help from anyone. Your dorm is clear across campus."

She repeated, "We can study at the library or your dorm. We can help each other. It will be fun. We can have some time to talk…"

I understood what she asked and suggested. She did not hide her interest, but I kept hearing, *She's LEAVING! I can't risk it. She is leaving.*

I made an excuse. "I'm busy with all my other tests. I don't have time."

She tried again, almost pleading, "I've had a tough term. I could use your help. I know you can help me, and I want to spend time with you."

I hesitated, feeling myself wavering, until I told myself, *Don't*. I refused her. She frowned, and her head dropped. We did not talk again that day.

She barely said a word to me in the next class, the last one before the exam. I knew I had done the wrong thing the moment I stepped out, but I couldn't do it. I could not risk it. I knew Hannah was leaving and the effect she had on me. It would take nothing, only an hour with her, talking, perhaps a little kissing, and I would fall hard for her. She would still be leaving, and I would have nothing but another heartbreak, probably worse than the last time. We had no time left.

The exam day came. I said, "Hello, and good luck" to her, but she did not respond. She had given up on me.

I finished first, faster than anyone else in the room. I always finished first.

I milled around outside for a while, waiting, thinking. I need to do something, something. Other students exited the auditorium, but not her, and I realized it was too late. I returned to my dorm.

I was restless that afternoon but forced myself to focus on my last exam the next day. I had my most challenging class still left. I needed to focus.

I had strange, restless dreams that night and woke from a nightmare where I saw Hannah sitting opposite me that April morning when she said, "I broke up with my boyfriend."

I reprimanded myself, *You stupid, cowardly fool! You missed your chance! You didn't even try. What's wrong with you?* I had no answer but tossed and turned until I fell asleep again.

The next day, I aced my last exam. I had a good quarter and made straight A's. When I returned to my room, I finished packing my car and returned my keys to the RA. I headed south to my home. I had no passengers this time, leaving me with no choice but to be alone with my thoughts.

I felt regret, even guilt, and then I thought of something worse: Hannah had asked me for help in her distress. She asked for my help, and I refused her. I only thought about my feelings and failed to help someone I cared about. This stung me, and I felt ashamed. I had done the wrong thing, and now I could do nothing to fix it. I had tried to be safe, but I only hurt myself and her. I owed Hannah an apology, but I had no way to deliver it.

I thought of Colleen. I had been the one who ended it. She wanted more, and I had been the one to say no.

I thought of Quentin. She had responded to my letter with a yes, but again I provided the no. I didn't even try.

I had been a failure with these women. All the no's had been my fault. Well, not all. Rosemary had been the one to break my heart, not me, but the rest were my fault. *But Quentin*, I thought, *that had been a success.* But I knew the success came from her, not me. She initiated all of it. I followed along, and I almost messed it up as well. But still, she had wanted to be with me and had singled me out.

I then realized the same thing about Hannah. Hannah had left me a gift that she did not intend to give. I had not meant to receive one, but there it was, and I opened it. Even a woman as wondrous and beautiful as Hannah had wanted to be with me. She had given me a gift of confidence. If I only tried, I could date a woman like that. I also thought I owed her something in addition to an apology. I owed her a thank you.

I resolved not to repeat this mistake. The next time with the next woman, I would try. There would always be another time. I determined that even if I had to stand on a stage in a spotlight with all eyes on me, I would try. I thought of Colleen. *I won't quit, either.*

I wouldn't give up and break it off without talking to the woman. The next one would get every chance, every opportunity. I would do what I could to make it successful.

I thought of something else. Never had I shared with a single woman my feelings. I tried to protect myself, but I failed. Heartbreak still came, most of it self-inflicted.

I thought of my parents. Before their marriage blew up, they never argued before us or fought. I thought they had an ideal relationship, but I remembered they never said "I love you" to each other or us. No one ever expressed their feelings.

I realized my failure to tell Colleen what I felt for her caused my problems. If I had told her, she would not have

invited me to that party, and we would have picked it up in January.
I will not do that again, either. The next woman, I will tell. I can do this better. I can learn from my mistakes. I thought of Quentin. I wanted more than sex. I thought of Colleen, Rosemary, and Hannah. I wanted much more. I needed something emotional, something personal.

I had denied what my longing that year meant and failed to acknowledge what drove and hurt me, but I would not pretend again. My heart had a hunger I could not restrain. I knew the truth and would act to get what I wanted and needed. In the future, it would all be different. I could and would act.

Chapter 11

Trudy

On my drive home, I stopped midway to grab a quick, cheap bite of food. After I finished and started again on my final leg home, I resolved to ask out one of the girls I knew in high school. Someone I wanted to date but did not. I considered several of them, starting with Ellen. I had been told she wanted to go to the prom with me, but I had two refusals already, and I could not handle a possible third rejection, so I didn't ask. She was Gregory's sister, and I remembered he'd mentioned she had a new boyfriend.

Debbie? One day, I sat with her outside the school against a wall, and we kissed for a while. Nothing followed because she acted uninterested in me.

Suzie? She still wrote me letters. We dated some in my senior year. I decided to respond to her last letter. Perhaps we could reunite.

On the first day home, I went into JB's Pizza in the early afternoon to tell them I had arrived and put in my request to add me to the schedule for the following week. I thought Sonia would be there, and I could confirm with her. She worked as one of the shift supervisors who ran the place.

A short, dark-haired woman, Sonia, greeted me with her usual affectionate teasing calling me "Christopher, Christopher" in her Brazilian accent. No one else ever called me by my full name. She thought it sounded funny. An immigrant woman in her late thirties with several kids, she worked at JB's Pizza to help support her family. I worked to save money for college. We had become friends in a teasing way. I was filled with a desire for girls, and perhaps the fact that I noticed her as a woman flattered her. This caused her to initiate this teasing, affectionate relationship we had. It was not a sordid relationship. We talked, and she teased me. All the ladies working at JB's somehow knew I was a virgin. I never told them that, but they knew it.

I had several girlfriends in high school, went out with multiple girls, and made out on several occasions but had resisted going over that line.

It had been almost a year since she had seen me. She looked at me with an appraising smile and questioned, "Christopher, Christopher, you are now a man?"

I understood what that question meant, and I nodded yes with a smile.

She gave me a somewhat sad smile as if to mark the passing of a child into a new stage that would mean separation between them. "You have a girlfriend?"

"No, no girlfriend right now."

She continued teasing me, "We have some new, pretty college girls working here this summer. They will be here on Sunday. You should come by and meet them, and you can see where you will be on the new schedule." Sonia always led the teasing but wanted to set me up with a girl. Our relationship resembled that of a parent/child as well.

I nodded and said I would come by. I got something to eat and drink and sat in the dining room.

Someone said to me, "Chris? Chris?"

I looked up and saw Trudy trying to get my attention. Trudy graduated the same year as me. I had known her since high school. She had short dark black hair, dark brown eyes, a pretty round face, and a dark complexion that had tanned a deep brown. She was of average height with a curvy, full figure.

We met at a swim party at the end of our sophomore year. The party had music playing, and some kids were dancing. She stood on the other side in a white bikini, and at an age when most girls had not developed, she already had full breasts and curves. She certainly caught my attention. I went over and asked her to dance, and she responded yes with a smile. We danced to several songs, including slow songs where we danced close together.

I wanted to kiss her. Did I mention she wore a bikini? I looked around for an opportunity. Kids jammed the place, and the school had brought many adults to chaperone. I thought I better not kiss her here in such a public place.

I did not ask her out as the evening began to wind down. I did not have my driver's license yet. It wasn't easy to date at that age.

I assumed I would see her in school, but I had never met her before, and our paths never crossed again for another year. She had a boyfriend by then, and I dated someone else.

I sat at the table next to her and responded, "How are you, Trudy? Did you have a good year in school?"

She beamed at me. "I had a great year!" she responded enthusiastically. "But I have even better news! I'm going to FSU in the fall. I'm transferring there and will live in one of the dorms. That's where you go, right?"

I smiled back at her and thought Trudy still looked good. "Yes, I live in Magnolia. Do you know what dorm you'll be living in?"

She hesitated. "I have the paper with the name, but I forgot now which one they put me into. I can't wait to start. Maybe you can show me around some when I get up there?"

I understood what that meant, and I thought, *What the hell? Ask her out.* "Maybe we can do something together this summer?" I suggested. "We don't have to wait until the fall."

"I would like that," she responded. "I have one small problem, however. My parents rented a cabin in the Smoky Mountains. We're spending almost the entire summer there. We're leaving on Sunday."

I replied, "We can still go out on Friday or Saturday. I don't start work until next week."

She beamed at me now. "I would like that. Let's go out on Friday."

I suggested, "We can go dancing. Do you know of a good disco place in Tampa? If I remember correctly, you like to dance?"

She responded again with enthusiasm, "I love dancing! That would be fantastic! I have been to a dance place in Tampa off Dale Mabry. It's a fun place."

I responded, "Sounds good. I need your address and phone number."

She gave me her number and directions to her house, smiling the entire time. We sat for a while, flirting with each other now that we had a date, until she had to pick up a sibling from some camp. "See you on Friday!" she said as she departed.

I stared at her as she walked out, admiring her shape. Yes, I always had a thing for those curvy girls. *Hey, I got a date in twenty-four hours! Summer is going to be good.* I finished eating and strutted to the front to talk to Sonia.

I bragged. "I got a date already, that girl who just left."

Sonia laughed. "Christopher, Christopher, already a ladies' man. I hope you stay a nice guy and treat them right."

"Of course!" I responded.

She went on, "You should come in on Sunday. I think you will like one of those girls. She seems so lovely and sweet."

"Okay, I'll come in on Sunday and meet her. Make sure the boss gets me scheduled."

She nodded and replied as I walked out. "I will. Goodbye."

Friday rolled around, and I put on the disco shirt I bought at FSU, dress slacks, and my best pair of shoes. I picked Trudy up and headed to the disco she recommended. She had casually dressed in a blouse and skirt with flat sandals. I thought of those girls who always dressed so well at FSU. They all wore heels to the disco. Still, Trudy looked cute, and her outfit showed her shapely figure.

She talked nonstop on the way over. I found it hard to respond.

We arrived to discover only a small crowd this Wednesday night in the summer. No one even danced. I got us two cocktails, and we found a table. We sat for a while, sipping our drinks and talking. Well, Trudy talked, and I listened and nodded.

She said, "You know you're the first boy I ever danced with."

I smiled at her.

She continued, "I was disappointed you did not kiss me."

My smile widened, and I responded, "I wanted to, but all the adult chaperones around watching us intimidated me."

She nodded. "Yes, we were being heavily watched."

A song that she liked started playing.

"Let's start the dance ourselves," she said and stood up.

I followed her to the dance floor, and we began to dance. Other couples soon joined us. I danced with enthusiasm but not any actual technique. Trudy danced well, and I tried to emulate some of her moves, no matter how clumsily. We danced to three or four faster songs before the DJ played a slow song.

I pulled her close, and we started gently swaying to the music. She pressed her breasts against my chest. As the song wound down, she looked up at me. I leaned down, and we kissed. I took her hand in mine, and we returned to our table for a break. The kiss had excited her, and she smiled broadly. The kiss also wound her up. Now she talked in overdrive, and I listened, responding with a nod or smile.

We followed this pattern all evening. We danced fast dances, then something slow, which always seemed to end with a kiss.

The kisses charged her, and she talked anytime we did not dance. The other couples dwindled again as it got late until we danced alone.

"I guess it's time to head back," I told her.

She nodded, and we headed out.

I parked in front of her house. All the homes in her neighborhood were dark. She did not leave the car but sat close to me, looking at me, waiting for me. I turned to her, and we kissed. We went at it with passion. We kissed long and full, expressing need and want. We kissed with open mouths, enjoying the taste of each other. I pressed her against me and moved my hands under her blouse. I pulled it up, exposing her full breasts in her bra. I worked on getting the bra off, struggling. *Why won't the bra come off?*

She giggled and undid her clasp in the back herself. Her large breasts fell out. She had big dark nipples.

I pushed her down on the seat and put my mouth on her breasts, tasting the salt from her sweat. After a while, I moved my hands down onto her skirt to pull it off.

She placed her hand on mine and said softly, "Not here. Not in front of my parents' house."

I had forgotten where we had parked. I thought, *Why didn't I take her somewhere else parking? How dumb could I be?*

I returned to tasting her large breasts, enjoying her sensual saltiness until she stopped me. "I need to go inside."

I got off, and she sat up. She pulled her bra onto her breasts and wiggled her blouse down. "Help me clasp the bra?" she asked. She turned away from me.

I hooked it together.

"I guess I won't see you until the fall at FSU?" she inquired.

"I guess not," I responded. "When you get to school, come to Magnolia and ask for me. Everyone there will know me and show you which room."

She nodded and leaned toward me for another long, expressive kiss. We finished, and she opened the car door. She said, "I had a really good time tonight. I'm looking forward to seeing you in the fall." She had been quiet since we started making out.

I nodded, and she turned to walk up to her house.

Chapter 12

Chloe

I met Chloe that Sunday and completely forgot Trudy. It had been a good evening with Trudy, but I did not have strong feelings for her.

I kept thinking about Chloe as I waited impatiently for the first day I would work with her. I arrived at work wearing a white shirt and black slacks and put on my red apron.

Surprised, Sonia asked, "Already here, Christopher? I wonder why? Tammie told me Christopher is already in love!" She teased, "I heard Christopher and Chloe generated so much electricity between them when they met that they caused the lights to flicker and little bolts to appear!"

I laughed. "Come on. We did not make the lights flicker."

She smiled and responded, "The girls are not in yet, but you can start grating the cheese."

My duties included pushing this extended horizontal package of mozzarella cheese through a mechanical grater to cut it up. I would put the entire grated cheese container into the walk-in refrigerator and wash and clean the grater parts.

I carefully reassembled it when I heard, "Hello, Chris."

Chloe stood in front of me. She wore the same work outfit of black slacks and a white top. Chloe was shorter than average, maybe five feet three inches. She had a shapely figure. I responded with too big a smile, "Hi!"

We both stood smiling at each other. Finally, she said, "I need to get my apron," pointing to the hanger just past me.

I realized I had blocked her way. "Oh, sorry." I moved to the side, looking at her as she walked past.

She glanced back at me as she put on the apron. She had her bandana in her hand and put that on as well. Once again, I looked into her pretty face, astonished to detect the warm glow of her skin.

"Are you going to USF?" I asked, seeking any reason to detain her.

"I will in the fall," she responded. "But I've attended the University of Kentucky for two years."

How could she be a year older but look three years younger than me? I asked, "That's a long way to go to school. Why did you go to Kentucky?"

"April, my best friend, really wanted to go there, and I liked the idea of going so far away from home. It's been great. I'll be sad to leave it."

"Why are you leaving?"

"They raised tuition, and my father says it's now too expensive. He will no longer pay out-of-state tuition, so I must transfer to USF. I'm going to miss UK." Her strong smile faded into sadness.

I felt this overwhelming urge to put my arm around her and comfort her, but I managed to suppress it.

I said, "I'm going to FSU. I like it up there as well. It's a traditional college town with a great atmosphere."

She responded, "That's the way UK was too. I have lots of friends up there now."

I had been moving closer to her as she talked. What an overwhelming pull she exerted on me. Wait, I needed to ask her something important! I blurted out, "Do you have a boyfriend?"

An embarrassed smile lit up her face. She wrinkled her nose and shook her hand vigorously, "No, no, of course not."

I followed with another question: "Are you dating anyone?" *There's no hope for me. Get it over with*, I thought.

She shook her head vigorously again, now embarrassed and excited by my questions. "No, no, not dating anyone right now."

So much suffering this past year could have been prevented with a few upfront questions. *Don't date girls with boyfriends! She doesn't have one!* I beamed at her, standing before me with her embarrassed and shy smile at my questions.

Sonia walked into this and said, "Customers are coming in. No time to talk right now."

Chloe turned and scurried to the front. She glanced back at me as she turned the corner.

Sonia said, "Christopher is in love!"

"Stop it," I said. "She'll hear you!"

Sonia laughed. "Christopher has left no doubt in Chloe's mind about his feelings. You can talk to her after work. Since we have many new people, Tammie is hosting a post-work party at her apartment. You can sit next to Chloe and talk to her all you want. Tonight, first, we need to work. It will be busy."

The crowds poured in, proving her right and keeping us busy all evening. My job involved hard, hot work, as I had to stand next to a hot oven and pull pizzas out when they finished cooking. Then, I cut them into slices and called out the customer's number for them to pick up their finished pizza. If I didn't pay attention, a pizza would burn.

The oven had a glass door on both sides. On the other side, they put the pizzas in after making them. I found myself looking through both glass doors at Chloe.

We made it through the rush and prepared to close for the evening. I had to wait until the end to clean the oven, so I usually left last. The girls finished first, and they followed Tammie to her apartment. She lived in a new complex off of Parsons just north of Clay. At that time, she lived in Brandon's only apartment complex. At twenty-two, Tammie went to the local community college, HCC, and worked full time at JB's Pizza. She seemed unsure of what she wanted to do with her life, as if she expected something else to happen. Everyone left except Sonia and me. She was responsible for locking up.

"Are you coming to the party?" I asked.

"Yes," she responded, "For a little while. It's nice to unwind after such a busy evening. I heard you ask Chloe if she had a boyfriend. Christopher, Christopher, you are so in love already. Did you ask her out yet?"

She teased me, but I had been obvious. "I have not had a chance to talk to her yet, but I will ask her out soon."

She nodded to me, and we headed to our cars.

I found Tammie's apartment, and Sonia and I met at the door. She knocked, and Tammie opened it. The three girls working up front sat in the living room, Sue on a chair, and Kelli and Chloe sat on a sofa. Chloe looked up at me and scooted to the middle to make space beside her. The other two girls looked at me expectantly.

I did not disappoint and headed straight to the seat next to Chloe and sat down. They were all drinking cocktails.

Tammie brought me one. "I made margaritas!" she said.

I took the glass from her and had a sip. "That's good," I said. "I've never tried a margarita before."

I kept trying to talk to Chloe, but all conversations were for everyone in such a small space. Still, I found myself looking at her at every opportunity. When she talked, her face constantly displayed expressive punctuation in every comment. She lifted her eyebrows, opened her eyes wide, tilted her head, wiggled her nose, puckered her mouth to make faces, threw her hands up, and opened her palms out. I had never seen anyone so expressive. Spellbound, I kept smiling at her, kept watching her. I got a sense that she enjoyed my attention. She kept looking at me when she finished talking, looking for my response to her performance and grinning.

As we talked and continued drinking margaritas, the other ladies kept asking Chloe questions. Sonia asked her, "Tell us about the bravest thing you've done."

I stiffened and interrupted, "Let's not discuss that."

Chloe gave me a curious glance.

Sonia said, "Yes, we need to hear that, as Chloe works with someone very brave here."

Chloe again glanced at me and answered, "I don't know how brave it is, but when I was in Rainbow Girls, my best friend Kelly was treated badly and passed over for an honor because she was poor, and her parents did not participate. I thought it very unfair that awards were given out not based on the girls' behavior but because of their parents. I stood up to get mine and, in my speech, I refused it and said how unfair they had been to Kelly, who worked much harder than the girls who had been recognized. That the parents should not be determining the awards. I basically told them off in front of all those adults and other girls. It was funny as most of them looked at me with their mouths open in astonishment."

My jaw dropped in amazement as I looked at Chloe.

Tammie interjected, "Wow, that took guts!"

Chloe responded, "I don't know how brave that was, but I am very loyal." She looked at me with my mouth agape and grinned.

Sonia said, "Let me tell you about Christopher's bravery."

"No, Sonia!" I exclaimed.

She laughed and continued, "Christopher is always so modest! Our Christopher was this skinny sixteen-year-old out bussing tables when it occurred one night. An obnoxious drunk customer in the dining area began shouting at his girlfriend, which he followed up by slapping her several times. Christopher intervened immediately and told him to leave her alone. This guy was huge compared to Christopher. He did not take it kindly and started punching our Christopher, who put his arms up and punched him back. This startled the guy so much that other customers had time to jump in and pull him down. Luckily a policeman was just down the street and quickly arrived to arrest this guy. Because Christopher intervened and was punched several times, they could convict this guy of assault. He had a habit of abusing his girlfriend, who never pressed charges. I will never forget when his girlfriend came inside after he was convicted. With tears falling, she thanked Christopher. She said he was her hero. That no one had ever stood up for her before him. Our Christopher is very courageous!"

I found the story embarrassing because the guy had kicked my ass and left me with two black eyes and a bruised jaw.

Chloe looked at me in wonder and said, "That was incredibly brave." She stared into my eyes.

I stared back into hers.

Sonia said to Tammie, a comment to the room, "Did you guys see lightning? I could swear I just saw it flash in here."

Everyone laughed at this inside joke except Chloe and me. She broke her gaze and looked at the windows, a little confused.

Sonia followed that up by asking me, "Christopher, Christopher, I thought you had to leave by one thirty. Too much enchanting conversation?"

I looked at the clock, and it read two. Damn, I did need to leave. I had committed to yard work for a neighbor in the morning for extra money. I stood up and said to Chloe, "I do need to leave."

Her cheeks blushed, and she nodded. "See you at work next week."

I headed out to my car in a daze and got inside. I could only think about Chloe sitting next to me. She had been so close I could smell her scent. When she looked into my eyes after that story, I wanted to sweep her in my arms and passionately kiss her.

I drove home and walked into the house and my room, dwelling on it. *How sweet would it be to kiss her? What is about her?* Something about Chloe seemed outright magical. I fell asleep and surely dreamed of nothing but her.

My alarm woke me up the following day, and I dragged myself up. Hungry, I wanted to eat before mowing the neighbor's yard. As I had some cereal for breakfast, I thought of Chloe again. *Next time I see her at work, I will ask her out. No more waiting. I've talked to her enough to think she likes me too.*

Then another word popped into my head: *special*.

I need to take her on a first date to someplace special. I can't just take her anywhere. It needs to be someplace special.

Last summer, I never wanted to go to work. It was just a job, but now I did. My next workday would be on Sunday. Sundays started slowly, and I had to be there before four p.m. I also wanted to know if I would be working with Chloe. If she worked, I would have had a chance to talk to her before we got busy. But I had yet to look at the schedule for anyone else for the coming week. Still, I prepared myself. *I'm going to ask her out. Where?*

While driving to buy me a drink at the convenience store, the radio advertised a big concert at the Tangerine Bowl in Orlando on August 5. There would be a lot of big bands: Steve Miller Band, The Little River Band, and Jimmy Buffett. It would be expensive, but it would be special. That was it! *I'm going to ask her to the concert.* I would ask early enough so I could get tickets.

Now, I had my plan and my resolve. I got to work early on Sunday, and as soon as Sonia let me in, I rushed to look at the schedule.

"She's not working today!" Sonia called after me.

She was not on the schedule today, Monday, or Tuesday. She worked Wednesday, but I was off. I kept looking. We did not work together until next Thursday! *Come on, seriously, next Thursday!* I slumped at waiting another week.

Sonia stood next to me now. "I wonder when you two are working together?" she teased me.

"Not until next Thursday, almost a week," I responded with disappointment.

Sonia laughed. "You missed all the excitement Friday night."

I asked, "What do you mean?"

She responded, "I think Chloe might be a wild girl, Christopher."

I stopped everything and stared curiously at her.

Sonia elaborated, "We stayed for a while and kept drinking margaritas. Tammie commented to Chloe that she looked younger than the other girls who were high school students. Chloe looked young and innocent. Tammie teased her, but she did not like that. Chloe told us, 'I'm not innocent. I've been with guys, multiple guys. I love to fuck, fuck, fuck.'"

I opened my mouth in astonishment.

Sonia went on, "We were all quite shocked. Chloe does look very innocent, but apparently, her looks are deceiving. She must be wild to say something like that."

I defended her, "I don't think she's wild. She seems very sweet, even shy, to me."

Sonia smiled at this and admonished me, "Be careful, Christopher. Be careful. Don't let your heart get in front of you."

I ignored her comment, but this piece of news disturbed me. I could not imagine her being wild. It did not fit her shy, embarrassed smile when I gave her attention. *No, it could not be true*, I told myself. *Doesn't matter. I'm asking her out next Thursday when we work together again.*

Sonia's comment about Friday night and Chloe kept buzzing around me all week like a pesky mosquito. I could not slap or shoo it away. Still, I did not let it bother me. It did not matter. I kept thinking of Chloe glowing with her amazing warm light. I wanted her. I liked Chloe above anyone else and would ask her out at the first opportunity.

I arrived at work early on Thursday. Only Sonia was inside. I returned to the cheese grater and started work on that while watching the front, waiting for Chloe.

Distracted, I did not see her enter, and she surprised me by asking, "Hi. How are you?"

I smiled back. "I'm great." I moved to let her access the aprons.

As she put one on, I looked back to the front. Sonia still busied herself preparing for customers. I asked Chloe, "Can I talk to you for a minute?"

She nodded yes while smiling.

"There is a big rock concert at the Tangerine Bowl in Orlando on August 5. Little River Band, Steve Miller Band, and Jimmy Buffett are performing. Would you like to go to the concert with me? I checked, and tickets are still available."

She opened her eyes wide and responded, "Yes! Yes! It sounds like a lot of fun. I want to go with you."

"Great. I will pick up tickets this week."

We stood beaming at each other. We were now dating. Sonia said something up front, and Chloe moved past me to walk up there. I turned, and my eyes followed her. When she reached the front, she glanced back at me. We smiled again at each other.

That night, I became a terrible employee. I used any trivial excuse to go up front and ask them—well, ask Chloe—a question. The crowd only trickled in, so it didn't cause any real issues though I could tell I had irritated Sonia.

Business slowed toward the night's end, and Sonia returned to talk to me. She wagged her finger at me, teasing me, "Christopher, Christopher, you still have to work no matter how happy you feel."

"I asked her out, and she said yes!" I said quickly.

Sonia smiled. "Okay. Where are you taking her?"

"We are going to a concert in Orlando on August 5. It will be a big concert and should be a special evening."

Puzzled, she asked, "August 5?"

"Yes, August 5."

"Christopher, that is over a month away. It's not even July yet."

I stood with my mouth open, stunned. I repeated, "A month away?"

Sonia laughed at my reaction and said, "Christopher is so hopeless, so hopeless." She turned and walked back to the front.

I thought, *Wait, I'll ask her out to do something else before that.* Anything else. But I realized I could not do that tonight. How stupid would I look asking for a second date before I even had the first date? I would have to wait until later in the week. I dashed to the back to check the calendar. We did not work together again until next Thursday! Who made up this schedule? Did they hate me?

Another long week and I had finally reached Thursday. It did not take long to ask her if I could talk to her momentarily. I started, "August 5 is still a month away. We could go to a movie this weekend?" I expected a quick yes.

She hesitated and anxiously said, "I can't go this weekend. It's the Fourth of July weekend, and my family is visiting Homosassa Springs."

"Oh," I responded. "Let's look at the schedule. We're both off next Wednesday."

She added, "I can't next Wednesday either. I have to go to dinner at my grandmother's house. We're celebrating her birthday."

For the rest of the week, we had to work. Recognizing reality, I said reluctantly, "I guess we'll have to wait until the following week's schedule is out."

Her anxious look disappeared, and she smiled. "Yes, we can look then."

Despite this disappointment, we worked together multiple evenings, and I spent them suspended in her orbit. No matter how busy we got, she inevitably pulled me toward her to look at and talk to her. She responded with a smile and an eagerness to speak to me. I did not attempt to do anything with her those evenings after work. Despite my assurances that she did like me, the two no's on dates had introduced some doubt, and I could not shake it. I could not handle an additional failure. What if I tried something and she refused me? I would wait until we dated.

The following week's calendar had us not working again until Friday.

Seriously? I thought. Then something else hit me. *They are doing this on purpose. They don't want me working the same nights as her unless we are busy! Come on!* I remembered Sonia's teasing and comments, but they always had an undercurrent of reminding me I had to work. I had to admit that Chloe did distract me. I would have to be more careful.

When Friday came, it greeted us with one of those hectic nights. It started busy and stayed active. I verified on the schedule that neither of us was working on Sunday but needed a moment to talk to her. We slowed down late in the evening, and she came into the back to take a quick break. I seized my chance and asked her, "Do you have a moment?"

She gave me an anxious look and nodded yes.

I did not like that look but proceeded anyway. "Neither of us is working on Sunday. Can we do something on Sunday?"

She frowned. "I'm sorry. I have to go to a family activity on Sunday."

I stood for a moment, looking at her. I said, "I'm off next Wednesday and Thursday. Can we do something one of those evenings?"

Her frown deepened. "I'm sorry," she said. "I'm not working the next two weeks starting Wednesday. I'm going to the Bahamas with my family. I won't be back till August 2."

I stood looking at her with disappointment filling me.

She added something else, "August 5 is all set for me. I already know I won't be working and have no other obligations. I'm looking forward to going to the concert with you." She smiled at me, trying to revive me.

Despite my disappointment, I smiled back. "Yes, I'm looking forward to it also. The concert starts at four, but it's a long drive. Traffic and the parking options are bad around the stadium, so I think we should leave at one thirty?"

"That sounds good," she said, and she gave me instructions on how to find her house and her phone number in case I needed to call.

Doubt taunted me, "Chloe just wants to go to the concert. She just wants to have a good time. You misread everything."

I tried to fight back, *No, no, I can tell she does like me. I can feel it.* But despite my assurances, I slumped with rejection. It would be over two weeks, almost three weeks. Still, I thought, with hope, we would go out on August 5. *We will see how this date goes.*

Chapter 13

The Date

While I did work with Chloe the Friday before August 5, I had no real time to talk to her because of the constant stream of customers. Fridays were typically the busiest night. She greeted me with a smile when I had a moment to chat. I reassured myself that she did like me. She certainly acted like it. We did reconfirm what time I would pick her up, and that was that. I would pick her up tomorrow for our date.

When I arrived, she exited her front door and headed to my car. I did not even have time to open the car door. Dogs barked in the background, so I assumed they must have alerted her. She wore a pale pink top with embroidered white daisies across the front. Her light wavy brown hair hung loose to her shoulders. Tight blue jeans hugged her hips and she wore red flip-flops on her feet. She had painted all her nails red. I had never seen her in regular clothes, only work outfits. I admired her feminine shape. She had a fantastic figure with full breasts and a thin waist. She opened the door, got in, and smiled at me. She had on eye makeup and red lipstick. The lipstick popped against her pale skin. I couldn't help but smile back, thinking, *Wow! She's beautiful.*

I started my car, and we headed out. A Florida August afternoon meant temperatures in the nineties. We had to keep the windows down because my car had no air conditioning. We talked anyway over the noise as we drove to Orlando. The drive would take at least sixty to ninety minutes.

Initially, we talked about the groups who would be there. I reviewed the concert list with her, discussing the various bands and the songs we liked. She did not know much about Jimmy Buffett.

I exclaimed, "He's the quintessential Florida beach guy! His early stuff is great! I have one of his albums on tape in the car. We can listen to it if you like here in a minute."

"Sure, that would be good," she said.

I followed with, "How about the Steve Miller Band? He was the patron saint of our cross-country team. We were all runners. Our team name was Eagles, so how could we not love a song called 'Fly like an Eagle'? We even had T-shirts made that said that."

She hesitated momentarily. "Well, I am not a fan of theirs. April's boyfriend Larry loved their music. He played their albums until I got sick of hearing them. Sorry."

"That's okay. They go last, so if we are not big fans, we can leave early and beat the crowd. I went to a concert here last year and got stuck for over an hour in the parking lot," I said.

"Sounds good to me," she responded.

"If you look in my back seat, I have a case with 8-track tapes, including a Jimmy Buffett one. You can plug that in, and we can listen to him on the way to the stadium."

She found the tape and inserted it.

The drive went faster than I expected. Leaving early allowed us to miss much of the heavier traffic. We were pulling off I-4 near downtown Orlando when the tape finished playing. She popped it out and put it in the case again.

I asked her, "You don't mind walking a little, do you? I can park toward the edge and avoid a bunch of the traffic."

She answered, "No, that's fine with me. I would rather walk than sit in traffic."

I found a lot on the perimeter, pulled into it, paid the attendant, and parked my car. The stadium stood in the distance. We locked the car up and headed down the street. She walked next to me. She placed her hand in mine, and I marveled at her small and soft hands. I looked at her, and she smiled at me. I smiled back and thought, *This is good, real good. She reached for my hand!* We walked the rest of the way to the stadium, holding hands like sweethearts. The doubts built up over the last couple of weeks evaporated. *She did like me!*

We got into the stadium and found our seats. The stage was in one end zone, and we sat opposite, so we had a clear distant view of the stage. The seats were hard with no padding.

I asked Chloe, "It's still hot. Do you want something to drink? They do sell beer."

"Too early for beer, but I'll take a Coke," she responded.

I went to the concession stand and got us two large Cokes. I handed one to her and sat down next to her.

We sat so close to each other that we touched. We had arrived early, and most seats around us still needed to be filled. We started talking, and I found myself smiling again. I focused all my attention on her. She punctuated everything she said with expressions across her face. I had never seen anyone like her, anyone else who did that. Her bright personality played her like an instrument hitting high notes with raised highbrows and pursed lips. She stretched out low notes with shakes of her head and extensions of her arms and hands. The whole thing came together into little faces she made when emphasis was necessary. She completely enchanted me. I hung on to every word. I jumped in when she paused to encourage her, as I would do anything to keep her talking. I only wanted to listen to her. I did not notice others filing into their seats. I did not hear any of their conversations. I ignored the music when the first act played and spent every moment with my eyes on her, talking to her.

My rapt attention seemed to delight her, and our conversations never wavered, never paused into silence. We kept talking. She asked me, "So you were on the cross-country team at Brandon? You must be very athletic."

I smiled at her compliment and responded, "Yes, I ran on varsity, and I was pretty good, top twenty, maybe even top fifteen in the county. Did you do any sports?"

"No." She shook her head vigorously to emphasize her no. "I was terrible at sports. I'm so bad I even got a B in my UK soccer PE class."

Astonished, I asked her, "You took PE in college?"

"Yes," she said. "It was April's idea. An easy way to get our grade points up. You need an excellent grade point average to make it into med school, but the plan didn't work. I got a B. I did find it hard to do the outside soccer part of the class. We took the course in the winter semester and were outside in shorts in the snow. I was freezing all the time. I made one hundred on all the tests, but he told me, 'You lack physical aptitude for the game. I can't give you anything but a B.'"

She mimicked his low voice with her face scrunched to emphasize his meanness. "However," she continued, now smiling. "I did once steal the ball from him. He dribbled downfield, and I managed, through sheer dumb luck, to steal the ball and kick it away. Everyone cheered for me. 'Go, Chloe, go!'" She laughed, her fists punching the air for emphasis. "He did get rather angry and ran off after the ball again. That was the lone moment of my athletic career."

We laughed together. "So it was cold up there?" I asked her.

"Yes, it snowed quite a bit the first winter. This past winter was not so bad, but it was pretty cold, with a lot of snow last year. I like that. Lexington has seasons, fall, winter, and spring. It's not like here."

"No," I answered. "We have summer and not summer, but it did snow here the winter of my senior year. The only time I have ever seen snow."

"Yes, I heard about that from my sisters. That was the same winter that it snowed a lot in Lexington."

"So you have gone to college for two years now?" I asked.

"Yes, I'll be a junior in the fall," she replied.

I said, "I just finished my first year. Did you graduate from Brandon High?"

"Yes, in 1976."

I replied, "I guess you are a year older than me."

She said, "Probably not. I'm nineteen. I turned nineteen in January."

My eyes opened in surprise. I said, "I'm nineteen too. I turned nineteen in April. How can you be a year ahead of me?"

She responded, "I went to Holy Innocents School for kindergarten and first grade. I was advanced, so they skipped me to first grade, so I've always been a year ahead of my age group."

"You must be smart to have skipped an entire grade."

She smiled at this compliment and shrugged. "I guess so. Are you a sophomore now?"

"No, I'm a junior. I took the CLEP tests and received enough credit for an entire year. I still had to take some requirements, but I finished those, so now I am a junior," I bragged.

She smiled and complimented me, "You must be very smart to get that much credit. I didn't take those tests because you must take all the requirements in pre-med. I'm going to guess you are making straight A's in college?"

"Well, I did make straight A's the last two quarters. I made one B in the first quarter. So you want to be a doctor?" I asked. She had impressed me.

"I did, but unfortunately, I got a D in physics, and you have to have such a high GPA that there is no way I can make it into med school," she replied.

"What happened?" I asked.

She related her sad story. "I took physics that semester. Denny had been assigned to be my lab partner. A really sweet guy whose father was a doctor. We always reviewed each other's lab notes before each class. He said he did not get a chance to complete his in one class. I told him to go ahead and take a look at mine anyway. Before the final, the professor called our names and said he wanted to see us after class. He sounded so serious and stern. It freaked me out. I could not understand what the professor wanted. We finished the test and went in to see him. He told me, 'You're getting a D, and Denny is getting an F. You guys cheated.' I couldn't believe this. I told him I didn't cheat, but he said, 'I saw him looking at your paper. That is cheating. There is no discussion here.'

"I could do nothing to stop him. I felt so upset that I went back to the dorm in tears. I had decided to quit college altogether! It seemed hopeless. The other girls in the dorm rallied around me and convinced me to keep going. I could do something else. They were so sweet and supportive, especially Patti May. She's also in pre-med."

As this story progressed, I took her hand into mine. I sat holding Chloe's hand. After she finished, she looked down at me, holding it. A perky grin lit up her face.

"So what are you going to do now?" I asked.

She did not remove it and shrugged. "I don't know. I'm still figuring it out."

I commiserated, "Professors can be such jerks. They act like they could care less whether you learn anything at all. They are perfect, and it is too bad for you if you don't understand something."

"I know," she replied. "You would think it is their job to teach us, but many don't care. They seem to think their job is to get rid of you."

I changed the subject and said, "So you said earlier you played soccer in the snow? Isn't it cold up there? Don't you miss going to the beach and things like that?"

She answered, "Not really. I mean, I like having seasons. It's funny how your body adjusts to a different climate. After a long winter, one day, we had a sunny day when the temperature reached around sixty. We all put on our bathing suits and went sunbathing on the roof. It did not feel cold at all. Down here, everyone would be wearing sweaters in weather like that. Though I did get the worst sunburn of my life that day."

"What happened?" I asked.

She replied, "I assumed I would not burn because I came from Florida. After an incident with my sister when I was eleven, we went to Brandon Swim and Tennis every year until I could drive. After that, I always went to the beach with my friends and always had a dark brown tan. I never burned, so I assumed the same applied, but I had not been in the sun for months. I ended up with such a bad sunburn that I blistered. The only time that has ever happened to me."

"Ouch, I have had bad sunburns too. That happened to me when we went to Wakulla Springs in May. My problem is that I'm fair, and I always burn. I turn red, then back to pale. I never tan." I said, "It's hard to imagine you tanned. You have such pale skin."

She smiled at me. "I don't go to the beach or hang around the pool much anymore. I have better things to do. It's not good for your skin anyway, too much sun."

I blurted out, "Your skin doesn't show any damage. You have such nice dewy skin."

She gave me an embarrassed grin and changed the subject. "Did I tell you about Patti May? She always talked about taking care of your skin. She was obsessed with it."

I commented, "Patti May sounds like a hick name."

Chloe continued, "She came from some tiny place up in the mountains. She was lovely, in any case. Patti May first introduced April and me around the dorm. She knocked on our door one day early in the first semester, introduced herself, and asked us, 'Do you want to party? I have a bottle of wine here, and I'm looking for someone to party with.' We invited her in, and she took it from there. She also had a problem with one of her classes, and we had to convince her not to quit. She ended up going into nursing. I'm thinking about that option too. She got engaged this past semester. I made her a present, a Groucho Marx lamp. She was a big Marx Brothers fan. I found it at some obscure store and painted it. The painting took me forever, especially getting his mustache right. She seemed to like it."

I complimented her, "That was very nice of you. It sounds like you spent a lot of time on it."

She said, "I did, but she did a lot for me. It seemed like the right thing to do."

It went on like this, continually sharing our stories, sharing ourselves. Our conversation effortlessly flowed. The only interruptions occurred when we went to the bathroom or I went to buy us something to eat and drink. I watched Chloe scoot down the aisle and then up the stairs to the common area when she took a bathroom break.

I remember thinking, *She's everything I wanted. She's smart. She's ambitious. She's independent. She's generous and sweet.* She disappeared around the corner. *Not to mention, she is absolutely beautiful. She is just beautiful.*

I had only talked to her for a couple of hours, close, talking. I had not even kissed her yet, but my feelings rose in intensity with every hour we spent together.

When she returned, we got into some of the crazy things we had seen in college. I told her about swimming in the

Landis Green fountain. She found that funny. I told her about nickel beer night and the FSU football games. We traded stories for a while until she came to the craziest one she had experienced.

"We had just won the NCAA basketball championship. I had watched the game with April and Larry at his apartment, and I was driving back to my dorm when the traffic suddenly stopped. I could hear people screaming, and then I saw this guy jumping from car roof to car roof. He landed on mine, and the whole car shook. He bounded off, and I jumped out to look. A giant celebration had closed the street altogether. I turned around to return to my car when another guy ran up, grabbed me, and kissed me. I couldn't believe it. I stood shocked as he ran off. Can you believe that? I had never seen this guy before."

I agreed, "That is crazy." I also thought *This would be the girl I would kiss.* I realized after that story that I needed to wait for better timing.

We talked through the first three acts, only taking a break to eat. Sitting in a giant cloud of marijuana smoke made us hungry. Fans had filled the stadium now, and everyone around us smoked joints. The whole stadium had a cloud of smoke hanging in the air. We did not need to participate; breathing in that cloud of smoke was making us high. When I went to get some food, I asked her, "Should I get some beer?"

She waved and gestured at the smoke. "I don't think we need it. After all, we both already have the munchies."

I laughed at this and headed to the concession stand. I got us both burgers and some more Cokes. We ate the greasy burgers, sipped our drinks, and resumed talking.

She mentioned, "I can cook much better than this. It's not very good."

I replied, "It's just greasy. So you cook?"

She responded, "Yes, I cook all the time. I used to cook meals for my family in Brandon in high school. I cooked most of my meals in the dorm too. I think my food is better. Everyone seems to like what I make. I know my desserts taste delicious." She smiled at me.

I remembered a girl I dated in the spring named Shelly and how good the food she made tasted. I wondered if Chloe cooked as well as she did.

Chloe asked me, "Do you cook any?"

"No," I replied. "I eat out or at the cafeteria. I can heat a can of barbecue chicken or make myself cereal or a sandwich, but I don't think any of that counts."

Chloe made a face, scrunching her nose, and said, "No. That does not count as cooking."

I changed the subject and asked, "You graduated in '76. Wasn't that the year Brandon had a streaker at graduation?"

Chloe laughed. "No, our boring graduation got rained out and had to be rescheduled for the following morning. I supplied the only excitement."

I asked, "You supplied the excitement?"

She grinned at me. "Well, the boys were allowed to wear maroon gowns, and the girls had to wear white ones.

A group of us thought that was very sexist. The girls are wearing virgin white! Seriously, offensive! Why couldn't we wear maroon also? So we planned to get maroon gowns and wear those. They even warned anyone who did that would not be allowed to graduate. I did not care because my parents were not attending. So I wore a maroon gown. The other girls chickened out on me. I tried to keep a low profile until the principal called my name. I had a short haircut then, allowing me to blend in with the guys. When I arrived, he kept looking at me, the list, then at me again. I almost laughed until he handed me the diploma and shook my hand."

Amazed, I exclaimed, "Wow! That took courage. I'm impressed you did that."

She made a face and shrugged as if she had done nothing important.

We kept talking to each other right through the start of Jimmy Buffett's portion when I recognized one of his big hits, and I said, "You know we did come to a concert. We should probably stop and watch a few of the performances."

She laughed but agreed. We paid attention to two, maybe three, songs, and then we were back looking at each other, talking to each other. I did not care about the concert. I just wanted to hear her. We talked right through his set and then into the final one when she looked up and said, "If we are going to leave early, we better get started. I think he is almost done."

I looked around. Most of the crowd stood up, cheering. We were the only ones sitting. I nodded at her to go, and we headed out, holding hands.

As we reached the car, she said, "I enjoyed tonight. I have never talked to a guy like this before. You are very, very easy to talk to. I really enjoyed tonight." She gave me a sweet smile and got into the car.

I got into the car, looked at her, and asked, "Do you want to go out next weekend? I know a disco in Tampa where we could go dancing. I want to take you someplace else special."

She responded, "I would love to do that. I want to go out with you again. It will be nice to get dressed up and go out someplace."

I felt so elated that I hardly heard her next question.

It came so quietly and softly. "Can I ask you something else?"

"Sure."

"Why did you ask me out and not April?"

Puzzled, I asked, "I don't understand what you're asking me."

"I've been best friends with April for over three years. We roomed together and went to lots of parties together. Boys always go after her first. I know she is prettier than I am, so I understand. No boy has ever gone straight for me in three years of doing things with her. She stood there when we first met, but you only talked to me. You only went for me. You only asked me out. Why?"

I responded, "I think you are much prettier than April."

She retorted, "No, I'm not."

I looked at her intently now. "I *think* you are much prettier than she is, and I found you much more attractive. There is something I like about you." I shrugged. She responded with a shy, embarrassed smile and added, "I'm glad you did. I'm delighted you did."

I scarcely remember driving home. We did not talk as much as we were tired after a long day, but I kept looking at her. She always returned my glances with a smile.

We managed to have an uneventful drive back. We had left early enough to miss the heavy traffic. When we arrived at Chloe's house, I parked my car and walked her to the door. We held hands for that short walk. She turned to me with a big smile and reached up to kiss me. She pressed her lips forcibly on mine, so hard against me that it did not feel like a kiss. She then turned and quickly walked in the door.

I thought about that kiss as I returned to my car and drove home. I understood what she meant. She meant to tell me she enjoyed our date, liked me, and wanted to give me a big passionate one, but that kiss…it had been wrong. Not emotionally, but technically incorrect. I then thought of something incredible. *Maybe she doesn't know how?* I thought, *How can that be?* But her kiss showed she did not know how. I thought of her comment while drunk at that after-work party to Sonia and Tammie. I thought about what she had said tonight, that she had never talked to a guy like that, and what she said about April. I realized this was a shy girl. She was just inexperienced. It did not matter, as the defective kiss had the desired effect.

I thought she did have feelings for me. I could not stop envisioning her all the way home. After I got into my house and undressed, I settled into my bed. I closed my eyes and remembered how she looked, that warm light that glowed from her skin, her expressiveness, and her smile.

It had been an incredible first date, an incredible day, but it had also been a long day. I soon fell asleep with her image floating around in my head.

CHAPTER 14

What is It?

Chloe's image still floated in my head when I awoke. I saw her as I made myself some cereal and ate breakfast. She hung around as I dressed and accompanied me as I pushed a mower down the street to mow a neighbor's lawn. As I walked up and down, trying to focus on cutting, she appeared at every turn, every straightaway.

I did not eat anything for lunch. I usually ate at every opportunity, but not today. I needed to study for a test tomorrow. I had reached finals week for my summer quarter, and the most demanding tests had been scheduled for Monday. I would have to drive to USF's main campus in North Tampa from my parents' house in Brandon early in the morning. My most complicated test would be held in philosophy. As I sat in my room trying to study, I looked up, and she sat beside me, shyly smiling. I looked at her image as if she was present.

I waved my hand at her as if to dispel her and said, "I need to focus. I need to study. Not now."

She shook her head. "No, you invited me. You want me here."

It went like this for the next hour. I would review my notes and focus on memorizing essential facts, but I looked up to hear her talking, smiling, and saw her amazing face. She sat right next to me.

"Stop it!" I commanded myself. "What is it? You will see her again soon. You have another date. It went extremely well. Why are you thinking about her all the time? Stop it!"

But I did not stop. At dinner, I hardly touched my food. I had no appetite. When my brothers or parents talked, I barely responded. I had entered a haze, enveloped not by smoke but by that warm glow that emanated from her.

I went out for an evening run. Despite it being hot and humid, I pushed myself hard until sweat soaked me, and I struggled to catch my breath. I would drive it out of me. I kept going, but when I finished and stood in front of my house, panting, trying to recover, I thought only of her.

I tried again that evening to study and review my notes for both tests. I tried to force myself to focus but constantly shifted my attention back to Chloe. I lay down on my bed. A strange ache pulsed deep within me. I asked myself, *What is it? What is wrong with me?* Exhausted, I tried to sleep but imagined Chloe lying in my arms, snuggling against me.

I wanted to smell her, kiss her, hold her. This longing overwhelmed me, and I descended into a fever. I could not dispel it, and the heat kept me from sleeping.

When the morning came, I gathered myself up. Exhausted, I tried to shake off this groggy, sodden state. I doubt I slept an hour or two, and the sleep did not revive me, as Chloe seemed to fill my very dreams. I staggered out after putting on my clothes. I needed to drive to school to take my tests. I did not eat breakfast. I didn't care about food.

I wandered into my first test, still in a haze, trying desperately to focus on the task. I tried to keep my attention on the questions, remember my notes, and enter the correct answers. Chloe always intervened and pulled my attention gently toward her. I finished one test and staggered into the second. It went no better.

When that ordeal passed, I slumped back into my car. I had straight A's going into these exams. I knew I had just blown two of them. I didn't care. I thought of her the entire way home.

It went this way the next day and the day after that. Luckily, the last two exams were easy, or I would have blown them.

The sense of relief after my Wednesday afternoon final exam did not last. Now that the quarter had ended, I spent all my time thinking about her. I surrendered to it. That haze of hers engulfed me. Everything not Chloe dissolved until I drifted on a sea of her. My life revolved only around her. From the moment my eyes opened to the dead of the night, I could only think of Chloe. Every thought, every desire, every impulse centered around her. I asked myself again, *What is it? What is this obsession?*

Looking at her image in that haze, she beckoned me, and I realized I would be with Chloe that night. I could stand close to her and talk to her. We would be working together.

I arrived at work early, still in her haze. I went to the back and put on my apron. When I turned around, she stood smiling sweetly at me. I know my entire face lit up with joy. The wind had dissipated all the haze, and now I basked in sunlight, her light. My happiness showed on my face, pouring out of my eyes and my smile. I was with her.

We talked quietly to each other. She told me, "I got a new dress. I'm going to wear it on our date Saturday. I think it's very pretty. I think you will like it."

"I'm sure I will. I'm sure you will look great in it."

Standing so close, an urge to pull her into me, abandon everything, and kiss her overwhelmed me. Sonia said something in the background, and I managed to restrain myself. I leaned toward her but stopped from reaching my hands out for her. It took all my willpower.

While working that evening, I danced around the oven when a song I liked played on the jukebox.

Late in my shift, Sonia caught me doing this and returned to talk to me. She said, "What is it that has Christopher dancing? I've never seen you like this. You dance at the oven. You dance back to wash dishes, and you dance around Chloe. What has made Christopher so happy?"

I shrugged in response.

Sonia gave me an appraising smile. She said, "Go up and talk to her. Have her make you something to eat. You two can take a break."

I bolted upfront. Chloe gave me a knowing smile. I made my request, and she responded, "I will make it extra delicious for you."

When I finished cooking the small personal pizza, she came into the back to talk to me as I ate. Chloe's presence stayed my thrashing. She made all my turmoil disappear. For the first time in four days, I ate something. I devoured the pizza. "You did an amazing job," I said between mouthfuls. "It's delicious."

She responded with a grin. "I see you like dancing."

"I do," I said. "I'm looking forward to dancing with you."

The time that night roared past. The last four days had felt like months, and these six hours passed like minutes. The closing time came. We parted, and she was gone. When I got home, I couldn't recall what I had done for those six hours. I don't remember cooking a single pizza or talking to anyone else. I spent the evening gliding around Chloe. Only she filled my memory, crowding everything else out. What she wore, what she said, how she smiled. I lingered over each one.

She provided the remedy for my suffering, and the calm of seeing her stayed enough that I soon fell asleep for the first time in four days.

But when I awoke the following morning, the calm had passed, and that thick haze of hers enveloped me again. I only thought of Chloe. It became worse because the evening before refreshed her image. Someone had suddenly focused a camera on a blurry view of her at a distance, and now I relished her in stunning detail. I cherished her facial expressions, her scent, and her voice. I did not eat. I did not think. Barely functional, my fever returned and soaked me with sweat. I spent another miserable, sleepless night in the heat of my delirium.

The following day rose no better as I did not eat or run. I did nothing but lay around in my bed, lethargic, physically sick, and hanging on to every bit of memory of her. I examined them again and again in my head. I sat next to her and listened to her talk. I lingered over that astonishing face with her expressions dancing across it. I held her hand in mine. This continued for hours until the day became night, and the time for sleep came again.

Sick of this ordeal, I interrogated myself, *What is it? What is wrong with me?* I had been heartbroken by girls before and experienced the agony of failure. I had made love to girls before and suffered when it ended. *But our date was successful! Why do I hurt so much?* I had nothing but success, yet I was wrecked.

Chloe sat close to me, smiling. She leaned forward and whispered, "You know what this is."

"No! No! I don't know!" Something popped into my head. Only one word formed. "No! No! How can it be?" I refused to accept it. I refused to say it.

She smiled and whispered, "It's okay to admit it. It's okay to say it."

Despite myself, it came from my lips: "Love."

She whispered, "It's okay to say it"—she paused, leaning close—"to me."

I closed my eyes, and her vivid image faded, leaving me stunned. I could not deny it because I had spoken the truth. I had fallen hopelessly in love with her, with Chloe.

Chapter 15

I Leap

My confession released me, and I fell asleep for the night. The following morning did not greet me with the same torment but with something new. I felt an intense excitement, an energized expectation, and anticipation for our evening date.

When I arrived to pick her up, she did not rush out this time. I parked my car, walked to the front door, rang the doorbell, and waited. An older gray-haired man with big ears answered the door.

I told him, "I'm here to pick up Chloe. My name is Chris."

He looked me up and down and stuck out his hand. "I'm Chloe's father."

I shook hands with him. He had a large hand and gripped mine as if to intimidate me.

He released my hand, turned, walked away, and shouted with a gravelly voice into the other room, "Chloe, your date is here."

Three younger girls poked out from around the corner in the other room and looked at me. They resembled Chloe but clearly, younger sisters. I looked back into their curious faces. They looked behind themselves, parted, and Chloe walked out between them.

The dark blue dress she wore looked expensive and fancy, with a white ruffle that ran at an angle from one shoulder across the top, leaving the other shoulder exposed. The length stopped just above her knees, and she wore a pair of black high heels. She had done her hair into a bun on top of her head, focusing attention on her incredible face, in full makeup with bright red lipstick. She saw me looking at her and smiled. I had been smiling since I had seen her. All her sisters behind her grinned at me.

She turned and introduced me to her sisters, "Carrie was the same height as Chloe, Cathy, a plump girl several years younger, and Charlotte, a pale redhead the youngest of all.

She opened the front door, and we walked to my car. I had the sense that someone was watching us from the windows. I opened the car door for her.

As she got in, she asked, "Do you like my dress?"

"Yes! You look amazing!"

She flashed a big smile and said, "Thank you. You look very nice also. I haven't seen you dressed up before."

I smiled at her and told her. "It's a bit of a drive to the other side of Tampa. It will take us about forty-five minutes." I started the car and pulled out. We chatted about work and the weather, and I asked her, "All of you have names that start with C?"

She wrinkled her nose. "Yes, my father's name is Carl, and my mother's name is Carol, so they thought it appropriate that we all have names that start with C."

I chuckled. "Kind of funny you are dating a guy named Chris."

Chloe laughed as well. "I did not really think about that, but yes, it is kind of funny."

"So all of your sisters turned out to meet me?" I asked.

She made a face. "Yes, everyone at home thinks they should be in the middle of Chloe's business, including my sisters."

I responded, "I met your father also."

She looked at me carefully. "Did he or my sisters say anything to you?"

"No, only hello."

She said, "Good, I've been getting the third degree all day. It's ridiculous. I've lived on my own for two years. They can't treat me like a little kid."

I agreed with her. "Parents, siblings, what can you do?"

She changed the subject. As we talked, I realized all my torment and agony from this past week had vanished. Happiness replaced it.

When we arrived and went into the disco, no couples danced. We found a table, and I got us two cocktails. We sipped our drinks and quietly talked to each other. We leaned toward each other as we spoke. A slow song came on, and I saw two couples walk to the floor. "Do you want to dance?"

She nodded. "Yes!"

We walked out to the floor holding hands. I put my arms around her, and she snuggled close to me. We danced slowly, swaying in a tight circle, embracing each other. Despite her heels, she seemed so small in my arms. I looked down into her face, and she responded with a bright smile.

Her eyes sparkled; her whole face shined. I bent down to kiss her. She pressed her lips hard against mine again, too hard.

I stopped and said quietly, "Too hard. It needs to be soft. Let me show you. Let me kiss you." I leaned back down and pressed my lips tenderly on hers, then released and looked at her.

Her eyes widened with surprise, and she showed delight on her face. She moved up to me to kiss me. We did it long and slowly as she demonstrated she now understood. We tenderly kissed again.

The song ended, and they played a fast disco song. We stayed on the floor and danced. She now became diffident, unconfident in how she danced. She looked around to check what others were doing. I just watched her. I didn't care how they danced. After the song ended, she indicated she wanted to return to the table. We held hands on the way back.

We leaned toward each other like conspirators concealing the conversation from those around them. She told me, "I'm not a great dancer. At least, not in this style of disco. I don't know the moves."

I responded, "I thought you did well. I don't know any steps either. It's just about having fun."

She nodded. "I took dance classes for years until my junior year in high school. I love dancing. Those structured classes teach you all the steps. I don't feel comfortable with the fast disco dances." She looked at me intently. "I like slow dances. Can we do all the slow dances?"

I grinned. "I love the slow dances," I said with enthusiasm. "We can do them all!"

Each time a slow song came on, we walked onto the floor and danced tightly intertwined. I pulled her hard against me, liking the warm feeling of her body. Inevitably, as the dance wound down, we kissed again. As I leaned down, she pushed up on her toes, her eyes wide with anticipation. She sank into the kiss by closing her eyes. She learned fast, and her kisses had become soft and sensual. Maybe I only noticed my desire, but I detected a longing in hers.

We had a second and then the third cocktail. Sometimes we leaned toward each other and kissed openly at our table. She took a break to go to the restroom. I turned and watched her walk. Her blue dress hugged her shape, displaying her hourglass figure. I thought she looked incredibly good. As she returned, I thought, *No, she looks beautiful.*

A slow dance greeted her as she returned, and we headed out to dance again. As we embraced and swayed together, I looked down into that shining face. I said softly, "You are so beautiful. You are incredibly beautiful." I had never given such a compliment to any girl before. I had told them they were cute, pretty, and attractive, but I had never told a girl before she was beautiful.

I saw the excitement on her face, even a thrill, but she shook her head no and said, "No. I'm not."

I did not expect this. I did not understand it. *Did she reject my compliment?* I emphasized again, "I think you are so beautiful, so absolutely beautiful."

Again, she shook her head and responded, "No, I'm not beautiful."

I stared at her in surprise. It never occurred to me that she would refuse my compliment. She pushed herself up and kissed me, and I returned it. I did not repeat my praise. I didn't say anything else, and I let it go.

We continued dancing until after one, and the crowd had thinned. We agreed the time to go had come. We headed out with my arm around her shoulders and her arm around my waist. I opened the car door for her, but before she got in, she turned to me to kiss me again. She kissed me long and sensually—a French kiss, tasting each other, hungry for each other.

I walked around the car and got in behind the steering wheel. She had scooted to the middle to sit next to me. I put the key in the ignition and looked at her. "I know a good place in Brandon where we can go parking. It's quiet and secluded. No one will bother us there." The car sat in the dark, the only light coming from a few dim lamps in the parking lot.

The darkness partially obscured her face, but she grinned. She nodded and said, "Yes, let's go."

I started the car and headed out.

She rested her hand softly on my leg.

This location sat behind an elementary school in a wooded area in Brandon. In those days, they did not enclose the whole school in fencing, and I could pull into the parking area. Woods covered the back half of the school's property. I could pull through the parking lot onto a short dirt road and drive into the woods. The trees obscured my car so no one could see it from the road.

Once parked, we turned to each other. We made out with longing, and we kept at it. Chloe leaned back and lay down on the seat, and I lay on top of her. When we paused for breath, I reached under her for the zipper on her dress. She leaned up so I could find it. I pulled it down as far as I could. We both sat up. She wiggled her arm out, and we pulled her dress down to her waist, exposing her bra. I put my hands behind her, seeking to undo it. I fumbled around, trying to find a way to open it.

I said to her exasperated, "Some father of daughters must have invented bras. They are so damn hard to get off."

She laughed and said, "There is a clasp in the middle. Just unhook it."

I found it, and the bra fell, and we lifted it off her. The clouds had cleared, and moonlight streamed through the trees, filling the car with light.

I looked at her breasts in that moonlight and admired their beauty. Each breast had a perfect round shape with large pink nipples that covered over a third of the breast. They had that same dewy, glowing skin. I thought, *Not even Playboy playmates have breasts this beautiful.*

She lay back down, and I pulled my shirt off and lay on top of her. I gently sucked her nipple on one with my hand on the other. I pressed my nose against her skin and inhaled her scent. She smelled better than anything I had ever known. I sucked on her nipples, tasting her. Her smooth skin tasted as wonderful as her scent.

I moved from breast to breast, enjoying one then the other. I lost all sense of time and made love to her breasts. She said nothing but caressed me with one hand on my head. When I took a break, I moved up, and we kissed long and hard again. Then I again returned to her breasts. I did not think anything as we did this. I just acted with her, on her.

After several hours, she said to me softly. "It's getting a little hot, and I'm thirsty."

I moved off, and she pulled her dress up but did not put her bra back on. I put my shirt on, and we both got out.

The air outside had cooled, and the breeze blew gently through the oak trees. The moonlight streamed down and splashed across her face. I stood close, stared straight into her eyes, and said, "You are so amazing. I can't stop thinking about you. I think I'm falling in love with you."

She opened her eyes and mouth wide with shock. She swallowed when she closed her mouth, and her eyes blinked as she stared back at me. A slight smile now appeared. She said nothing. We stood staring into each other's faces. I said nothing. I don't know what I expected. I had not planned this, and even now, I did not think. It just came out.

After a while, I said, "I know a twenty-four-hour convenience store nearby. We can go and buy some Cokes."

She nodded, and we both got back into the car. I pulled out and drove to the convenience store. I went inside and got two bottles of Coke. We opened and drank them in the car, looking at each other. Neither of us had said a word since we left the woods. She seemed to be searching for something to say but came up empty. She glanced at the clock in the car, which read four thirty.

Finally, she talked, and this earnestness was displayed on her face. "I had a good time tonight. I thoroughly enjoyed dancing with you." She smiled ruefully. "I especially liked the kissing and…" Her voice trailed off, and she shrugged, blushing.

Relaxed, I smiled at her and said, "I enjoyed spending an amazing evening with you."

She responded, "We don't have to go somewhere so expensive next week. We can go to a movie or grab a bite to eat. I can pay my part. I know this place, and the concert was expensive. You don't have to pay for everything. We can look at the schedule tomorrow since we are both working and can pick the time for our next date. We don't have to wait for next weekend. The first night we are both not working, we can go."

I nodded at her, entranced by that expressiveness that always danced across her face. I had my first thought in hours. *There is no thinking, no falling. I am in love with her.*

Chapter 16

Net?

I dropped her off just before five and did not reach home until after five. As I drove home, I wondered about my behavior. Why had I not tried to pull her dress the rest of the way off? I was confident she would have let me. It never occurred to me. I kept going for the last couple of girls until we had sex or they stopped me. I did not even try with Chloe. *Maybe love does change everything.*

That evening my mind emptied as we parked. I just sat there with her. I only wanted to be against her and needed her against me. I struggled to describe my feelings. I hesitated. I just wanted to love her. That explained it. I only wanted to love her. I did not need anything else. I thought about her standing in the moonlight with her beauty shining through. My feelings for her overwhelmed me, and I told her. I can't believe I told her. *She must think I am insane.* It didn't matter because I told her the truth. *I do love her.*

I had no problem falling asleep and woke up after one p.m. I remained calm as I got up, dressed, and searched for something to eat. I thought how strange it was that things had changed so much in a mere week. I spent last week in complete agony—and now, calm. I didn't know why I remained relaxed.

The kitchen clock read two. I had to be at work by four. I thought about her and how we would determine our next date together. Yes, I smiled at that. I had thought of us as *we*.

I did not arrive early this time, but just before four. I glided across the parking lot as if I floated while thinking about the girl I would meet on the other side of that door. Chloe was there before me, and already she had on her red apron and red bandana. She had been waiting for me. She greeted me with excitement on her face. I motioned to her, and we walked back together to the schedule.

She said, "I already looked. We are both off Tuesday and Saturday." She paused and looked at me intently.

"That works. Tuesday is good, just two days from now."

Her smile deepened at that comment. She studied me intently as if she had searched my face for something.

She said, "We can meet here on Tuesday. I can drive my car here, and we can go out to eat and to a movie. No need for you to pick me up at home."

I nodded. "Okay."

"Saturday, you can pick me up again at my house."

I nodded again.

She said, "We can figure out where to go on Saturday when we are on our date on Tuesday."

Sonia said something in the background. We both looked up at her. She asked, "What are you two conspiring about? I see you leaning so close to each other." She smiled at us.

Chloe blushed and walked back up front.

After she had walked out of hearing range, Sonia asked, "So you and Chloe are dating?"

I said, "Yes, we are. Just planning our next dates."

She replied, "I made sure both of you had off next Saturday again."

This surprised me. "Thank you!"

She raised her finger and wagged it at me. "Christopher might be in love, but at work, he works."

I grinned at her. "Yes, yes. I will be good at work."

She returned my grin. "I'll be watching you two."

The customers came steadily all that evening, so we only had a little time to chat. When Chloe got a break late in the evening and went to the back, I had a chance to tell her what Sonia had said.

She blushed and frowned simultaneously. "You mean everyone here knows we are dating?"

I said, "Uh, yes. It's a small place."

She looked around. "I guess that's okay." She then looked at me and, with a slight smile, said, "I don't think it's me wandering away from their post. I've noticed you often come up front when I'm working."

I shrugged. "I plead guilty. What can you do when you're in…" I paused and did not finish.

She opened her eyes wide with excitement. She said, "I'm on the early shift this evening. I'm not closing, so I'll see you on Tuesday at six." She stepped closer to me, and we kissed. My gaze followed her out the door.

I arrived before her on Tuesday and parked in my usual spot by the highway away from the building. I got out and stood next to my car. This small boxy red car whipped into the parking lot from the road. It turned and pulled in next to me, and Chloe got out. She drove a small square red Fiat. The car had been painted a bright red except for a white roof. I had to laugh. The small vehicle fit her with its unusual but attractive style.

She asked, "Are you laughing at my car?"

I responded, "I can't help it. It suits you. Small and agile, but attractive."

She grinned at me as she walked closer. When she reached me, she stood on her tippy toes to push up to me. She gave me a soft, full kiss.

When she stopped, I exclaimed, "I'm thrilled to see you too!"

She had dressed casually in shorts and a T-shirt with flip-flops. She then gestured toward her car. "Do you want to take my car or yours? I don't mind driving, but I do drive fast."

"Okay, let's take your car then."

We returned to her car, and she unlocked her side, got in, and unlocked my door. I climbed in and thought, *Hmm, this is a small car. It would take a lot of work to park in this car. Maybe this is a mistake.*

She looked over at me. "Seatbelt on and be ready!" She looked at me more intently and, leaning toward me, said, "It's not a good car for parking, but we can still kiss a lot in it."

I leaned toward her, and we kissed to prove her point.

After we parted, she said, "Let's go to Dog N Suds. I love their root beer and hot dogs."

Brandon had few dining options in those days, only a few fast-food restaurants that served hamburgers or pizza. We got all the pizza we could already stand from work.

She backed her car out and headed over. I would describe her driving style as zippy. We zipped out. We zipped down the highway. We zipped into the parking lot. We ordered our hot dogs and root beer. She got a hot dog loaded with chili and all the fixings. I got mine plain except for mustard and ketchup. We both got root beers.

After we ordered, she asked, "Only mustard and ketchup? You are not a very adventurous eater. You should try mine with the chili. Delicious!"

I tried to change the subject. We discussed food during the many hours of talking on our first date. I found out she liked to cook, and I liked this trait in Chloe. But as we spoke, I realized she had no fear of cooking or eating. An adventurous girl, she seemed to have tried everything. I found it intimidating. I ate boring stuff. I ate junk. I had never attempted anything more exotic than pizza or Taco Bell. Her comment on the hot dogs showed that she had decided to work on this with me. I made excuses about the chili, but she would not accept a no. I would have to try it.

The root beers came in frosted mugs, and they did taste delicious. I tried her chili dog and thought it didn't taste bad.

She showed her pride at this breakthrough. "See, there are lots of good things to eat. You just have to try them!" As we finished eating, she said, "We have a little time before the movie. We can talk a little. I must tell you that after the movie I have to go home. I can't stay out late tonight."

Disappointed, I nodded at her.

She smiled. "We can smooch during the movie and in the parking lot afterward before I have to leave."

I had discovered she liked to kiss.

She leaned toward me, and we kissed again for a long time. After we parted, she asked, "Can I ask you something?"

"Of course!" I replied. I wondered if she would ask me about what I told her Saturday night.

She asked, "Am I your girlfriend? It is our third date, and we have a fourth one planned."

This question surprised me. "Yes!" I said. "You are my girlfriend."

She smiled and responded, "You have not asked me, though?"

I asked, "Will you be my girlfriend?"

"Yes!" she exclaimed, leaning to kiss me.

I thought, *What is this all about?*

She leaned back and said, "You are my first boyfriend. I've never had a boyfriend before."

Another surprise that I found shocking. "Really?" I asked.

She explained, "I have dated guys, but typically only one date. I didn't want to go out with most of them again. You are the first guy to take me out three times!" She threw her palms up for emphasis.

Still finding this hard to believe, I asked her, "So you have only dated a few guys, just once each? You didn't date anyone in high school?"

Chloe said, "I have always been extremely shy. I never even talked to any boys until I got into college."

"You don't seem very shy to me."

She grinned, shrugged, and pushed her head toward me to emphasize her point. "My first boyfriend is very easy to talk to!" She puckered her lips, and I pressed mine on hers for a quick peck. She then asked, "How many girlfriends have you had?"

This question stopped me for a minute. I hesitated, not sure how to answer this. It depends on how you define it. I confessed, "I guess about half a dozen."

She opened her mouth wide and exclaimed, "I'm your seventh girlfriend!"

I laughed at this reaction and hedged, "Well, probably my fifth or sixth girlfriend. I mean, many of them we only dated for a little while. Only a couple were actual longer girlfriends."

She asked a follow-up question, "By a little dating, you mean you dated more than three times?"

"Yes, all of them I dated at least five or six times."

She nodded and said, "Well, that explains it."

"Explain what?" I asked.

"Why you're such a good kisser! You've had a lot of practice!" She raised her eyebrows and tilted her head forward to punctuate her comment.

I started to laugh, but she leaned to me again. I met her, and we had another long, lingering kiss.

After she pulled away, she pursed her lips into a rueful smile and made a face. She exclaimed, "Yes, you are a really good kisser!"

I held off an intense desire to say, "I love you!" I did not want to scare her. I thought it, though, as I sat smiling at her making a face at me.

I changed the subject and talked about Brandon High School, what cliques we belonged to, and who our friends were.

She said, "You know, I think we met once at Brandon when I was a junior."

I responded, "I don't think so. I would have remembered meeting you."

She smiled brightly at my response but continued, "I sat in the car and didn't get out. Camilla was driving."

I stared at her. Surely, she did not mean the same Camilla.

She continued, "She told us she needed to stop by a boy's house. She bragged that she broke his heart but had to break it up with him because he was getting too serious, but this boy still loved her. His parents loved her, and everyone in his family loved her. She stopped the car and got out when she spotted him running near his house. He seemed annoyed.

He didn't want to talk to her at all. He kept looking to escape. She chatted with him briefly, got back in, and said, 'See! He still loves me.' We looked at her and thought she was crazy. I'm pretty sure that guy she stopped was you." She now grinned at me. "Were you Camilla's boyfriend?"

I nodded in embarrassment. "Yes, I have to admit I was Camilla's boyfriend. We met in the spring of eighth grade, and she was my girlfriend until the end of ninth grade when *I*"—I paused to emphasize the I—"broke up with her. She did not take it well, but her rollercoaster emotions exhausted me. She would break up with me every two to three weeks and then get back together. I couldn't take it anymore."

She laughed. "So you were her boyfriend!" She teased me, "She was two years older than you? Pretty impressive!"

I smiled back. "I guess I have a thing for older girls." I gestured at her.

Still grinning, she nodded at me.

I did not tell Chloe I broke up with Camilla in response to my parents' problems. After what happened between them, I vowed never to let a woman hurt me like that, and I concluded that Camilla breaking up with me over every little issue made her untrustworthy.

Chloe interrupted this thought by insisting on splitting the bill at the restaurant. "We are girlfriend/boyfriend. We should split costs as we do things together."

I did not argue and even admired her independence.

The theater sat in a small standalone building and only showed second-run movies that had been out for a while. I don't even remember what was playing on the screen that night. We strolled in holding hands, and I headed to the back row. I looked around. Only a few other people were in the theater.

Once we sat down, I put my arm around her, and she snuggled close to me. The lights went out, and they began playing previews. She turned to me, and we kissed. We spent the entire movie making out. Passionate, tender, French, any kissing you can imagine. Chloe wanted to experiment and try them all out. I even made a small hickey on her neck because she wanted to experience that. We departed with my arm around her shoulders and her arm around my waist.

She checked the time when we reached her car and said, "Plenty of time for more smooching!"

After we finished and she drove me back to JB's Pizza, she kept smiling. I floated with only the seatbelt holding me down. It had been another fantastic date.

As she drove us back, we talked about Saturday. She said, "I want us to go to a restaurant in Tampa. I want you to try something new."

I asked, "What do you mean, new?"

"Just someplace you haven't been before. Trust me, you will like it, and it will be good for you to broaden your food horizons." She smiled at me as she said that.

Apprehensive, I could not tell her no. "Okay, I'll try it."

She continued, "You must come in when you pick me up Saturday evening. My mother wants to meet you." She made a face.

I replied, "Okay, I'll come in on Saturday."

She pulled into the parking spot next to my car and rechecked the time. She leaned toward me and said, "We have time for a little more smooching!"

So I responded to her enthusiastically, and we spent the last minutes of the evening passionately making out.

We would work together again on Thursday and Friday before our date on Saturday. I would see her every day of the week except Wednesday. I also considered visiting JB's Pizza to visit her that day but realized I needed patience. Yes, she had become my official girlfriend and displayed enthusiasm at every opportunity. She even initiated most of the kissing. She liked me a lot.

But I found myself asking the question. Did she love me? I told myself to calm down and be patient. Because you leaped off the cliff does not mean she will jump with you. You shocked her, even scared her, but I thought I also thrilled her. I tried to push this question out of my mind. I thought about how I had almost told her again. I needed to control myself and wait a while. She needed to get to know me. Good thoughts filled me with joy over being with her, but I also kept thinking about that question. Yes, I did imagine saying it to her again as she stood bathed in moonlight and hearing her response "I love you too" come back. But she didn't say that, and a ripple of doubt eroded my calm.

I did not have any doubt when I saw her on either Thursday or Friday, and no doubt came from her. She eagerly greeted me daily by motioning me to the back for a hello kiss.

I complied with pleasure. She closed Thursday with me and asked me to walk her to her car. I did so, and she took my hand. We turned to each other when we reached her car and began making out. She did it with enthusiasm, passion, and even longing. I returned it with as much love as I could push from my lips.

"I can't stay too late," she said, and she parted reluctantly, and we drove off to our homes.

The next day, Chloe started work two hours after me. I was getting the cheese ready in the back when Sonia returned to tease me. "Christopher is so, so in love with Chloe. He and Chloe kiss every chance they can now."

She smiled at me, and I shrugged with a yes.

"I wonder," she said, pausing, "does Chloe love Christopher?"

My mouth dropped open with astonishment, and I turned to look at her. How did she know what I was worried about? Did the girls talk? Did Chloe say something to some of them?

Sonia's smile turned kind, and she told me, "Christopher has a big heart. That always wins the girl in the end. Chloe did ask me a funny question about you, though."

I asked, "What?"

"She asked me if you were honest."

I stared at her. "What did you say?"

"I said you were sincere. I told her Christopher is one of the good guys with a big heart and just needs the right girl to open it up." Sonia grinned at me. "I told her she should grab you with both hands and keep you."

I opened my mouth and exclaimed, "You did not say that!"

She laughed. "Somebody has to help Christopher! I wonder what Christopher said to Chloe to cause her to ask such a question?"

I blushed.

Sonia studied me. "You need to be patient with Chloe, however. She has had a hard life at home." Sonia turned and walked off.

I stood thinking about Sonia's comments and remembered that Chloe's best friend April worked there. Maybe Chloe discussed what I said to her. Had I been exposed? I did not like that thought. Every word had been meant for Chloe alone. I had leaped without thinking and had not even bothered to check for a net. But why did Chloe ask Sonia that question?

Chapter 17

Doubt

When Chloe arrived on Friday, I wanted to talk to her, but we only had time for a quick smooch. She walked in with all smiles. As I cooked, I kept looking at her again through the glass doors of the oven. When she caught me, she grinned. Customers kept us busy that night without time to talk or chat. Chloe did not close that evening, so we had no opportunity to talk after work either. She left after sneaking in a quick goodbye kiss to me and confirming when I would pick her up on Saturday.

She told me to wear something decent on Saturday but not too nice. I struggled with that for a while but decided on a collared shirt and a pair of jeans. When I arrived at her house to pick her up, I stood outside for a second, studying her home. I had not paid attention to it before. The house had been built of all brick construction in a ranch style so popular in the 1970s and sat on a large piece of property with giant oaks everywhere. I looked both directions from the door and assessed the massive size of her home, about four times the size of mine. Chloe and I both acted like poor students. But entering the house of someone with this much wealth made me feel a little uncomfortable.

I rang the doorbell, and her youngest sister, Charlotte, opened the door.

She grinned at me and ushered me toward the living room. She said, "Chloe is waiting for you inside here. She's all ready to go!"

I followed her directions and walked into it. Chloe sat on the couch next to an older woman I assumed had to be her mother.

Chloe stood up as I approached, and she smiled at me. She gestured toward her mother and said, "This is my mom."

I approached her and said, "Hello, I'm Chris."

She said, "Nice to meet you, Chris. You look familiar. Have we met somewhere? Maybe I know your parents?"

I responded, "I don't think my parents know you, but I don't know. I cook at JB's Pizza, and many people have eaten there. Maybe you saw me there?"

"Maybe," she said as she continued to study me. She then looked at Chloe and me and asked, "Where are you guys going tonight?"

I looked at Chloe, who answered, "We're going to a Chinese restaurant and then to a movie. We might stop for a Coke or a snack afterward, so don't wait up for me."

Her mother looked at Chloe and then back at me. "Don't stay out too late," she said, looking at me.

I nodded, and Chloe stood up and told her, "We need to go, Mom." She grabbed my hand.

I told Chloe's mother, "It was nice meeting you."

She nodded at me with a smile.

As we approached the door, a couple of her sisters squealed, "Have another *good* time, Chloe." They both laughed as we walked out the door.

Chloe said nothing to me until we were in the car, and I drove it around the corner from the house. She said with emphasis, "The hickey was a terrible idea! My mother saw it and gave me a hard time about it." She lowered her voice slightly and mimicked her mother, "'What are you doing? You need to be careful! Is this boy trustworthy?'" She returned to her normal voice. "You would think I was freaking fifteen, not nineteen!"

"I'm sorry," I said.

"Don't be," Chloe responded. "I wanted it and thoroughly enjoyed it. I don't care what they think! I'm an adult and can do what I want with my boyfriend!" She made a face as she said this. She smiled widely and instructed me, "Stop at the stop sign and kiss me properly."

After I stopped, she greeted me with a long, lingering kiss.

"That's better," she said, smiling afterward.

"So, we are going to a Chinese restaurant?" I asked.

She flashed me a smile. "Yep! There's a dish I think you will like."

Skeptical, I said, "I've never had Chinese before. I don't know."

She responded, "Don't worry, nobody will poison you. You will like it, trust me."

What could I say to that other than, "Okay."

She directed me toward the restaurant off Fletcher Avenue in North Tampa near the University of South Florida. I found it in a small bland strip center. Other than a Chinese letter sign, it could have been any store. We pulled into the parking lot and entered the restaurant. The hostess sat us in a booth facing each other and gave us menus.

I perused the menu with alarm when Chloe said, "Look at number B5. I think you will like that one."

It read, *Butterfly Shrimp with Bacon*. I studied the description and replied, "That does sound good."

She smiled, "Try it. You'll like it."

I ordered that, and she ordered some items that didn't sound appealing. It featured many vegetables in some sauce over rice. When our food arrived, the meal delighted me as they wrapped bacon around the fried shrimp and served it over rice. After eating some shrimp, I complimented her, "You were right. It's delicious. I like it."

She beamed at that and offered me some of her food.

I hesitated, but I agreed to try a small bite. I admitted, "It does taste decent."

She smiled some more at that. "I will help you eat better food," she said.

I nodded and commented, "I do like this restaurant."

After we finished our meal, split the bill, and reached my car, she leaned over to me and said, "Smooch!"

Grinning, I complied. We watched a movie at University Square Mall, located near the restaurant. We found the theater crowded with many eager to view this recently released movie. We ended up in seats in the middle of the theater in the middle of a row. I put my arm around her, and she snuggled up to me.

She smiled ruefully and said, "I want to watch this one." She looked around. "It's too crowded for other things."

I nodded and agreed we would watch the movie. After the movie, we walked out to my car, holding hands. Once in, we turned to each other and started to kiss long and slow, full of hunger for each other.

After a while, we paused for breath, and she said, "Let's go parking."

"Yep! Let's go," I said, grinning in response.

I headed my car to the exact location we used last week. We arrived at almost two. Again, we had the place to ourselves.

I parked the car in the trees, and she said, "Let's roll the windows down this time."

I agreed, and we both rolled our windows down. A breeze entered the car, making it appreciably cooler.

We poured ourselves into each other with enthusiasm. I kissed Chloe's neck and hands when we parted for breath. I put my hands on her T-shirt and began to lift it. She helped me, and we pulled it off, revealing her bra. She unclipped the bra herself and removed it. Her large breasts hung with that dewy pale skin and large pink nipples. She lay back on the seat, and I lay on her. I moved my mouth and hands between her breasts. After a while, I moved my hand to her jeans. I unbuttoned them. She did not resist and sat up to wiggle them off. She removed her panties as well. I took my jeans off, and she looked at my erection. She lay back down, and I climbed on her again, kissing her lips, our bodies full against each other, and tasting her breasts.

I got ready to put it inside her when she paused me with her hand. "Condom?" she asked in a soft voice.

I just looked at her. "I forgot to bring one."

She frowned at this and asked, "Can you sit up?"

I did, and my erection dropped. She said apologetically, "I think we need a condom. I'm not on birth control. I don't want to get pregnant."

"You're right," I responded with disappointment. "I had not planned on anything."

She smiled. "Well, I am your girlfriend now."

Her directness surprised me. I sat staring at her. She looked beautiful sitting there naked. Those amazing breasts, her dark bush against her pale skin. I motioned toward her bush with my hand. "I can taste you, at least. Do something for you."

She considered this. "Hmm, well, I guess so."

She started to lie back down, but I stopped her.

"I don't think we can make it work logistically like that. I have to lie down, and you climb on top of me."

She nodded. We moved around, and I lay down. She climbed on top of me and moved up to my face. I first kissed her, put my tongue on her, then inside her. She tasted sensual, silky, warm, and wet. I looked at her face in the moonlight, but she showed no expression, just impassiveness. I kept moving my tongue around until she suddenly tensed. I focused on that area. I moved my tongue rhythmically like a windshield wiper, back and forth. Chloe slightly adjusted herself and rocked gently. After a while, she gasped and lifted. Chloe moved off, and I sat up. She looked down at my erection, then back into my face but said nothing. She had no expression on hers.

I asked, "Was it okay?"

She nodded yes.

We sat for a while, looking at each other. Chloe picked up her bra and began getting dressed. I started putting my clothes on. Once dressed, she opened the door and stepped out. I walked around the car and hugged her tight.

A strong breeze blew through the trees, rustling the branches. The moonlight streamed down through the trees and bathed her in the light. Overwhelmed again by her glowing beauty, all restraint fell away, and I said, "I love you."

Her impassive expression changed to surprise and excitement. She searched my face with her eyes opened wide but said nothing.

I waited, but when no response came, I said, "I'm thirsty. Let's go find something to drink."

She nodded, and we both got back into the car. She stayed quiet, and I did not talk either. We drove in silence to the convenience store. This time a thought popped into my head. *She doesn't love me.* I felt doubt roar to life inside me. Tormented and restless, I admonished myself, *You said you would wait to tell her again!* But holding her so close in the moonlight, my feelings spilled out, and I told her.

At the convenience store, I bought two Cokes again. We sat silently, drinking them. The time had almost reached four.

She said shyly, "That's the first time anyone has done that to me."

I said, "I've only done it once before this. I did it okay?"

This time she opened her eyes wide and nodded her head up and down vigorously. I thought she even blushed a little. She finished her Coke and leaned toward me. "Kiss me again," she said softly.

I leaned into her, and we kissed, long and slow. My doubts stilled, and I swam in her scent, taste, and soft body against mine. I sunk into it, filled with her.

We lost track of time and only checked again when the time had reached five.

"You better take me home," she said.

When we arrived, she looked at her house and saw the light inside. Concern displayed on her face. She kissed me goodbye, got out, walked to the door herself, opened it, and entered.

Chapter 18

Frustration

The following day I slept till almost two. After I got something to eat, I thought about last night. I admonished myself, *Why did I tell her again? You said you were going to wait! Give her some time!*

I knew why I did not wait. I saw Chloe in the woods, bathed in the moonlight, and my feelings erupted. I did love her, but her lack of response worried me. She liked me, but did she love me? I did not know. She had said nothing.

We both worked again that day. I got to work early, and she stood outside waiting for me.

"Wait," she said. She motioned me to her car.

I got in, and she leaned toward me to kiss me. She gave me another extended one, and it seemed full of affection. After we finished, she told me she had gotten into a heated argument with her parents. Her mother confronted her when she got home and told her how upset she was that Chloe had stayed out till five a.m. Her father started yelling at her.

Chloe told me some of what they discussed. "My parents didn't trust me and accused me of being wild and out of control. They even wondered if I had already gotten pregnant. I told them to stop being ridiculous. I had lived independently for two years, and they tried to force me back into being a child. It wasn't fair to me. They wanted me to stop dating you, but I refused and told them I would keep dating my serious boyfriend."

I felt hope when she said this.

She said, "After a while, I started crying, and my father left. My mother then agreed that whom I dated was my decision, but I didn't have to stay out so late. So, we compromised on one a.m. She also decided I could move into a dorm at USF instead of living at home." She looked up at me. "Lots of drama at my house today, but I'm used to it."

I hugged her to comfort her and said, "We need to get on inside."

She nodded, and we headed to work. We went back to put our aprons on and check the schedule. We both were off again next Saturday. Unfortunately, one or both of us worked every other day of the week, leaving us only next Saturday.

I told her, "I can't believe they gave us Saturday off again."

She responded, "I asked Sonia to do that. I told her that we were serious and needed a day off together each weekend."

I looked at her in surprise at her use of the word serious again. I liked that word from her.

She then said, "Unfortunately, I had to agree to go with my parents to Homosassa Springs on Labor Day weekend."

She shrugged. "Sorry. I had no choice." She did not hide her disappointment.

I responded, "Well, we have next Saturday at least. Labor Day is two weeks away."

She nodded and turned to walk back up to the front.

We worked together three times, but Chloe closed only on Wednesday. I walked her to her car at the end of her shift. We immediately fell into each other's arms when we reached it. We made out as long as she could dare timewise. When we parted and I headed home, I again thought she filled her kisses with emotion for me.

I wondered again whether she put love in them. After each time we spent together, I would sift through, searching for clues about how she felt. I found only positive things. She always wanted to be around me and showed her affection for me. I did not think of this when we were together, as everything else disappeared in her presence. My happiness and love for her swamped every other thought or emotion.

On Thursday, she brought brownies and rushed back to give me one. I bit into it and looked at her with wonder. "Wow!" I exclaimed. "They taste fantastic!" I took another and ate it as well.

She reminded me with a smile, "See, I am a good cook."

I nodded at her and thought again about what a marvel she truly was.

She added, "I want to make you something delicious. I want to cook for you, but everybody is in Chloe's business at my house. No hope there." She raised her palms toward the ceiling to emphasize her point. She asked, "Do you like pineapple?"

"Yes." I nodded.

"Good! I make a delicious pineapple upside-down cake. I'll bring you some next week."

I smiled, and she leaned toward me and kissed me. She did not even look around at first.

Later in the evening, we had time to discuss our date on Saturday, and she told me, "Let's do Dog N Suds again and a movie out here. That will leave us time for other activities before I have to be home by one."

I smiled at this comment. I leaned close to her and said quietly, "I got what I needed. I have some in the glove compartment, and I'll have some in my pocket."

She grinned at me and said, "Oh! Also, put a blanket in your car. I think it will be more comfortable on a blanket outside."

I agreed. The evening ended for Chloe at ten, and she closed it with a long goodbye kiss to me in the back.

We had little time to talk on Friday because we were slammed with customers. The business was always heaviest on Friday. We did manage a quick kiss before she left.

Afterward, as I thought about our date on Saturday, I instructed myself, *Don't tell her again. You need to give her some time.* I needed a cloudy night without moonlight. Chloe, in the moonlight, leveled my defenses, and I blabbed everything. Every inhibition would fall away in her presence. All doubts and anxiety disappeared until only my happiness remained. I needed and wanted to be with her. My love erupted out of me. It came out in my smile, my rapt attention when she talked, my embrace, my kissing. It poured out of me toward her. She overwhelmed me, and I wanted to tell her how much she meant to me. I did not intend to pressure or push her. I just loved her. My emotions always spilled out.

When I pulled in to pick her up on Saturday evening, she opened the door and came out. This surprised me as it meant no inspection tonight.

She said, "They all went out to eat in Plant City. No one is here right now." She followed that with a smile as she leaned toward me for a kiss.

I embraced her, and we kissed for a long time. Afterward, I started the car and noticed she wanted to say something.

"What is it?" I asked her.

She frowned and made a face. "I have some bad news."

I turned and looked at her.

She continued, "My period started, and it's heavy. I want to wait on any sex until after it finishes."

"Oh." I thought that was terrible news.

She added, "We can still make out, however. Lots of smooching." She gave me an encouraging smile and puckered her lips.

I laughed. "Yes, that's always good with you."

She beamed at this and nodded her head vigorously. As I pulled out, she said an enthusiastic "Me too!"

I said, "You don't seem very shy. Always eager to make out!"

She laughed, "Well, I worked very hard on my shyness, but back in elementary school, after I transferred to Seffner Elementary for second grade from Holy Innocents, I did not talk to anyone for the first two years I went there. I refused to talk. Only if a teacher directly asked me something did I talk."

"Wow."

She said, "When I got up to my teen years, I decided I needed to do something about my shyness, so I started to work on it. I joined every organization I could, like Girl Scouts and Rainbow Girls, forcing myself to interact with others. Also, it gave me an excuse to be out of the house. Of course, those clubs all involved talking to other girls, but it was a big step in the right direction. I slowly got better and better. I still feel uncomfortable talking to someone I don't know, especially guys, so I never went on a date until my freshman year in college. Even all my initial dates were set up by other girls." She stopped and looked at me. "I was serious that you are really the first guy I could ever talk to. You are the first guy I dated that was not set up by someone else."

I looked at her, and her cheeks blushed.

She said, "I'm really happy you did."

I decided to ask her about something I'd heard several times now. "Are things that bad for you at home that you want to be away?"

She replied, "Absolutely. My parents fight all the time, and my dad is always trying to force me to do things. He thinks he can yell at me enough, and I'll cave. Years of that have made me very resistant to anyone bullying me. I refuse to bend to pressure. That infuriates him, and he yells some more. The easiest solution is not to be there. That's also why I have worked since I was old enough. It keeps me away from home."

"I'm sorry it's so bad," I said. I reached over and pulled her to me to hug her.

She replied softly, "Thanks." She squeezed me tight.

When we parked at Dog N Suds, she quickly kissed me before the waitress arrived. We ate and talked. That incredible expressiveness flowed across her face punctuating everything she said, enchanting me. She raised her eyebrows, tilted her head, shook it, lifted and flung out her hands, made little faces, puckered her lips, and even blew me a kiss once. I sat spellbound, rapt in her performance, willing to spend hours staring at her.

When we got to the theater, I parked in the far corner, away from other cars. We poured ourselves together and passionately kissed. We had thirty minutes, and we meant to use it all. Only the clock managed to break our embrace. We walked into the theater, my arm around Chloe's shoulders and hers around my waist. Another almost full theater, but we did find some space in the back. As soon as the lights went down, we kissed again. Yes, we did watch some of the movie. Okay, we hardly watched any of it. Maybe five minutes and only when someone coughed and commented about getting a room. I mean, seriously, Chloe wanted to kiss. All I could do was respond with "Yes!"

When the movie ended, we ignored our heckler and walked outbound with our arms around each other. When we reached the car, we were still parked alone with no one near us. We fell back into making out.

Only when we took a break to breathe did she say something. "Should we go parking?"

I looked around and saw no one in sight. "Well, considering we have limited time, this does work here. We don't waste any time driving."

She grinned at me, and we fell back to kissing. We did it with open mouths, tasting each other. At other times we did it with tenderness. We pushed ourselves together, and we caressed each other's hands. The warmth of her body radiated against mine. Her scent poured over me. I thought of nothing. I sat with her, lazily floating in her, everything else but her forgotten.

After another break for air, she checked the clock. "Oh, it's past midnight. We need to start heading back." She moved away from me and back to her seat.

I said, "Let's buy a Coke on the way back. I'm thirsty."

She agreed with a coy smile. "Kissing makes you thirsty."

I responded, "A lot of kissing does make you very thirsty!"

She chatted happily as I drove us to the store. She kept laughing as she talked. I desperately wanted to look at her, but I had to keep my eyes on the road. She informed me, "I asked Sonia to make sure we both have the same weekday off next week so we can go out. We can't go out next weekend because I'm leaving with my parents."

I had forgotten about that. "Good idea," I said.

She said, "You know it's only a few weeks until you return to Tallahassee."

My expression dropped. Somehow, I hadn't even thought about school. I had to leave in only a few weeks, and she would be down here, not up there with me.

When I pulled up to her house, no lights were on except on the front porch. She studied the house, then leaned toward me. "Kiss me goodbye!"

I complied, and we locked together for a long time.

When we parted, she smiled sweetly. "See you tomorrow. We can check the schedule to figure out next week."

I nodded. On the way home, I went through the evening. It had been another incredible date. Chloe swept away any doubt, any reservation. There seemed to be no doubt from her either. We fell together at every opportunity. I wondered if I'd ever had a girlfriend who wanted me like she did. I had to admit that a few had shown a lot of affection for me, had kissed me with intensity, and wanted me to kiss them every chance. I thought of Colleen. She always seemed so happy to see me.

But with Chloe, I felt something more, some greater intensity from her. I had not had a girlfriend who initiated most of the kissing. She always wanted to do it with me. Since I had become her first boyfriend, maybe she made up for all those years without one. I benefited from years of pent-up demand. I laughed at that, but I wondered. Perhaps it all happened in my head. I made it seem more intense because I had fallen deeply in love with her. I didn't know. Did she love me? She had not said a word about my feelings or hers. She did call me her serious boyfriend. That thought brought me hope.

I then thought of something else: I would be leaving in a few weeks for college. I looked forward to that last year, but now it filled me with dread. Chloe had changed everything, and I had filled my life with her. I did not want to leave without her.

On Sunday, she beamed at me. What a lift I got seeing her. Every concern fell away, and I let my smile speak.

Chloe kissed me intensely and afterward took my hand. "Let's check out the schedule!"

When we looked, we both worked together on Tuesday and had Thursday off.

"Perfect!" she said. She looked at me, narrowed her eyes, and pursed her lips. "Thursday, everything should be good."

I understood what she meant and smiled at her. We decided to go to a Chinese restaurant again on Thursday and then go parking. She reminded me about the blanket. This planning and her intent pleased me.

On Tuesday at work, she sealed her greeting with a kiss. She carried a small paper plate in her hands. When we got to the back, she told me, "I baked you some pineapple upside-down cake."

She handed me a fork, and I took a bite. I looked at her with astonishment. "Jesus, Chloe! Maybe you should be a chef. This tastes so good."

She laughed and asked me, "So you like it?"

"Yes, I love it."

She smiled ruefully at that comment. "That's one of my best dishes. I came up with the recipe myself after experimenting. I make it extra gooey."

I looked at her with admiration.

She closed that evening. Afterward, we sat in my car, embraced, and made out for a long time. I thought, *Damn, this girl loves kissing me.* I left with hope, and I looked forward to Thursday. I told myself, *Control, control. Don't blabber it out to her. Just control yourself.*

When I picked her up on Thursday, she immediately came out of the door before I opened mine. She dressed casually in shorts, flip-flops, and a T-shirt with a square cutout over the chest, showing some cleavage. I liked that shirt. She looked terrific in it.

The door behind her opened, and her three sisters stepped into the doorway. They waved to me, and they all laughed when I waved back. Chloe glanced back in time to see them before they shut the door. She rolled her eyes.

She told me, "I got a boyfriend, and all anyone can talk about in the house is my boyfriend. Geez, they are all driving me crazy!" She smiled at me and leaned in to kiss me. She whispered afterward, "I do have to please my audience."

I laughed and started the car.

After we turned the corner away from her house and reached the stop sign, she asked me, "You have everything you need, right?"

"Yes! Including a blanket in the back seat."

She looked into the back seat then at me with a coy smile.

I cannot remember what we talked about at dinner. Typically, in Chloe's presence, time stops, and I am only in the present. But I had something else to look forward to tonight, and I was anticipating that.

We got to the car at almost nine p.m. I worried we would be too early in pulling into the parking area. Someone might see us. It had been a great spot so far, so I reassured myself it would be fine. Still, when we arrived, I waited to pull in only if the street had no other cars. I saw no other vehicles, drove back, and parked. I noted that the evening had been cloudy, and no moonlight streamed through the trees.

She unbuckled and leaned toward me, and we kissed for a while. She kissed me so tenderly that I thought she conveyed love in those kisses. After a while, she said, "Let's try the blanket."

I nodded, and we got out and laid the blanket on the ground next to the car. She sat down, and I sat down next to her. She lay back, I leaned into her, and we kissed again. This time we kissed with more passion, even urgency. I moved my hands onto her and started to lift her T-shirt. She stopped me, and we both sat up. We pulled her shirt off, and she undid her bra herself. I looked at those amazing full breasts hanging there and immediately reached my hand and gently cupped one.

She smiled at me and reminded me with a comment, "Your shirt."

I removed my hand and took my shirt off.

She lay back down, and I pressed my face to her breasts, putting my mouth on her. I loved how she tasted, but even more than that, I loved pushing my nose close to her and inhaling her incredible scent. It always provoked my insatiable desire for her.

I moved my hands to her shorts, and again she stopped me, and we both sat up. She removed her shorts and panties, and I stood up and removed my shorts and underwear but took the condom out of my pocket before taking my shorts off. I stood holding an unopened condom in one hand while erect. I looked down at Chloe. A breeze blew through the trees rustling the branches and leaves.

It must have moved the clouds as the moonlight streamed and splashed across her. I looked at her. Her naked skin glowed in that light. I thought, *How can anyone be so beautiful?*

I knelt close to her, and I said it. Not once, not twice, but three times. "I love you. I love you. I love you."

She stared at me intently, and a touch of distress flashed across her face.

This shocked me, and doubt rose in me. I admonished myself, *Shut up, idiot!*

She looked down at me. My erection had dropped. She looked back into my face, hers now impassive again. She lay back down, and I climbed on her again, tasting her breasts, inhaling her scent, but now a line of desperation ran through it, and I did not respond. Instead, I worried about her look of distress and her failure to say anything.

I knew I had ruined it this evening and stopped. I sat up and looked at Chloe. She studied me. She sat up and embraced me. She gave me a long kiss, full of want. After she finished, she looked at me again. She then leaned away from me and began putting on her clothes. I got dressed as well. Chloe said nothing about what happened, and I did not explain. I knew why it happened, but it did not stop my frustration. I said, "Let's go get something to drink."

She replied, "Okay, I'm thirsty."

Inside the car, I realized midnight had passed. We had been parking for a while. Time always stopped when I kissed her, and tonight it all had stilled until I told her and shattered it. I had broken the spell.

We chatted a little about meaningless things to avoid discussing what happened. When I arrived at the convenience store, I bought us two Coke bottles and took them to check out. I looked at the clerk, and he smirked at me. I realized he recognized me. He was a heavyset guy with long greasy hair.

He said as he checked me out, "Back again, huh? You must like this parking lot." He smirked.

I ignored his comment and did not respond, but I took my change and left. I realized he must have noticed us making out. When I kissed her, everything else disappeared, including our surroundings. I got in the car with the two Cokes and handed one to her. I told her I would pull into another place down the street because the clerk had said something about us sitting in the parking lot. She nodded to show she understood.

I found a small real estate office a few blocks down with no lights on. It had parking on the side as well. I parked and turned to look at her.

She took a sip from her Coke. "I enjoy going out with you. I like spending time with you. I feel happy when we are together. I had a great time tonight." She continued, "I'm sorry I have to go with my parents this weekend. I would rather stay here and be with you. I won't get back until Monday night. I told Sonia to put me on the schedule for Tuesday and next week. I also told her to ensure we both had off next Saturday since that would be your last weekend before you head to school. I'm going to miss you."

I looked at her closely. Her eyes had become moist with tears. I could not handle that, and I leaned toward her, pulled her against me, and kissed her. I closed my eyes this time as I did not want to see her tears. We kissed for a long time, and it felt so different. She seemed to be putting her feelings in it for me.

Chapter 19

The Last Date of Summer

I spent all weekend frustrated because of what I had done. Why couldn't I keep my stupid mouth shut? We would've had sex! I was ready, and she was ready, but I had to go and blurt out my feelings. I kept thinking of that distressed look on her face. Why did she have that expression? What did it mean? I shrank from the worse interpretation: *She does not love me.* I told myself she felt something for me. She told me that afterward.

I hectored myself repeatedly, *I had to keep harassing her. I had to keep pressuring her. Leave her alone!* I defended myself. I knew I had not meant to pressure her. I thought of her lying on the blanket, naked, glowing in that moonlight. *Of course, you told her. You do love her.*

Thankfully, I worked all weekend, so I had a chance to break from this internal debate each day.

When I arrived Sunday, Sonia said, "I took care of you and Chloe. You will be happy."

I checked the schedule and saw we had off next Saturday. Chloe would be closing with me on Wednesday and Thursday. Sonia had taken care of us. She now stood with a kind smile on her face.

"Thank you," I told her. "The schedule works well for us."

She responded to me, "I know you will miss her. She is going to miss you as well. I was wrong about her, Christopher. She is a very nice girl; she has real feelings for you."

I looked at her. *How does this enigmatic woman know what worries me?*

She said, "Have faith. You will find a way to make it work despite the distance."

I asked her, "The other day, you commented on Chloe having a hard life at home. What did you mean by that?"

She asked, "Chloe has not said anything to you?"

I shook my head no. "Just that her father yells a lot."

Sonia said, "I heard all of this from April. Apparently, Chloe's parents have been on the brink of divorce for several years. The only hold-up is he is concerned about the money."

I replied, "I know lots of people who are divorced. It's not that terrible."

She frowned. "April says that when Chloe's father drinks, he blames her for all his problems. He is not a good man. He cheats on his wife and does not even hide it." A customer came in, and Sonia turned and headed up there.

What she said disturbed me. I spent the rest of the weekend worried about Chloe. It added to my concern that I was leaving the following weekend. I was leaving her here.

We had our date on Saturday, and I would leave on Sunday. Classes would not start for a week, but I had committed in the spring to give Bill a ride up to FSU when the dorms first opened in the fall. I could not renege on it now. Then, I thought of something else. This last date must be memorable.

I spent all day Monday trying to think of something special. I thought of concerts. I had already done that. How about going to the beach and spending the sunset together, followed by dinner? I knew a restaurant on St. Pete Beach where my parents had taken me on vacation. I thought of another place I had read about in the *Tampa Tribune*, the Kapok Tree restaurant in Clearwater. It was rated as one of the best restaurants in Florida and famous as a tourist attraction. Chloe would find it an extraordinary place. We would have to dress up, and it would take all evening, but I also knew she would see it as an excellent way to conclude our summer. Yes! That location would work perfectly.

I knew Chloe worked Tuesday night, so I went and talked to her. I knew I needed to take every chance to be with her before I left. I surprised her, but she greeted me with enthusiasm. She walked up to the counter and kissed me across it. Delighted to see her, my smile spilled out. I told her about my idea for a memorable date at the Kapok Tree. She liked the idea. She had heard of the restaurant but had yet to eat there. She enjoyed dressing up and told me about a new dress she had purchased herself that she would wear for me. We did not talk long since she had to work, but even those few moments lifted me.

On Wednesday night, she greeted me when she came in with a warm, full kiss. This sense of my impending departure weighed on her as well. We talked about it some.

She said, "I'm going to miss you when you leave. Will you write me letters? I will respond. We can at least keep in touch that way."

I replied, "Yes, of course, I will write back—anything to keep in touch. Maybe you can come up later in the fall and attend a football game with me. You could see my dorm and meet my friends."

She answered, "I would like that, but I'm not sure my car can make it. I wonder how much it would cost to fly?"

I responded, "I don't think it's costly. I know kids from Miami who fly back and forth. I can pick you up at the airport and check you into a cheap motel."

"I'll look into it," she said. "I do have some money now that I'm working."

We discussed the date on Saturday, and she mentioned that her parents had been there. They thought the restaurant had excellent food, and the décor amazed them.

When we finished closing, we walked out together, hand in hand. She got into my car, and we kissed with intensity. Surely, she put her feelings again in them. I tried to prolong our embrace as much as she dared, but eventually, she had to go, and we departed.

We repeated this on Thursday, talking together at every opportunity and after closing, spending the remaining time in each other's arms, making out in my car. Sunday was rushing upon me, and I kissed her with the full intensity of my feelings to express them before I departed. When I thought about these evenings, I thought she showed nothing but affection for me. Surely, she did share my feelings. Still, she said nothing, and I did not ask.

I grew up in an environment where no one ever discussed their feelings. Even when my parents came to the brink of divorce and reconciled. No one said anything. They acted as if nothing had ever happened. I finally asked my mother about what had happened a month after they got back together. She told me, "You don't need to worry about it. It was just a misunderstanding. Everything is back to normal. No need for us to talk about it." She cut me off immediately after that. There were times after their problems that I outright hated my mother. But as time passed, I suppressed it and all memory of what had happened. I learned never to talk about it or my feelings.

I knew I should have talked to Chloe, but I believed she thought I pressured her. I did not ask because I feared she might pull away. Better to be unsure than to receive a no. While doubtful, I always had hope. It wasn't like we had a problem. We got along well. Other than not saying something back to me, she acted like I was the greatest thing ever to happen to her.

I put on my silky disco shirt, best pants, and shoes for our date. Chloe did not rush out when I arrived, and I walked up to the door. Her sister Cathy answered and let me in with a grin. She ushered me into a formal living room with lush blue carpeting and heavily stuffed blue upholstered sofa and chairs.

Chloe's mother came and told me, "She's almost ready. I think you will like her dress."

I smiled at her mother and thought she seemed friendly.

She said, "I hear you're going to the Kapok Tree."

I responded, "Yes, I'm looking forward to it. I hear you have been there."

She answered, "Yes, several times. The food is excellent, but explore the place, including the gardens. It is spectacular, with lush foliage, beautiful fountains and statues, and a kapok tree. We thoroughly enjoyed each time we went. It's a special place to go."

I looked at her and thought, *Is her mother complimenting me?*

When Chloe entered, she wore her hair up. I had indicated to her several times how attractive she looked with it up, and I know she did it for me. She had black eye makeup on and wore bright pink lipstick. Her dress dazzled me as it hugged her shapely body. She wore a dark red and black plaid dress with a ruffle on the bottom and a white collar at the top. A tan vest covered her chest with a ribbon tied across her waist. The entire thing looked quite formal. She finished it with black high heel sandals with thick heels. She had painted her nails pink as well.

I gave her my dazzled smile. "You look great! The dress does look good on you!"

Her mother was still sitting there, but I didn't care. I wanted to sweep Chloe into my arms and kiss her. Chloe beamed at me and motioned me to follow her to the door. I said goodbye to her mother, who smiled at us.

"Have a good time," her mother said.

We walked to the car holding hands. We got in the car, and we kissed in the driveway. There was no need to drive around the corner first.

Chloe asked, "So you do like my dress?"

"Yes, you look beautiful in it."

She smiled again and told me, "Thank you." She looked at my clothes and ran her hand across my silky disco shirt. "I see you are slick again this evening."

I looked at her quizzically.

"Slick like your shirt." She made a face at me, and I realized she had teased me. She said, "My boyfriend, Slick, is taking me to someplace special tonight!" She grinned at me and raised her eyebrows.

I laughed.

It took us over an hour to drive there. As we drove, I told Chloe, "Your mother acted rather friendly to me tonight."

She smiled. "My mother likes you and says you have nice teeth."

I asked, "Nice teeth?"

"Yes, my mother has this weird thing about teeth. You have nice teeth. Also, my mother is delighted I have a boyfriend. Since I was a teenager, my mother has always encouraged and pushed me hard to date. She always wanted to know why I didn't have a boyfriend. It was very uncomfortable for me sometimes as my mother would buy me these wild clothes and expect me to wear them."

"What kind of clothes?"

"Super short shorts, tops, and dresses that show lots of cleavage. I sometimes think my mother must have been quite wild. She always pressured me to dress sexy. It didn't work, as I refused to wear anything I thought was inappropriate. My mother says I am very stubborn." She made a face and stuck her tongue out.

When we arrived, it took a while to find parking, as cars filled the lot. We followed the signs to check in, where a long line met us. It took almost twenty minutes to check in. The hostess told us it would be another forty minutes before we would be seated. She gave us a map of the grounds marking a spot where you could buy a cocktail to take with you as you explored the gardens.

We headed first to the cocktail bar and ordered the planter's punch. The drinks came in fancy glasses with the Kapok Tree logo and flowers on the top. We sipped our drinks and decided to first look at the tree. We followed the map and the signs until we exited into the gardens and found our way to it. It towered over a small wall that guarded it against curious tourists. The trunk had to be five or six feet across, and the tree spread high and wide. Looking up, I could not see the end of it.

I said, "Wow! That's a big tree."

Chloe nodded in agreement and added, "My mother said red blossoms cover it in the spring."

We then explored the gardens, sipping our drinks and holding hands, two sweethearts enjoying each other's company while playing tourist.

Everywhere you looked were lush plants and classically themed statues. One garden had an entire row of statues interspersed with fountains. We strolled, admiring the place. We stopped in front of a small pond with a massive fountain in the center.

Chloe turned to me. "This is a special place. Thank you for taking me here." She then leaned toward me, and we kissed.

Thunder rumbled in the distance. I looked at the sky and saw the dark billowing clouds headed toward us. It thundered again but closer. I indicated the darkening sky and told her we should go inside before it started raining.

We walked hand in hand, exploring the interior. We even entered the gift shop. They called our names, and we returned to the hostess station.

They sat us in a dining room filled with hanging plants, lush foliage on one of the walls, and fancy chandeliers suspended in the center. Thunder boomed outside, and the rain fell so hard it pounded the glass roof that extended over part of the dining area. We ignored the rain, but it gave the atmosphere a sense of closeness as if even the world outside pushed us together. We each ordered another cocktail and studied the menu.

Chloe decided on stuffed flounder with crabmeat. I decided to order the seafood platter so I could try several things. I asked her, "Should we order an appetizer?"

She answered, "No, we should save space for dessert. My mother said they have delicious desserts here."

"I like that plan." After we ordered, I said, "It feels so strange that summer is already over."

Chloe said, "Let's not talk about that. Let's enjoy this evening together."

"Well, what did you use to do in summer?" I asked.

She replied, "We went to Brandon Swim and Tennis for most summers starting when I was eleven. That's why I became so tan. It was boring. How much time can you spend swimming?"

I said, "We never went to Brandon Swim and Tennis. Too expensive. My mother used to take us to Lithia Springs once or twice a week before she started working. I loved going there. It felt so cool floating in the springs with the water welling up beneath you."

"We used to go to Lithia Springs, too, until my sister almost drowned. Maybe we met each other there," she said.

I responded, "That would have been weird. Did you say your sister almost drowned at Lithia Springs?"

Chloe said, "Yes, I was eleven when it happened, and she was five. It had started as a bad day on which my father yelled at me in the morning. We got to the park, and my mother told me to take Charlotte to the water as she brought my other sisters and a picnic. I resented taking care of her and dragged along as she sprinted to the water. Of course, she stupidly jumped into the deep end. I looked up, and she disappeared beneath the water with her hands flailing around. Panicked, I started running but did not yell, even though they had lifeguards. Before I reached her, some boy swimming nearby pulled her out of the water and carried her to shore. The lifeguard showed up and checked her out. She coughed up a little water but was okay. I felt so guilty and upset I started crying."

I stared at her and asked, "It was your red-headed sister, right?"

Chloe nodded. "Yes."

I asked, "Were you wearing a light blue two-piece bathing suit?"

Chloe's eyes opened wide. She replied, "Yes, how did you know that? Wait, what are you saying?"

"That boy had a buzz cut and freckles on his face."

Chloe now stared back at me.

"He hugged you and told you, 'It's okay. She's all right. It's not your fault.'"

Chloe's mouth dropped open. "I can't believe it. What did I do after the boy hugged me?"

I chuckled, "You realized a boy in a bathing suit was hugging you, and you suddenly jumped back. Your eyes were so wide as you stared at me, but you did stop crying."

She stared back in amazement and finally said, "That was you? That's unbelievable."

I grinned wider and replied, "So we did meet each other earlier. First time I ever hugged a girl. I don't know what came over me, but you seemed so upset that I just did it. After that, I had a worse crush on you and kept looking at you for the rest of the day until we left. Every time we returned, I looked for you though I never saw you again."

Chloe finally grinned. "You really rattled me when you hugged me. The first time a boy had ever done that. I saw you looking at me and wondered if you liked me. We never went back because my mother put us into Brandon Swim and Tennis so we could all take swimming lessons. I confess I found myself thinking about you a lot after that too. How strange we meet later, and now we're dating."

"Maybe it's fate," I said and shrugged.

Chloe stuck her tongue out at me, and I laughed.

We spent the rest of the dinner enmeshed in each other. As we talked and she enchanted me again with the dance of expressiveness across her face, the tilting of her head, and the gestures with her hands, I thought I detected something new. I studied her closely, rapt as usual with her performance, and realized what I now felt. Love flowed from her, warm and generous, through her eyes, smile, words, and gestures. It washed over me, embraced me, and told me the truth. She did love me. All my doubts and even my departure tomorrow fell away. I sat present with her, filled with love. I reached my hands across the table and took her hands.

She paused talking, and I told her, "You are so beautiful, so incredibly beautiful."

She did not verbally refute my compliment but smiled ruefully as she shook her head no. She disagreed. She didn't deny it hard, as my comment thrilled her. She leaned toward me, and I met her with a kiss.

Chloe shared some news as we talked, "My mother said I could fly to Kentucky next week. I have a bunch of stuff I left up there. I can pack it up and ship it back home. I will fly up there on Tuesday and return on Sunday." She paused for a moment, looking at me. "Do you think you can come up and stay with me over the weekend? We would have three full days together if you came up on Wednesday. I had planned to share an apartment with April, and my bedroom remains unoccupied. You could stay there with us."

Surprised, I said, "I like it. How long will it take me to drive up there?"

She replied, "Well, it takes us almost eighteen hours from Brandon, so probably thirteen to fourteen hours. The school year doesn't start until Monday, so it should work."

I said, "I like this plan. I'll do it. I will arrive there Wednesday night."

Chloe smiled at me. "It should make for a very fun weekend. Also, it means we can spend a lot of time together before you are in school all fall."

I nodded at her.

When the food arrived, I was famished and had already devoured the bread they had brought. The food tasted amazing. Chloe delighted in my enthusiasm and pressed portions of her food upon me, which I also admired. We ordered desserts. I got Key Lime pie, and she ordered a chocolate dessert.

We tasted each other's dishes, and I finished any leftovers. We got our bill, and I paid it, despite Chloe's insistence that we split it. I said, "Not tonight. Tonight is my special treat for you. No splitting."

Chloe reluctantly accepted this, and we headed out to the car.

When we reached the car, we turned to each other and kissed for a long time. When we parted, Chloe said softly, "We have some time to go parking."

After I arrived and parked the car in the trees, I noticed the rain had also moved through that area earlier. Water saturated everything. I looked at the blanket and told Chloe, "I don't see the blanket working. It's so wet out here."

She shrugged. "I guess we'll make do with the back seat." She moved into the back.

It was a dark night with clouds blocking any moonlight. I got in and sat next to her. We kissed with urgency, hunger, and happiness. I caressed Chloe's cheeks and her soft hands. I pulled my shirt off, and she wiggled around and removed her dress. It took some work to remove it with the vest. She sat back next to me, wearing a bra and panties. I put my hands around her and worked to remove her bra.

Again, it took some effort until she said, laughing, "Find the hook, and just unhook it." She laughed until I successfully removed her bra, revealing her incredible breasts.

She stopped me and motioned for me to remove my pants. I took the condom out, sat it next to us, and took off my shoes and pants.

Both of us were now in our underwear. Chloe lay down, and I buried my face in those breasts, inhaling her scent and tasting her. I moved from breast to breast, sucking one while cupping and caressing the other. After a while, I put my hands on her panties and removed them. I then pulled my underwear down and off. I stood erect, extremely excited. Chloe handed me the condom. I opened it and put it on. She lay back down and adjusted her legs.

As I knelt between them, I looked into her face and said it again. "I love you."

Her face froze, and she turned her expression impassive and said nothing.

I knelt, looking at her face, waiting. She said nothing. I had told myself not to tell her, but it came out again. No moonlight either. She continued to say nothing, and I dropped. I sat back and looked at her. She returned my look. After a long moment, I removed the condom and started putting on my clothes. She looked up at me. Nothing was displayed on her face. That normally expressive face now suppressed any emotion or comment. She sat up and got dressed as well. Once she finished, she scooted over, pressed against me, and gave me another long kiss.

Neither of us discussed what happened. We never talked about it.

I knew why it happened—I had done it on purpose. I had broken the spell and stopped myself because I needed to know. I needed to know if Chloe loved me.

Tonight, for the first time, I thought she did love me, but I needed more than my intuition. I needed to know. I knew I had to depart tomorrow and needed the truth. I had spent the last month suspended since I declared my love to her. I had never landed, and I had suffered for it. I found myself now needing a resolution, an answer. One did not come.

Chapter 20

Trudy

When I arrived at Bill's house on Sunday, he came out before I even made the front door. Bill carried his stuff out, ready to leave. We crammed his things into the back seat of my car and headed off. Bill had been a runner in high school as well. Another skinny guy, Bill stood a little taller than me, with straggly brown hair and brown eyes. Bad acne had left many scars on his face, far worse than mine. He would not be described as attractive, which affected his confidence with girls.

"Man, I am so ready to return to school! Do you know how boring it is here, living in the middle of nowhere? I did nothing all summer but work. Time to have some fun!"

I looked around as we pulled out. He did live in the middle of nowhere, rural Pasco County, somewhere in the center. I had no idea exactly what they called this area. I responded to him, "Yeah, you live in the middle of nowhere."

He gave me directions from one winding small road to another until we finally intersected with US 41.

Once we got on 41, Bill asked me, "You know how many girls I dated this summer?"

I replied, "I don't know, two?"

He exclaimed, "Zero. Zero! There are no freaking girls around here, okay? I need to get back to school where there are many girls, and we are the older guys. The freshman girls will love us!"

I laughed at this. I hadn't thought about it, but yes, we would be the older guys this year.

Bill asked, "Okay. How many girls did you date this summer? Three? Four? Five? Come on, tell me."

I laughed again. I said, "I dated just two girls this summer."

"I knew it. I knew you would get lots of action. Man! How do you do it?"

I laughed again. "Bill, you just talk to them, and—ready, here's the secret—you ask them."

He laughed and asked, "How many did you have sex with? I bet it was all of them."

"Dude! I'm not going to tell you something like that. Come on, man. I don't talk about girls I dated like that. Just for the record, I do not have sex with every girl I go out with. I mean, seriously, I'm not Ed."

He ignored my comments and said, "Oh yeah, you are starting to be like Ed, man. That blonde you made out with at the Hawaiian party, man, she was gorgeous. You showed capabilities like Ed, dude."

"Okay, enough of that. Anyway, it will be different this fall. I have a girlfriend."

Bill exclaimed, "What!"

"Yes, I have a serious girlfriend. Her name is Chloe, and she's from my hometown. She is going to USF this fall, making it a long-distance relationship. But I am going up to see her in Lexington on Wednesday. She has been attending the University of Kentucky and is transferring to USF. She went to say goodbye to her friends and invited me to spend the weekend with her. I won't be back until Sunday night."

Bill whistled. "Wow, a whole weekend." He said nothing for a while and then added, "Long distance? That can be hard. It never seems to work for anyone I know. With all the parties and all the freshman girls at FSU, I don't know, man. It sounds like you're setting yourself up for trouble."

I did not respond to this at first. I had not faced the fact that distance now separated Chloe and me and the difficulty that posed. I knew some of the people Bill referred to, and yes, they all broke up. Several girls I dated had boyfriends back home. It did not work out well for anyone. I responded, "I know, but I'll figure something out. She's not that far, and we'll find a way to visit each other."

Bill said, "Wow, you must be serious. Good luck." Bill wanted to keep talking, but I responded with only short answers. After a while, he got the hint and fell silent. I had not recovered from getting in at almost two a.m. last night and did not want to talk.

We made it to the dorm around five p.m., and I parked near the back door to unload our vehicle. We found the RA and got our room keys. My new roommate, Mike, studied art and wanted to be a painter. He'd even painted a picture with me in it. I stood in a phone booth, looking depressed. It must have been last winter. Mike had reached his junior year, and I appreciated rooming with a more mature, laid-back roommate. He did not pester me about girls. He had a girlfriend he had met at FSU. We got along well last year, and we decided in the spring to room together this year. When I got to the room, Mike had yet to arrive. I picked one of the two beds and started unloading all my stuff.

After I finished, I lay on my bed and thought about Chloe and what had happened. She acted as if she loved me at the Kapok Tree. Finding out we had met before did seem like fate had brought us together. She acted like she found me the most fantastic guy in the world when we made out. And she clearly wanted to have sex with me—I messed that up. But when I said it to her, she froze and said nothing. Maybe she didn't love me. She just wanted to have a good time. Perhaps she just wanted the boyfriend experience. I knew I couldn't resolve it, lying there, picking apart our time together.

Maybe some relief, some understanding of what she felt for me would come this weekend. I resolved to take plenty of condoms, and this time I would keep my stupid mouth shut. I would let her say something first. If not, we would have lots of sex. I fell asleep with that thought in my head.

I awoke early afternoon the next day. It was the first time I had slept late in a few days. The rising afternoon heat in the room woke me up. I decided to buy a burger for lunch. My local bank was adjacent to Wendy's, and I could deposit some checks after I ate. I could check on my student loan request if I had enough time.

Someone knocked on my door. I opened it, and there stood Trudy. I looked at her in surprise. I had forgotten I'd told her to look me up here when she settled in her dorm. She stood smiling at me. She wore a tight blouse with cutoff jean shorts and flip-flops. I invited her in, and she looked around the room.

She made a face. "Wow, these are not very good rooms, are they?"

I laughed. "No, this is a cheap and poor dorm. No frills here at all. But it is a cool place to live. We do have a lot of fun here."

She nodded and smiled at me again. "I live on the other side of campus. The dorm even has air conditioning, and my roommate is a sophomore. You should come by and look at my room. My roommate will be gone tomorrow afternoon. Why don't you come by after lunch?"

I looked at her closely and thought that sure sounded like an invitation. I responded, "Sure, I will be by around two p.m.?"

She smiled again and nodded. "That works." She then walked up to me and surprised me with a kiss.

She kissed me so quickly that I did not think to stop her. She had last seen me on our date, and I had been all over her.

After she pulled back from our kiss, I told her, "I was heading out. I have to deposit some checks and care for some financial stuff."

She nodded and said, "Well, I'll see you tomorrow afternoon."

I walked her to the door and let her out. I thought, *Why did you kiss her? That was stupid.* I know she surprised me, and I did not think about it. I reconsidered whether I should go to her room tomorrow. It would be awkward. She told me where she lived but did not give me the dorm phone number. I could only reach her by going over there. I would have to be on my guard and quick about exiting.

My stomach growled. I had nothing to eat since last evening. I headed out to eat first.

After I finished eating, I stopped by my local bank. I deposited three checks: one for my scholarship, a check my parents had given me, and one I had written myself from my home bank account. I did not save nearly as much money as the previous year. I had spent too much of my work money on Chloe that summer. But I had already applied for a student loan, which would give me more money than I had any quarter last year. I should have plenty of money.

The next day, I found myself standing at the door to Trudy's dorm. Someone exited the dorm, and I walked in and looked around. She lived in a newer dorm, one with air conditioning. This dorm had someone in a window at the entrance. I told them whom I came to meet and displayed my student ID. She directed me down the hall and to the left to find Trudy's room.

I knocked on Trudy's door, and she opened it. Barefoot, she wore a tight top that showed the cleavage of her full breasts and small tight shorts on those soft, tanned legs. She did look good. She walked over and sat down on her bed. She looked back at me and signaled me to join her. I hesitated. I thought sitting on her bed next to her would be a mistake. Instead, I walked over to the desk chair, turned it around to face her, and sat down.

She gave me a puzzled look and asked, "What do you think of my room?"

I looked around. "It's nice. I see you and your roommate decorated everything." The windows had curtains, and posters covered the walls. The hard floor had a rug covering most of it, and decorated bedspreads covered the beds. Girls always had such neat rooms compared to ours.

Trudy said, "My roommate will be gone all afternoon. Why don't you sit here with me, and we can talk?" She patted the bed next to her. "My roommate's schedule leaves me with the room by myself Monday, Wednesday, and Friday afternoons." She smiled encouragingly at me.

I stood up. Did I intend to sit next to her? Trudy tempted me. I mean, she looked damn good. Yes, I wanted her. Something caused me to stop, and I decided to tell her the truth. "Trudy, I have a girlfriend. I met her after we dated, and she became my girlfriend."

Disappointment replaced Trudy's smile.

I said, "I'm sorry, Trudy. I am sorry."

She nodded and looked at me as if considering something. "Is your girlfriend a student here?"

I replied, "No, she's back at USF. We met in Brandon during the summer."

Trudy sat there still considering something, then she grinned.

I knew what that meant and added, "I'm meeting her in Lexington tomorrow. She used to go to the University of Kentucky and went up there to get her stuff. We are going to spend the weekend together."

Trudy's smile faded. She stood and said, "We have terrible timing, me and you."

I nodded in agreement. We did have terrible timing. She walked me to the door and did not hide her disappointment. I had ruined her plans for the afternoon.

As I returned to my dorm, the side wanting Trudy started complaining. *What is the matter with you? You have turned down sex twice with two girls in three days. Are you stupid? That's it! You're stupidly in love.*

Stop it, I told myself. No, love did not make me stupid. Love opened my eyes to the world as it existed. Love showed me what I wanted, what I needed. Now, I needed to be patient. Still, I sighed, thinking about how good Trudy looked sitting on that bed. I had wanted her. She did tempt me.

Chapter 21

The Weekend

I planned to leave by eight thirty or nine a.m. on Wednesday for my trip to Lexington but overslept and got on the road just after ten. Mike had arrived the evening before, and I told him about my plans. Mike understood because he had become close to his girlfriend.

The trip took me almost fourteen hours driving to Lexington, getting me to her late. It was approaching midnight when I got off the interstate and followed Chloe's directions to the apartment. Chloe greeted me at the door with a warm smile. She said, "You made it! Give me a smooch."

I leaned forward and gave her a quick kiss. She escorted me inside and directed me to the sofa.

April stood in the living room. "Hi, Chris."

I waved at her. "Hey, April." Looking back at Chloe, I said, "I'm sorry it's so late. It took me over fourteen hours to drive here. I've never driven that far by myself. Talk about exhausting."

Chloe said, "I know, especially if you hit traffic. I made some brownies for a snack, and we have beer."

"Sounds good."

As she went to get the snacks, I looked around the living room. The small apartment had an entertainment center with a record player, speakers, and a stack of albums. A round dining table and chairs sat near a bar in the kitchen. I sat at one end of the sofa, and on the other, they had placed a pillow and a blanket.

Chloe arrived with a plate of brownies and a can of beer. She sat beside me, smiling at me and talking as I ate the brownie, drank the beer, and finished a second of each. The beer relaxed me, and I yawned. I said, "I'm so tired, Chloe. I really need to sleep some to recover."

She nodded. "I understand. I'm tired too. See you in the morning." She leaned over and gave me another quick kiss before turning out the lights and heading to her room. I lay down on the sofa and fell asleep.

Chloe woke me up by kissing me on the lips the following morning. I opened my eyes to see her shining face beaming down at me. She said, "I have things to do today, so wake up! The bathroom is down the hall, and after you finish, we can go get lunch."

I sleepily nodded and went to the bathroom for a shower and a change of clothes. When I came out, it was almost noon.

Chloe said, "There's a new Wendy's nearby. I know you like their burgers so we can go there."

"Okay," I replied.

She said, "April left to meet her boyfriend, so it's just us for lunch."

The cool, overcast weather surprised me when we stepped outside to go to my car. It even rained a little from a cold front blowing into the area. The temperature had to be in the low fifties. "Wow, I did not expect it to be cold. I only brought shorts and T-shirts."

Chloe chuckled and snuggled up to me, "Here, I will keep you warm." She had on a pair of jeans and a sweatshirt.

Still, I scurried to the car to get out of the cold.

On the way, Chloe said, "We're celebrating April's birthday this evening with a party at the apartment. I need to pick up a cake, some decorations, and some alcohol and mixers to make cocktails this afternoon. My friend Elizabeth is coming over to go with me. Do you want to join us or hang around the apartment? April will be gone all day too."

Still tired from the drive, I replied, "I'll just relax in the apartment."

At Wendy's, we got our food and found a table. She sat opposite me. She kept beaming at me and appeared extra perky. She said, "I got to pack my stuff up yesterday. I can't find my boots, though. They were these really cool boots for winter." She made a pouty face at me.

I grinned and said, "April didn't borrow them?"

"We don't wear the same size."

"Maybe they are at home, and one of your sisters took them."

She shook her head no. "I always left them up here over the summer." She made another face, rolling her eyes, and gave an exaggerated sigh. "Oh well, it's not cold in Florida."

As she continued talking about her friends, her accomplishments, and my drive up there, I found myself again rapt at her performance. That dazzling face with those expressions dancing across it warmed me, and I basked in it with delight. The joy poured out in my smile. I reached across the table and held her hands. She pursed her lips into a bemused grin. I tugged on her hands, and we leaned toward each other and kissed. Everyone else in the restaurant had disappeared, and we sat engrossed only in each other. My love for her flowed from my eyes, smile, and attention across that table to her.

Chloe seemed especially happy as she made faces and smiled back at me. She said, "I think you already missed me!"

Someone eating at the table next to us made a loud comment directed at us. "It must be nice to be a young couple so in love."

I turned and looked. An older woman with short gray hair, she nodded and smiled at me. I nodded at her in return. Chloe did not look at her, but her smile turned rueful and embarrassed. She continued talking as if the woman had said nothing.

I found the woman's comments exhilarating. She did not say I was in love. She said *we* were in love. I had proof from someone else, a stranger, and she agreed Chloe loved me!

This woman provided external evidence of what I believed. Chloe did love me.

That woman's comment changed everything and released me from my doubt. I walked out of the restaurant hand in hand with Chloe and kissed her with intensity when we reached the car.

She patted me on the chest and said, looking into my eyes, "I missed you. I'm so glad you came. We will have a good time this weekend."

I met that comment with another kiss.

When we reached her apartment, Chloe's friend Elizabeth had already arrived. Chloe introduced me. "This is my *serious* boyfriend, Chris."

Elizabeth studied me for a moment then smiled. Chloe let me inside, but they had to go, so she directed me to the stereo and a stack of albums if I wanted to listen to music. She departed with her friend, promising to return in a few hours.

I reviewed the albums and found a Loggins and Messina album. I knew this was Chloe's favorite group, so I listened. The live stage album contained the extended version of "Angry Eyes." I liked that song not because of the anger but because of the intense emotions. Extreme emotions filled me, and the album fit. I also thought of Chloe while listening to it.

They returned with alcohol, cups, mixers, and a giant cake box. Chloe and Elizabeth motioned me over, eager to show me the cake and smirking. I did not understand why and said, "It's just a birthday cake."

They laughed together, and Chloe waved me over. "Come look, come look!"

I strolled over as Elizabeth opened the top of the cake box. When I looked inside, I laughed. The cake had been baked in the shape of a penis. Both girls erupted in laughter at my reaction.

Soon after that, April arrived with her boyfriend, Larry. They introduced me as "Chloe's serious boyfriend." Larry was a tall guy with shaggy blond hair and a beard who appeared a couple of years older than April.

The girls kept the lid on the cake box. No peeking until the party started. A few other people arrived. We ordered some pizzas, and the girls set to making cocktails. We all sat around talking and drinking. After a while, Chloe brought the cake to the middle of the table. We all stood around it, and April's mouth opened in shock when she opened it. We had a good laugh at that. We sang "Happy Birthday."

Elizabeth cut a piece from the head and handed it to Larry. "Okay, Larry, you need to feed April the tip of the dick!"

Everyone laughed. The girls kept making jokes as they handed out the rest of the pieces featuring the penis. "Every girl needs some dick!"

After the mirth of the cake faded, we all sat around again, talking and drinking. Eventually, the other guests departed, leaving me, Chloe, April, and Larry. After several cocktails,

April and Larry headed into her bedroom, leaving Chloe by me on the sofa.

Once they entered the bedroom and shut the door, we turned to each other and kissed. I kissed Chloe intensely, with my overwhelming love for her. That woman in Wendy's had done this. She had opened the gates to the dam that blocked us, and I roared through them, unrestrained, full of strength and passion, sweeping everything before me. I kissed her neck, her hands, and her mouth. She pushed herself against me and returned my kisses and caresses with her own. I took off my shirt, and I helped her remove hers. I unhooked her bra, this time with relative ease.

She said, smiling, "I'm impressed. You're getting better at that."

She lay on the sofa, and I got on top of her. I tasted her soft, round breasts with their flawless, dewy skin again. I sucked on her big pink nipples, pressed my nose to her skin, and inhaled her scent.

After a while, I stood up and removed a condom from my pocket. I took my clothes off and stood by the couch. Chloe watched me put on the condom. She undid her jeans and pulled them and her panties off. She lay back on the sofa, and I moved on to her. She touched me and helped me adjust to get inside her. I pushed in until fully inside. She felt so soft, warm, and wet.

I began to move on her, in her. She kissed me insistently, with hunger, and I moved, pushed, and thrust. She kept kissing me, and I kept moving. I thought nothing and glided across her soft body underneath me.

When the eruption began, I groaned. Chloe touched her finger to my lips to silence me. I released inside her in total ecstasy.

We lay together for a long time afterward. She did not want me to pull out. We kept touching, kissing, and enjoying the feel of each other's skin.

Afterward, we sat quietly next to each other. Chloe said, "Here, take my hand. Let's go to my room. You can sleep with me."

We stood up and walked down the hall naked to her bedroom, holding hands. We lay down together, and she rolled over onto me, putting her head on my chest. She rested on my arm that lay underneath her. I drifted asleep with her warm body pressed against me.

The sunshine streamed through the shades in the morning. I got up and peeked out. The sky was pure blue without clouds or rain. I looked back at Chloe, sleeping still naked from the evening before, and I thought she had done that. She made the sunshine flood my morning. She filled my morning with her light. Looking at her lying there with her soft glowing skin, that warm haze she emitted, I wanted nothing more than to be enveloped, sink into it, and lose myself.

She stirred now and opened her eyes. She gazed at me and beckoned me back to bed.

I shook my head no and said, "Bathroom."

She understood and lay back down. I searched the room for my clothes but then remembered they sat in a small bag in the living room. I had no clothes on, no clothes in the room at all.

I could hear her roommate and boyfriend talking and moving around the apartment. I looked around some more and spotted a towel draped over a chair. I wrapped it around me and walked out. As I made my way to the bathroom, I passed April. She grinned at me, a knowing grin, and I returned it.

After I used the bathroom, I went into the living room with only that towel around me to get my clothes. Larry also gave me a knowing grin, and I responded. Yes, I would not deny any of it. I had sex with her and would have sex with her again shortly.

As I returned to the room, clutching my clothes and the towel around me, Chloe exited in a robe and said, "Bathroom."

I nodded my head and grinned at her as well. She returned a rueful smile.

I did not put my clothes on in the bedroom but instead searched for my jeans. I found the condoms, pulled them out, and put them on the nightstand beside the bed for easy access. I lay back down on the bed and waited for her. She soon entered and saw me lying there. She looked at the pile of condoms on the table, then slid her robe off and joined me in bed. She moved close to me until we touched.

We stared into each other's eyes. I placed my fingers on her and softly touched her. I wanted to feel her beneath my fingers, to understand her skin under my caress. I wanted to embed her into my memory.

She now did the same to me, running her fingers across my skin, touching and exploring me. We kept looking at each other without talking, just feeling, constantly caressing. We even stroked each other's hands and fingers.

I placed my fingers on her breasts on her nipples and kept gently pulling until each nipple hardened beneath my fingers. I marveled at how soft, how warm, how silky she felt. Her fingers wrapped around me now, and I had hardened beneath her hand.

Neither of us could take it any longer, and we rolled together. We kissed as we had touched, slow, gentle, full of curiosity, wanting the full taste of the other. I needed the same understanding of Chloe's taste as my touch required. When we parted for breath, she rolled over onto her back, and I climbed onto her and slipped inside. As we kissed, I kept it slow and steady. Now that same curiosity and need to understand filled this as well. I wanted to prolong, sink into, and remember it forever. While inside Chloe, I felt her warm glow swell, lift, and envelop me. I sank into it, joined it entirely. My words can never capture the joy of that experience.

The pleasure overwhelmed me, and I quickened.

Chloe placed her hand on the small of my back and said one word in my ear: "Slow."

I slowed down my pace. She wanted to linger in this as well. I kept moving until it overwhelmed me, and I gasped in ecstasy and released inside her. She did not quiet me this time.

When I started to pull out, she stopped me with her hand on my back and one word: "Stay."

I stopped and instead put my mouth on hers. When I finished, I put my face against her neck and kissed it. She gasped, stopped, and did the same to me, putting her face on my neck and kissing me. My whole body tingled with the stimulation. Too much stimulation. I had to lift my neck away. We looked at each other and laughed. I pulled out and lay back down next to her. We embraced.

We lay for a long time in each other's arms, enjoying the warmth of each other.

After a while, she said, "We need to get up. I want to show you around Lexington and the campus. I need to say goodbye to some of my friends as well."

I reluctantly agreed and joined her in getting dressed.

She said, "I want you to try a local specialty for lunch. It's called a hot brown. There's a place near campus famous for them."

I asked, "A hot brown?"

"It's a Kentucky specialty, an open-faced sandwich made with turkey, cheese, bacon, and tomatoes."

I said, "I don't like tomatoes."

She replied, "You can have one made without it."

"Okay. Tell me how to get there."

We headed out of the apartment to my car, and she gave me directions. The restaurant was inside an old formal-looking hotel in the center of town near the campus. We ordered, and they did allow me to order mine without tomatoes. Chloe commented that the tomatoes made it taste better. Still, I remained adamant that I would not eat it with them. When the sandwich arrived, I thought it tasted good. It was homey with the turkey, cheese, and bacon over the white bread. As we sat eating, we talked. Chloe appeared to be even happier today than she had been yesterday.

She smiled at me as we talked, and those smiles warmed me, and I felt loved. I said, "You are determined to expand my food horizons."

She laughed at this. After we paid our bills, we walked out holding hands. She leaned over to kiss me when we got into the car. Affection spilled out from her in everything we did.

She directed me to the UK campus. We parked at the stadium and went out for a walking tour. She took me past the two dorms she had lived in, and we stopped at the second one. A few of her friends who still lived there came out, and she introduced me as her serious boyfriend. That term, again. I wondered if she made fun of me. But she did not say it as a joke. She told her friends, "Here is my *serious* boyfriend."

I liked that interpretation. As we continued the tour, I asked Chloe, "Why do you call me your *serious* boyfriend?"

She greeted my question with another big smile. "I never had a boyfriend before. I like to brag on you and inform them I now have one."

I smiled at this as well and leaned over and kissed her.

She then added, looking into my eyes, "We are serious, aren't we?"

Before I answered, she leaned in and kissed me, but I liked how she asked me that.

We stopped at the university center where she had worked in the cafeteria. I did not work at FSU. The small size of Tallahassee compared to the size of the university made it nearly impossible for students to find jobs near the campus. I did not want to work in college either because I wanted to have the time to enjoy it.

I asked her, "Why did you work both years?"

She replied, "I did it to earn money for my expenses. I did not want to depend on my dad for that too. I don't know. I had the time and always worked. I worked in high school." She smiled at me. "After all, we met at a workplace. Good thing I liked to work!"

I returned that smile and said, "Yes, indeed!"

She told me about her job and said, "I met lots of people. All the basketball players came in at one time or another. It made me feel so tiny. I stood at their navels, taking orders or delivering food. Those guys were all giants. Of course, we are a basketball school and the current NCAA champions, so it was a big deal to know some players."

I nodded to that. She continued her tour, and we eventually ended up back in my car. Walking around took three hours, but we had nothing else to do. I did not care what we did if I did it with her.

We got back to the apartment around four p.m. We did not say anything to each other, but I found us walking hand in hand into Chloe's bedroom. She closed the door, and we fell into each other's arms.

It did not take long before we removed our clothing and got into bed naked together. Something new possessed both of us: a hunger, a voracious appetite for the other. We touched, we caressed, and we pressed ourselves against each other. We wanted to be together. We needed to be together. It did not take long until Chloe helped pull me on top of her, inside her. Nothing now stopped me from trying to quench my insatiable hunger. I gave in to it. We both gave in to it.

Something more potent than sex animated us and drove us together into each other. We needed to push two into one. Of course, I ended in ecstasy. That part always happened easily to me. But it did not seem to be the point. A deeper hunger propelled us against each other, into each other. Afterward, we lay together, our arms around each other, still naked, enjoying the warmth of our skin-on-skin contact. We lay intertwined like that for a long time, not wanting to break the spell. April broke it by knocking on the bedroom door.

Chloe rose, put on a robe, cracked the door open, and peeked out.

April asked, "Okay, can you lovers break away to get something to eat?" I could see April grinning. She added, "I know you wanted to take Chris to try some chili. Larry wants to go too. We can all go together then stop and meet some friends at the bar afterward."

Chloe responded, "We will be ready in a few minutes." She shut the door, looked back at me, and motioned for me to climb out of bed.

I stayed in it, staring at her. She dropped the robe off and moved to put on her clothes. I loved looking at her naked. She had such beautiful skin. I said, "Naked is a good look on you. It really works for you."

She laughed and motioned again for me to roll out of bed. I reluctantly did.

We decided to take my car because Larry and April had smaller cars. Chloe sat with me, and Larry and April sat in the back. We first went to a local chain called Gold Star Chili. Other than the chili, it was a typical fast-food restaurant. After we finished, Chloe gave me directions to a bar near campus where we would meet their friends. Chloe explained that most of their friends had moved out of the dorms for this school year, so we could only meet a few when we toured the campus.

At the bar, we ended up with around twelve girls who had been friends of Chloe's and April's, with a couple of guys and boyfriends who had been dragged along. Chloe introduced me to all her friends. This time she smiled at me when she called me her serious boyfriend. I sat right next to Chloe. Throughout the evening, she would sometimes hold my hand or kiss me. She seemed determined to have some public display of affection for her friends. I helped this along by sometimes passionately kissing her when she initiated one. A couple of her curious friends spent some time talking to me, an experience I found akin to meeting someone's family. They seemed to be sizing me up. Beer, however, gradually erased the awkwardness. Once we became well-lubricated, we joked and laughed, having a good time.

April teased, "You guys are so lucky you could meet Chris, as I had to pry these lovers out of the bedroom to drive over here." The girls all laughed at this, and when I looked at Chloe, she laughed. She displayed no sign of embarrassment and acted proud.

April gestured at me. "Since he arrived, all I hear is constant squeaking noises out of the bedroom. I found him walking around naked in a daze in the morning, wearing nothing but a towel after Chloe wore him out."

Everyone and Chloe again laughed. Her friends considered it good news that she had gotten a boyfriend, and they all congratulated her, even in jokes.

When Chloe took a bathroom break, her friend Elizabeth leaned toward me and said softly. "I've never seen Chloe this happy. Other guys never treated her very well. They always just took advantage of her, but it seems like you really like her. Be good to her. She deserves some happiness."

I replied, "I do like her. She is very special to me, and I will never hurt her."

Elizabeth nodded at me in approval. When Chloe returned, she said, "I like your serious boyfriend, Chloe. He seems like a good guy."

Chloe beamed at that, and I hugged her tight.

The group dwindled as it got to be around midnight. Soon after, we broke up completely, and the four of us returned to the apartment. When we arrived, Larry and April headed to her bedroom, but not before April threw Chloe a broad grin. I entered Chloe's bedroom with her, again, hand in hand.

Again, we fell into each other's arms. The beer had removed any inhibitions we still had. We kissed, touched, and caressed with absolute abandon. We pulled our clothes off and tumbled into the bed together. I put my mouth on Chloe's skin and her breasts, hungry to taste her. She kept putting her hand on me, gently pulling me. After a break for air, she motioned me to roll over on my back. She then moved down to my groin and put my erect dick in her mouth. She moved her head up and down. Her lips clamped on me. She did not do it for long, but I found it exhilarating and gasped. The whole time she fixed her eyes on mine.

When she stopped, I offered to do the same to her, but she refused and told me, "I needed to taste you. You have tasted me before."

I nodded in acknowledgment.

She then asked, "Can I be on top this time?"

"Yes."

She swung up on top of me and put me inside her. I liked this position. It allowed me to focus on her breasts while she moved up and down on me. I always had my hands on her. She would sometimes pause to lean down and kiss me. The beer had released her inhibitions, and she moved on me with urgency. I don't know if the condom affected me or the number of times on the last day, but I lasted and lasted. Chloe made no noises, but she suddenly quickened. Her eyelashes flickered rapidly. She looked at me with wide eyes and then kept steadily moving. I soon released, groaning.

I always made a noise. Chloe leaned down on me and kissed me insistently. This time she did not linger on me but pulled off. She rolled over next to me and put her head on my chest. I moved a little to remove my arm from under her and put it next to her.

I thought of what Elizabeth had said and asked Chloe, "Elizabeth told me other guys had treated you poorly. I heard this from others as well. What did they do?"

Chloe replied, "When I started here, everyone knew I was a virgin, and they kept trying to set me up and encourage guys to approach me. I found it humiliating, but I don't like pressure, so I rejected them all. By late in the winter, it had started to bother me. I drank until thoroughly smashed at a party at Larry's fraternity, and one of his frat brothers kept flirting with me. He seemed like he did like me, and I was so drunk that I let him take me to his room. I barely remember it other than being sore the next day. He remembered it well and bragged around the dorm that he had plucked my cherry. The next time I saw him, he acted like he could command sex from me anytime he wanted. In front of me, he told some of the other guys what great tits I had."

"What a jerk!" I exclaimed.

"Yes, so I stopped talking to him. Late in the spring, we were at Larry's apartment, and he invited another friend, Brian, over to set me up. This guy was cute and very friendly. I thought he genuinely liked me. Once again, I drank too much, and when Larry and April moved to the bedroom, I did not resist this guy. I saw him a couple of days later on the weekend. I went to talk to him, thinking he did like me, only to find him on a date with another girl. He treated me like I was no one."

"Jesus, all of Larry's friends seem like jerks."

"It seems like all I attracted was guys who wanted to screw me, nothing more."

I responded, "I want more, a lot more."

Chloe grinned. "I know."

I asked, "So that was it?"

"No," she said. "There was one more guy. I did not date for a while after that, but in May, April introduced me to someone she swore was a nice guy. He showed up at Larry's for a double date. We had some cocktails, and I will admit that Tom was charming and very good looking. I was attracted to him. I made sure not to drink too much, but when Larry and April entered their room, he started kissing me. I thought this guy liked me. Afterward, he kept talking nicely to me and arranged for me to meet him at another party at his dorm a couple of days later. When I showed up, he was quite friendly again and kept flirting and dancing with me. After a while and several beers, I went to his room with him. I felt happy and thought I had finally met someone. I asked him when we could meet again, but he avoided giving me a clear answer. He never contacted me or asked me out again. After a couple of weeks of not hearing anything, I asked April about Tom. She talked to him, and he told her that while he had a good time with me, he did not like me that much and was not interested in a relationship. April learned from someone else that he had a terrible reputation as a guy who just screwed many girls. She apologized to me as he had fooled her as well. Between those guys and my father, I've learned not to trust men. I know I am frustrating, but letting go is hard."

I pulled her close and hugged her. I whispered in her ear, "I'm not going to hurt you. I meant what I said."

She responded, "I know you're different." She shook her head and said, "Enough of these tales of woe. I'm having an amazing weekend. We have another day together. I don't want to talk about bad things anymore. Just hold me tight and make love to me again in the morning." She stopped any response with a kiss.

I soon fell asleep with her head on my chest.

When I awoke the following day, she lay close to me, touching me. I stayed against her for a while, enjoying the feeling of her warm skin. She began to stir, to move around. She opened her eyes and looked at me. I smiled at her. I moved to her and gave her a quick smooch.

She said, "Let's spoon." She rolled onto her side and snuggled her back up to me, her rear end against me.

I put my arm around her and snuggled up tight to her. Again, we lay clasped together, enjoying each other. She began to move against me, and I grew excited. She moved a little more until I became firmly excited.

I kissed her shoulders, her back, and her neck. My hands caressed her breasts. Soon she rolled onto her back, and I put myself inside her again. We did not repeat the hungry fury of last night, but I moved on her, in her, a constant insistence. This time she leaned up and put her mouth on my nipples as I continued to move on her. Her act sped me up, and I did not last long. My whole body tingled, almost vibrating, a feeling of overwhelming sensation.

I looked at her, my eyes wide with astonishment. Afterward, we rolled back to each other, against each other, again wanting to linger in that feeling of skin against skin. I lay there with her, feeling relaxed. A deep, warm joy infused me. I did not want to disturb that satisfying feeling.

We lay like that for a long time until my stomach growled with hunger. Chloe moved away and looked at me. "I'll make you some breakfast," she said. "I got some eggs, bacon, and bread for toast. I'll cook for you."

"Sounds good," I responded. We got up, dressed, and walked into the living room. As we walked in, I looked around the living room and saw no sign of April or Larry.

Chloe quipped, "They had to leave early today. They went hiking in some park. Just you and me, us lovers." She raised her eyebrows and made a face at me.

I smiled. She bustled around in the kitchen cooking while I got a glass of water and sat at the table.

She asked, "What kind of eggs do you like?"

I replied, "Scrambled."

She produced a plate of food for us, and we ate breakfast together. We slept late and stayed in bed long after we'd awakened. We discussed what we should do in the afternoon and decided to watch a movie.

I remembered seeing a newspaper machine at the entrance to the apartment complex. I went down and got a newspaper. We checked what movies were playing and the show times. I suggested Cheech and Chong's latest film, but she did not like their movies. She enjoyed mysteries and comedy, so we settled on *Foul Play* with Chevy Chase and Goldie Hawn at three fifteen. She wanted to take me to a local pizza restaurant famous for its garlic bread sticks that evening. Going to an early movie would allow us to go to it immediately afterward. She said it could be crazy busy on Saturdays, so it was best to be there early.

After we got into the movie, I put my arm around Chloe, and she snuggled against me, but we watched the movie this time. We already had plenty of alone time together. We left the cinema feeling slightly disappointed overall. The mystery and most of the movie's comedy fell flat. After we exited, she gave me directions to Joe Bologna's Restaurant and Pizzeria.

They did not take reservations, and we waited an hour in line. When seated, we ordered a pizza to split, garlic bread sticks, and a pitcher of beer. We drank the beer slowly and took our time eating and talking. When we finished, we headed back to the apartment.

Chloe quizzed me, "What did you think of my food tour of Lexington?"

I complimented her, "I enjoyed it. I liked the pizza best, but I found it all interesting."

She reminded me, "See, trying different things to eat can be rewarding."

I smiled. "Okay, you're right. Thanks for taking me to these different places."

She said, "I know it's still early, but my flight tomorrow morning is fairly early at nine a.m., so we can't stay up so late tonight."

I groaned, "Nine a.m.? Man! That's so early."

She laughed. "You do need to drive back too."

I agreed, "I know. I know, but I hate getting up early."

She sighed. "Tonight's our last night. I'm going to miss you."

I looked over at her.

She said, "I'm going to miss you something terrible. It's been a great weekend."

We both sat quietly for a while. I had not considered the future the entire time I had been there. All the love I poured on Chloe kept me in the present.

"We still have tonight," I reminded her. "Let's worry about that tomorrow."

She nodded. "Well, I will need to turn the alarm on. I know what a late sleeper you are."

When we arrived at the apartment, we found April there. Larry had returned to his apartment for the evening. We all sat around chatting for a while. Chloe interrupted this by announcing that it was getting late and that we needed to go to bed due to her early morning departure. I stood up to head back to the bedroom. April gave Chloe a quick look and a grin. I did not suppress mine.

When we got into the bedroom, Chloe first focused on packing. I put together my small bag, leaving out what I would wear tomorrow. When I finished, I watched her. She didn't seem to have that much stuff. I asked her, "Where's the stuff you left up here you came to get?"

She replied, "I already packed and shipped it before you arrived." She soon finished, and she looked at me.

She removed her clothing and lay down on the bed, her eyes on me. I looked at her lying there with that incredible glowing skin, her soft, feminine body full of curves draped naked on the bed. I would remember her image for the rest of my life. I removed my clothes and climbed into bed with her. We rolled together and kissed for a long time. The knowledge that we would soon part affected it. We kissed to remember this weekend and each other.

I had grown excited by having her against me. She always excited me. Soon, I put myself in her, and she winced. Alarmed, I looked at her, but she chased that quickly by pulling me down and kissing me. I moved steadily in her, and this time we mainly kissed. I kept moving with that same steady insistence until she provoked my ecstasy. Again, I gasped and released into the mindless bliss she had brought me.

Afterward, we rolled together again, seeking that intimate touch and mutual warmth. An ache rose in my groin, a dull pain. I said, "I'm sore down there, really aching."

She responded, "I'm sore too, so sore."

We both chuckled.

She went on, "This will be the last time this weekend. I can't take another in the morning. I need some time to recover."

I nodded at her. "We don't have time in the morning anyway."

I also thought painfully that there would be too much time to recover. It might even be a few months. I shrank from that thought. I could not wait till Thanksgiving, two months away, to see her again. I pushed myself closer to her and placed my face against her breasts. I wanted to inhale and remember her scent. She stroked my head with her hand. When I finished, we nestled against each other, intertwined in the warmth of our bodies. She said softly, "This has been the happiest couple of days of my entire life. I don't want it ever to end."

I pulled her tighter and responded, "Me too, and I'm never letting go."

We did not talk after that and stayed tight against each other until sleep took us.

The insistent beeping of her alarm awakened me. Sunday morning had come, and we needed to move. I had to drive her to the airport for her flight.

Chapter 22

Despair

We got our stuff together and headed to the front. April's door was still closed, and I glanced at Chloe as we walked past it. She put her finger to her lips to stay quiet. I assumed they said their goodbyes last night. After loading the car, I followed her directions to the small airport and parked in a surface lot beside the terminal. We found her airline and got in line to check her bags and check in for her flight. The short line moved quickly, and we soon finished and followed the signs to her gate. We walked together, holding hands as no airport security prevented friends and guests from going to the gate.

We found two seats in her gate area and sat down to wait as her boarding time drew near. She leaned against me and put her head on my shoulder. She would soon be gone, and it would be two months until Thanksgiving. Pain rose within me. We had not even been together for two months. I could not comprehend being separated from her.

She raised her head and turned to me, and I kissed her. We did it in front of everyone else in the waiting area. We kissed to stop the departure. It did not work, and they began boarding the plane. The line dwindled, and she stood. I walked with her toward the gate, holding hands. The time to depart had arrived.

She turned to me. "I have to go. I am really, really going to miss you. Will you write to me? Will you write to me soon? I'll write you back."

I could barely comprehend what I felt, but it overwhelmed me. "Yes, I will write to you. I don't know how I can take this separation. I love you, Chloe. I love you."

Chloe's expression froze, and distress appeared. Tears showed in her eyes. She shook her head no and said, "I have to go." She turned, walked down the line, gave her ticket and ID, and passed into the gangway toward the plane. She did not look back.

I stood watching her, not comprehending, not believing. Pain rose and rose in me until it expressed itself from my eyes in tears and flowed down my cheeks. I turned and walked toward the exit. Others looked at me with curiosity, sympathy, and alarm. I ignored them all and kept walking. The pain kept pushing the tears out, and down they fell. I made no noise: no weeping, no crying, just silent tears falling. I walked out of the exit, over the crosswalk to the parking lot, located my car, opened it, got in, and started it. I followed the signs to exit the airport and the direction to I-75. I just followed the signs.

She did not love me. The tears kept falling. She did not love me. How? How? I saw the distress on her face and the shaking of her head.

The tears kept silently coming.

I loved her with everything I had. I had given all my heart, all of myself. I held nothing back, and there was nothing more I could give, but I had failed.

Chloe did not love me.

I had poured everything I had out over this weekend. It was the greatest three days of my entire life. Happiness so deep I could not describe it, much less comprehend it. I had loved her without restraint.

She did not love me.

How? How? No answer came. The tears continued falling silently as I drove onto the interstate and headed south.

I thought of something terrible. I thought of what she had said to Tammie and Sonia at that party before we even dated about sex. Had it just been that to her? Had she just deceived me? Is that all I meant to her? No, I had done more than that. I loved her. I loved her with everything I had. It had only been love from me. It had not been enough for her. I had failed. She did not love me.

What am I going to do? Should I give up? Was it over? Hopeless? Could I give up? These thoughts stoked the pain, and that expressed itself as silent tears. No, it was too late. Once I had fallen, I had fallen in love forever. My feelings persisted past any pain she provoked. I stood before her defeated, but I would not surrender. I had moved well beyond quitting. I loved her, and I would always love her. Even if she ultimately rejected me, I would still love her. What was I going to do?

I thought about the weekend we had just spent together. She had accepted my love. She had enjoyed it, showed it off to her friends, and even bragged about it. I did not understand. How did she not love me? I thought, at least, she did allow me to love her. That she had said I made her happy.

An answer occurred to me: I would just love her. She accepted my love. She enjoyed and basked in it. She let me love her. It would be enough to keep loving, seeing, and being with her. It did not matter if she did not love me back. I would love her. It would have to be enough.

The tears stopped. Despite its bitterness, I had an answer that released my pain, stopped my tears, and left me with a curious relief. I say curious because I felt numb.

The miles ground beneath my wheels as I drove south. I stopped thinking, turned on the radio, and listened to music as I drove. When I moved out of range of the station, and it crackled and faded, I found another. I had nothing left to express, nothing left to feel. I drove in a monotonous haze grinding the distance underneath my wheels.

Someway, somehow, I made it home. The day finished fading, and the skies had darkened. I had made it home just past eleven p.m. I felt exhausted, and in the morning, classes were starting. The weekend was over.

Chapter 23

Sue

Mike was sitting on his bed when I entered. We talked for a little while, and he asked about the weekend.

I said, "I had an incredible time. I stayed in the apartment she shared with her roommate. We spent three days and nights together. But that long freaking drive has left me exhausted today. I drove thirteen damn hours by myself. Man, I am tired. I got a morning class, too, at ten a.m."

He nodded and said, "My first class starts early too."

I replied, "Ouch, that's tough. Did the freshmen act crazy this week?"

Mike laughed. "Yeah, you know it. Lots of stupid kids running around acting like fools."

I laughed and asked, "I bet Nelson told them about the fountain. You can't live in Magnolia without taking a dip."

Mike laughed again. "I don't know. I'm sure he will if he hasn't yet."

We continued chatting about if anyone else had left and any other dorm news. Mike had installed a big fan in one of the windows. Our room faced Landis Green, and we had windows. The dungeon rooms lay directly below our floor.

I commented, "Fantastic fan, man. It helps cool the room."

Mike nodded. "Yeah, my dad spotted it this summer, and we got it for the room. It helps a lot, especially in the afternoons and evenings."

I replied, "I like it. It feels a lot cooler with it on. Well, I would like to call it an early evening. I know it's only twelve thirty, but I need some sleep to recover from the drive and prepare for classes."

"Works for me." Mike walked over to the lights and flipped them off. It did not take long for me to fall asleep listening to the purring sound of the fan blades in the window.

I spent the next few days settling into the whole school routine and ensuring I had all my books for my schedule. I also got the money from my student loan and headed to the bank to deposit that check. I stood looking at my balance afterward with sheer wonder. It increased by almost fifty percent of what I had last year per quarter. Last year I burned through all my savings, and by the time I made the final quarter, my situation had become challenging. I struggled to make sure I had enough money to eat. I got sick of eating peanut butter and jelly sandwiches. *I will do well this year*, I thought. *I could eat off campus more frequently.* I hated the cafeteria, as did most guys, but it remained the least expensive option. Buffets worked well when money grew tight. I paid my tuition that week as I did not need to drag it out this quarter.

On Friday, after I finished my classes, I realized I needed to write Chloe. I had put it off and tried not to think about her, but she always occupied my attention. Now I had that image of her lying naked on the bed for me in my mind. I knew I did not have an answer. The answer I produced occurred only when emotion overwhelmed me. I needed a release from that pain.

The answer could not be accurate. I thought, *There's no way she does not have feelings for me. I mean, she acted all weekend as if she loved me. I received it. I returned it. You can't fake that. I don't know why she couldn't say it. I don't understand why she shook her head. Maybe it meant, "No, I don't want to part."*

I did not understand her or why she acted that way. When she was with me, she did nothing but love me, nothing but yes.

I thought for a long time about what I should write to her. I started with news about my classes and told her some stories about the dorm and the coming football game. After writing two pages, I began to put my feelings into it. I described how I missed her something terrible already. I included a poem about us that I told her she inspired.

I speak through the racket of effort,
the dust of motion,
to find you're listening.
Can you hear past the congeal of habit,
the glare of desire,
to meet my seeking?

Reach out your hand for mine
groping for a way between us.

Including the poem relieved my feelings, and I thought if I could not discuss them with her, I could at least express them in a letter. I ended the letter with a paragraph about what I felt.

> *I'm sorry I keep saying I love you. I just can't help myself. I'm so much in love that I have lost all control. Mine is a sticky love. I cannot throw it away. I cannot pull it from me. I cannot stop it from wanting to stick with you. I don't know what you are feeling or thinking, but my love will not give up. It will still be here when you are ready.*
>
> *I love you forever.*
>
> *Chris*

I needed to know what she felt, and I considered asking her in the letter, but I remembered the distress on her face at the airport when I said it. Maybe she just needed more time. I mailed the letter in time to make the final pickup for the day on Friday.

Confessing my feelings in the letter released most of my anguish.

Over the next week, I stuck to the dorm and did little until Friday. After two weeks of moping, I needed a release and decided to party. I had not received a letter from Chloe, which added to my desire to drink. I went into the common area to meet my dorm friends and drink beer. We plotted our plan for the football game on Saturday. We would have a keg before kickoff and the after-game celebration. A bunch of guys in the dorm kicked in so we would have a full barrel, and a few guys went over to get it when they opened on Saturday. Drinking from our keg costs much less than getting drunk on the in-stadium beer.

After the game, well, you had to have a keg or something to drink. How would the freshmen drink enough to swim in the fountain? I mean, we were all just being thoughtful. We decided to go to the game as a group and sit together. We called ourselves the Drunk Magnolia Cheering Section. It seemed like a perfect plan. What could go wrong?

It started well. We popped the keg and started drinking two hours before the game. We had to arrive early to sit together in the student section. We drank our first beers, stashed the keg for the party later, and headed over. Before we got seated, we had been intermingled with a bunch of girls from Reynolds. I managed to sit next to my roommate Mike and his girlfriend, with Dave on the other side of me, but two freshman girls from Reynolds sat behind us.

On the left sat Becky, a petite girl with dark black shoulder-length hair, dark eyes, and a pale oval face. She had some curves on her too. She had a white top with a flower print, white hemmed shorts, and white sandals. She had smooth tanned legs. Okay, I admit the girl looked attractive.

Okay, she was gorgeous and sat right behind me, looking at me, talking to me, asking me questions. On the other side sat Linda, a tall thin girl with light brown long hair down to the middle of her back. She wore a casual blue dress and wedge sandals. She dressed better, and she had on full makeup and painted nails. Yes, she also looked pretty, though not as good looking as Becky. She also kept talking to me and asking me questions.

I got both of them beers from the concession stand. Attending college football required partying, so I instructed them. They appeared to be eager students wanting to learn how one behaved at a college football game. I got them both a second beer in the second half. Oh yeah, I got myself a beer each time as well. We screamed when we scored, cheered wildly, and joined in enthusiastically on chants. Our team won easily, so the game became a little boring. I tried to ignore these two girls. I did not want to be tempted by another girl, but they kept talking to me. Dave complicated my situation by inviting them to our after-game party.

A bunch of girls streamed into this impromptu party. The keg got rolled out, and we all started drinking. Someone set up some music. The next thing I knew, a bunch of couples started dancing. Mike had brought his girlfriend, and he had already reserved our room for himself that evening. After all, I didn't need it. He danced close to her. I kept moving around the room, talking to my old dorm friends, but when I paused and sat down, the next thing I knew, those two girls were sitting beside me.

Becky asked me to dance with her. We swayed slowly together to the music, and she pressed herself against me. When the dance ended, another slow song played, so I asked Linda to dance. When we returned, we talked. Both girls kept flirting with me.

I became aware of something. They both expected something. What did the girls want? Both girls expected me to kiss them, but they wanted something more. I realized these girls were competing. They competed for me. They expected me to make a choice: one girl or the other. I refused. I would not pick a girl because I did not want a girl. But they kept sitting there, kept talking to me, kept dancing with me, and I kept drinking beer. I came back with Becky after one dance, and Linda departed. The girls made a choice. Becky now sat really close to me as we talked. Her eyes were on mine. I tried to break this spell but found myself thinking about the room. Thank God Mike had already gone back with his girlfriend.

Someone told us the freshmen had walked out to swim in the fountain. I could escape, but I found Becky walking out with me. We stood around the fountain, laughing and cheering as different freshmen took the plunge. Dave joined them and initiated himself into Magnolia.

When the swimming stopped, Becky asked me to walk her back to her dorm. I did so reluctantly. When we reached her dorm, she turned to me, leaning toward me. She expected me to kiss her. I succumbed and did so. She delivered her kiss with a sensual intensity, and I enjoyed the hunger in it. When we paused, she asked, "Should we return to your room?"

"My roommate has already gone in there with his girlfriend," I replied.

She seemed disappointed, but I did not tell her I had a car. She lived in Reynolds. Thank God she lived in Reynolds, a dorm I could not enter.

I had not planned on kissing another girl. I had been remarkably passive in all of it. She had done everything, including charming me and wooing me. She chose me and initiated the kiss. I'm surprised she didn't ask me out afterward as well. I should not have kissed her, but intoxication reduced my control. We separated with a "See you again soon."

After I said goodbye and turned to walk back, I met Ed with this drop-dead beautiful blonde with tousled hair. Ed had enjoyed himself again, and he grinned at me. He had seen me with Becky, and I returned his smile. It seemed the right thing to do.

When I returned to the dorm, the RA started chasing visitors from it. Mike came out with his girlfriend and started walking to her dorm. I headed to our room and plopped down on my bed. I remained intoxicated and don't remember Mike coming in, as I soon fell asleep.

The next day, when I thought about Becky, I thought about how strange it all went and how she played the aggressor. She had some will to her. She chose me. She made it happen, not me. She was dangerous—not physically, but risky to my plans with Chloe. I decided to avoid her. I would not let what happened Saturday happen again. I had too much at stake. Thankfully, our football team had the next

Saturday off. I would easily avoid the temptation by avoiding parties on the coming weekend.

Something else about what happened with Becky struck me as odd. I did not feel as guilty as I should have. Why didn't I feel guilty? It had been just one kiss she initiated, and she surprised me. But I kissed her. I thought about that and realized I felt angry at Chloe. She left me hanging out there. Why couldn't she say something? Why couldn't she admit to her emotions? I had done all the work. I took all the risks. She had not once said how she felt about me. She had to do something if she wanted a claim on me. I could not do it alone.

The after-game party on Saturday was so successful that we discussed having a full-scale dorm party. We scheduled it two weeks later on a Saturday when the team played away. Of course, it would have to be a toga party. We lived in the age of *Animal House*. The movie had an enormous effect on our party-crazed college life. We would party as they did in togas! Someone acquired the album from the film so we could dance to it. Now, we had no togas, but everyone had sheets. Just wear shorts and a sheet wrapped around you.

A bunch of us went to the movie again. It played for months at a theater close to campus. We went stoned and drunk. Undoubtedly, the film would be better drunk, and we needed ideas for our party. It did seem funnier.

That weekend, I relaxed and hung out. A group of us went to the cafeteria for lunch. After lunch, I decided to check my mail. It had been two weeks, and I might have had a letter from Chloe.

In my mailbox sat a letter from her. I stashed it in my shorts and would read it back in my room. I had the space to myself that day. Mike went somewhere with his girlfriend and friends and would not return until the evening.

I inspected the post date and discovered Chloe had mailed it before I sent my letter. She had put the wrong box number on it, delaying it from getting to me. I opened the letter and read it. The letter did not say anything personal except one *I miss you* at the end, followed by *Chloe*. Most of it only provided basic info. She wrote me a cautious letter as if she tried to avoid saying anything too personal. I reread it, parsing her words.

Come on, I thought. I tossed the letter down on my bed with irritation. When we were together, she always treated me with such affection. Someone reading this letter would have thought she was not even my girlfriend! Her letter exasperated me. Despite that, I went ahead and wrote her a reply. I made it as personal as possible to differ from her letter. I provided news, but I also included how much I missed and loved her. Yes, I said that in the letter. I talked about how much I enjoyed the weekend we spent. I told her I longed to hold her and kiss her again. I also added another flowery ending. I ended it with *Endlessly, eternally, loving you, Chris*. I did not want Chloe to doubt my love.

When I returned from mailing my letter, some dormmates had already obtained a keg and popped it open. Mike had also returned and told me he wanted the room for the evening. I decided to join the guys with the beer in the common area. They were getting ready to order pizzas. I joined in and threw my financial contribution into the pot.

We had an evening to kill. I knew I was staying in the dorm that night, avoiding any parties and avoiding any temptation from girls. Only about a dozen guys hung around initially, but it swelled until we had close to thirty guys. By then, I had drunk multiple beers and smoked a few joints. We had several freshmen who were real dopers. They always produced joints for group enjoyment when we partied now. I usually kept the smoking of marijuana to a minimum, but here in a party situation, already drunk, a "no" slid easily into a "yes." I spent the evening talking and drinking in the common area until Mike departed with his girlfriend. I went into my room. The beer, combined with the marijuana, soon had me fast asleep.

The following week I kept my focus on school and running. I tried not to think of Chloe, but by the end of the week, it had been four weeks since I last saw her. I was accustomed to doing something with her all the time. I had also been used to doing something physical with her all the time. Even if it only started with kissing. I missed that personal interaction and needed it. My sexual desire for girls kept rising in me. The girls in my classes all looked better at the end of four weeks than at the beginning. My lust goaded me more than it had last spring. Now, knowledge lay under it. I had enough real experience to know how incredible a girl could make you feel. I wanted that badly, and I wanted it now.

On Friday, I checked my mail. I had a letter from home but nothing from Chloe. I tried mightily not to think about Chloe, but she always popped up. When she did appear, she provoked this incredible longing to be with her, hold her, and kiss her. This intense longing tended to interrupt anything else I had been doing. I tried to avoid it, but she would repeatedly appear to me. If I did not keep myself busy, she soon occupied me.

I checked again on Saturday afternoon for a letter from her. The last one I received came on the previous Saturday. Nothing appeared in my box at all. I was worried that her lack of writing meant something. Her previous non-emotional letter and this failure to write accurately reflected her feelings. I worked hard to stuff this terrible feeling down and away, but it kept hanging around me the rest of the afternoon through dinner until it came time for the party. I decided to drink it away.

A buzz had been building all week in the dorm as we got near our toga party. We would have a keg of beer and create a spiked punch. Everyone kept experimenting with the sheets. It turned out to be damn difficult to keep them on as a toga. Mike's girlfriend, Emma, came to our rescue. She showed us how to pin them up with safety pins. Everyone complimented Mike on having such a smart girlfriend.

Luckily, we had a bunch of safety pins left over from road races we had used to pin our numbers on our shorts. I wore a pair of shorts under my toga and flip-flops. Emma helped us put our togas on for the party. The three of us walked down to the common area for the party together.

The beer keg had already been tapped, and some guys had finished the punch. They got Emma to taste it. She assessed the punch as tasting good. I headed to the beer and started drinking, hanging around with other early arrivals. It did not take long before others began streaming into our party.

I mixed with the girls, meeting more freshman girls. I danced with one, then two, then a third. Drunk and happy, I had successfully chased the dark feeling that bothered me in the afternoon. Dancing to "Shout" from *Animal House* released everything. The whole place went wild every time we played it. Everyone jumped up and started dancing and shouting. After another rendition of that song, I met Sue.

She was a tall, thin girl with short wavy blond hair, pale skin, and intense blue eyes. She had long legs. *Pretty, very pretty*, I thought. She was tall, almost as tall as me. She had to be five feet ten inches. She stood tall enough to look me in the eye. Despite her thinness, she did have a feminine shape. She was almost wispy, fairy-like. I found her femininity attractive. I flirted with her. She did not react much, though she responded to my flirting with friendliness, even a touch of warmth.

I got both of us beers, and she sat next to me. We were talking to each other. She came from south Florida, the Ft. Lauderdale area. Her thinness indicated she might be a runner, but she had done no sports.

A slow song came on, and I asked her to dance. I pulled her close to me. I found her lightness surprising. Despite being close to my height, she settled so small and lithe in my arms. I also found her warm and soft against me.

We walked back to our seats holding hands. We leaned close now when we talked. I gave in to what I wanted and kissed her. She responded so softly. We sat close, talking to each other. My desire for her rose. Something in this girl triggered and aroused me.

A slow song came on, and we again headed out to dance. I pulled her close to me. Her warm, soft body and small breasts pressed on me through the improvised togas.

As the song wound down, I kissed her and took her hand. Looking around the common room, I did not spot Mike and Emma and concluded they had already departed for our dorm room. I sighed, and we headed back to our seats. I wanted to go down the hall to my room, but it would not be tonight. My car was too far to walk as I had run an errand during the week and returned to only find parking at the stadium.

We spent the rest of the evening dancing, kissing, and talking until it came time for me to walk her back to her dorm. Some of the guys in the common area stared at us as we walked past. We exited the dorm, holding hands.

Outside, the air had become cool. Another front had blown in, and the temperatures had dropped rapidly this evening. She shivered at the cold, and I put my arm around her. We strolled across the green toward her dorm, where we stopped and kissed for a long time. I held her tight for a while. I wanted to linger in her soft warmth.

When we paused, she inquired, "Can I ask you something?"

I nodded yes.

"My sorority is hosting a formal dance here in early November. Would you be my date? Would you take me to this dance?"

I smiled at her. "Of course, I will take you."

She looked into my eyes and said, "I like you, Chris. I like you a lot." She embraced me in a hug.

I stood hesitating, then said, "I like you too, Sue. You're such a sweet girl."

She then took out her purse and wrote a phone number on a slip of paper. "I have to be at my sorority every Sunday and Tuesday afternoon. You can reach me more easily with this number than at the dorm. I had a very good time tonight, Chris." We kissed again, and she returned to her dorm when we parted.

A nearby couple embraced and kissed as I got ready to walk back. Ed had Becky in his arms. Becky flashed me a smile. I grinned at her and turned to walk. I strolled, savoring the crisp evening. Someone behind me called my name as I got near the dorm.

I turned to see Ed walking toward me. He had a grin on his face. "Some girls, huh?" he asked.

I nodded. "Yes, some girls. That Becky you had is gorgeous."

"Yeah, I liked that tall blonde you had, too."

We nodded at each other, grinning. We did not talk much the rest of the way and soon parted after we got inside, but some guys noticed Ed and me entering together.

I turned and headed down the hall. Thirsty, I needed to get a drink of water from the fountain. I looked at the common room as I walked past. Most of the people had departed, and the RAs were chasing the remaining visitors from the dorm.

I checked for Mike and wondered if he and Emma had left our room. I stopped and asked Todd. He said yes, he had just seen Mike walking his girl out. He commented to me as I walked past, "I see you made another conquest, dude."

I ignored that and headed to the room.

The following day I tried to push what I did out of my head. I would not rehash it, would not analyze it. Things just happened. That was it, no more. At least I hadn't gone over the line. Still, I had to acknowledge how sweetly Sue treated me. She did seem like a nice girl. I thought about the date I had agreed to with Sue. I thought of the number the girl gave me. *Should I contact her and cancel, or should I take her to the dance?*

I still did not know what really would happen with Chloe. She had not said anything at all about her feelings in her letter. Maybe I meant nothing to her. I tried to push that ugly thought from my head, but her lack of a letter introduced doubt. I did not know what future I had with Chloe.

I decided to wait a while until I received another letter. Surely, another would arrive soon.

CHAPTER 24

Yes

I woke up the following morning in a restless, disturbed state. To ease my anxiety, I ran with some other guys. Todd asked me about Sue, but I deflected. I would not discuss this with anyone and pushed the pace of our run hard after that question. A hard afternoon run relieved my anxiety, and I relaxed some, helped by physical exhaustion. I ate in the cafeteria, to the disappointment of many who wanted me to go off campus with them. That evening I went to the library and studied.

I had a few tests that week and focused on those subjects. I needed something to distract me. Too many guys in the dorm wanted to talk about last night, but I needed to suppress the previous night. When I did think of her in my arms and her mouth on mine, it flooded me with anxious guilt.

Monday brought the welcomed distraction of classes. When I finished midafternoon, I headed to the union to check my mail. In my box sat a letter from Chloe. She had not sent it to the correct box again, delaying it a week from reaching me. She had addressed it not to Chris but to Slick, and she had drawn a little heart on either side of the name.

I stared at it for a while. What did that mean? I found a bench away from the student union in a quiet spot, and I opened the letter.

> *Honey, I missed you so much. I only think about my sweetie and how much I miss him. I keep thinking about the weekend we spent together in Lexington and how happy you made me. I got your letter, and I cried when I read it. These three terrible long weeks apart made me realize how I feel about you. Last night while closing with Sonia, she talked about how wonderful you were. I burst into tears again and told her I know you're amazing. I told her I miss you something terrible. I'm sorry I've been so cautious. I need to see you again soon.*
>
> *Even my mother realized how much I missed you and suggested I visit you in November. She said I could call you long distance. When would be a good time for me to call so you can be near the phone? I need to hear your voice again.*

The letter went on like that for a full page. At the end of the letter, she wrote, *Love always with all my heart, Chloe.* I stared at that. Did she say what I thought she said? Did she mean that? Hope rose and rose in me. I reread the letter and knew I needed to see her in person as soon as possible. I decided I would go down this coming weekend.

I tore a piece of paper out of my notebook and quickly wrote her a short reply.

> *I got your letter. I am so happy to hear from you. I need to see you again as soon as possible. I've decided I will come down there this coming weekend. I can arrive on Friday night and stay until Sunday afternoon. I will stay at an inexpensive hotel by the interstate in east Tampa. We can spend all the time we can together. You can call me at four p.m. on Thursday. I will make sure I am near the phone.*

I ended it with a *So completely in love with you, Chris*. I also told her she was sending her letters to the wrong box number, delaying them.

I rushed back into the post office, got an envelope and a stamp, and mailed my letter. Chloe should have received it in time to call me on Thursday.

I walked back to my dorm with my steps light. I thought the response I had wanted and expected for so long would finally come. I imagined saying I love you and hearing her say it followed by passionate kissing and lots and lots of sex. Okay, so I spent most of my time imagining in detail the sex, but during it, we were saying "I love you."

The next three days took the equivalent of three months until the time arrived for her call. I worried that my letter might not reach her in time. I focused on school and running and tried to push everything else out of my mind. It did not work well—I kept thinking about Chloe. I must have read her letter a dozen times.

On Thursday, I went to the common area and sat by the phone at three thirty in case she called earlier. I told the RA seated in the window that I had a call I expected around four p.m. He nodded at me. I sat close to the phone and reviewed some of my class notes from that day. At three forty-five, the phone rang, and I jumped up. The RA answered and waved me away. It was for someone else in the office. They talked for a long time. I resisted an impulse to burst in, tear the phone out of their hands, and hang it up. Finally, they finished, and soon after that, the phone rang again. The RA answered it and waved me over.

"Chloe?" I asked into the receiver.

"Yes, it's me, sweetie. I'm so happy to hear from you. I missed talking to you."

I lowered my voice and responded, "I really missed you too. So, you got my letter?"

"Yes! I am so looking forward to you coming. I got off Saturday night, but I have to work Friday and Sunday nights. Sonia told me I could leave early on Friday, around ten p.m. So where exactly will you be staying?" she asked.

I told her the name of the motel and the exact location so she could find it. I told her about the ten-minute time limit on the phone.

Before I said something emotional, she jumped in, "My mom just walked in, so I can't say anything personal. I miss you."

I responded, "I miss you and will see you tomorrow." Then we hung up. She would arrive at ten thirty, so I needed to be at the motel before that. My last class on Friday ended around three thirty, so if I left soon after that, I could easily make it to Tampa before ten.

As I walked back to my room, I thought about her voice. I heard something new in it. Did I detect tenderness in it? Did I imagine that? Why did she call me sweetie? Her nicknames struck me as odd. Still, I would see her tomorrow! No waiting till Thanksgiving. The excitement of her letter chased what had happened on Saturday night.

I told Mike my plan for the weekend so he knew he had the room.

He smiled at me and said, "Sounds like you are in for another great weekend."

I grinned and said, "Yes, I think it will be."

On Friday afternoon, I got my small bag ready with clothes before my afternoon classes to head out immediately. When the class dismissed, I swung past my room, grabbed the bag, and said my goodbyes.

I soon found myself hurtling down the highway out of Tallahassee toward Tampa. Traffic was light, and I made good time, soon reaching my motel. After I entered my bland, nondescript room, I checked the time. The clock read nine p.m. I called JB's Pizza and asked to speak to her. I told her what room I stayed in so she could find me. She confirmed again that Sonia was letting her leave at ten, so she should be there by ten thirty.

Ninety more minutes, I thought. I turned on the TV and tried to find something to watch. I found nothing interesting after checking through all the channels, so I turned it off. I would have to wait. An hour still to go. That hour took a long time to tick off. Around 10:25, she knocked on the door. I opened it, and she stood smiling, holding a bag.

I pulled her into the room, grabbed her, and kissed her with all the longing of five excruciating weeks.

"Oh, sweetie!" she exclaimed. She handed me a bag and said, "Hon, I brought you something to eat."

I opened it, and inside I found a melted ham and cheese sub, still warm.

She motioned to me. "Go ahead and eat, sugar."

I found it strange that she called me these affectionate nicknames. I sat at the small table and ate the sandwich. She watched me quietly and seemed to be waiting for something. When I finished, she moved away from me to the bed. I stood up and walked toward her.

She looked at me and said, "Are you going to say it?"

I stared back at her, hesitating, thinking, *Did she say what I thought?*

She stood up, stepped close to me, and said softly with a warm smile, "It's okay to say it"—she paused, leaning close—"to me." She stopped and waited.

"I love you," I said quietly.

She smiled at me and exclaimed, "Sweetie, I love you too!"

We both stood looking at each other. I thought how strangely anticlimactic it felt because I failed to grasp that I had not reached the end but stood at the beginning. She opened a door into her world and invited me inside.

I looked into her eyes and said, "Chloe, I love you. I will love you the rest of my life."

She raised her hand and tenderly touched my cheek. She responded, "Chris, I love you with all my soul. I will love you forever."

She leaned toward me, and we kissed. Not a usual one, but something more, as if we wished to seal our declarations of love with evidence of authenticity. When we parted, I looked into that face shining for me. She gave me a coy grin and said, "Enough talking. Let's get naked and make love."

I removed mine, and she did the same until we stood face to face. We fell into each other, our bodies warm against each other, hugging, touching, and caressing. We needed to seal that declaration of affection with something more physical than words. We needed to close ourselves together and break down the distance between us.

I needed to not just speak about love but to experience it. In this new state, we needed to press ourselves together and act to make two into one. We needed to confirm that our words had a deeper meaning and entangle ourselves physically together until she and I became us.

We tumbled onto the bed, full of exuberant passion. My desire roared with this incredible hunger to touch Chloe, taste her, and swim in her wonderful scent. I pushed myself on top of her, tasting her. My hands were all over her, my mouth on her nipples. She caressed me with her hands and returned my kiss with intensity every time I raised my head.

I throbbed with readiness. Chloe helped me enter her. I let myself go completely. I sank into her, feeling her skin against mine, her silkiness. We kept pausing and kissing, then I would resume. As the pleasure took over, I quickened my pace, moving faster and harder on her, in her. The ecstasy of her dissolved my control entirely, and gasping, I felt my world disappear until only she remained. She captured my mouth with a kiss full of love when I regained myself.

She whispered as I stayed inside her, "I love you, sweetie. I love you so much."

I said, "I love you, too. God, I love you."

We kissed again, long and soft and full. When I pulled out, I rolled over and lay close to her.

She rolled her head onto my chest and put her hands on me. We lay for a while, enjoying the feel of each other, savoring the understanding we had indeed confirmed. She and I had become us.

I broke the silence. "I am so glad you finally said it. I have waited so long for this day. It doesn't seem real to me."

She moved her head off and smiled softly at me. "I'm sorry, sweetie. I'm sorry it took me so long to say it. I didn't know, and it was so hard for me to trust. I didn't have your experience. You were my first boyfriend. I've never been in love before. I didn't know how it felt."

I responded, "I've never been in love either."

She nodded and continued, "At first, I didn't believe you. Everyone always told me boys would say that to you. They will say anything to you. I didn't believe it for a long time."

Shocked, I sat up and stared at her. "You didn't believe me?"

She kept talking. "When we first met, you reminded me of Tom. You were charming like he was, and I thought you just wanted sex from me."

"Like *Tom?*" I asked incredulously.

Chloe responded, "Of course, you are far more intense. The way you focused on me. I never had anyone treat me like that. It swept me away, so I decided I liked you so much I would say yes to whatever you wanted. Then we didn't do it, and you kept saying it to me." She paused and glanced at me. "I started to think you really meant it, and that scared me. Could I trust you enough to let myself love you and believe you would never treat me like my father does my mother—"

I interrupted, "I will never do that to you, Chloe."

She nodded. "I know, but it's hard to get past the pain I've experienced. I finally realized as we kept dating that you did mean it. You did love me. I knew I felt incredibly happy with you. That weekend, I thought, *Chloe, maybe you do love him.* It upset me so much when you said it to me at the airport. I could see I had hurt you. I rushed to board the plane so you would not see me crying. As I cried, the woman beside me gave me some tissues and said, 'It's so very hard to part with someone you love.' That made me feel ashamed that I didn't say something. This last month with you gone, I found myself feeling terrible. I couldn't believe how much I missed you and thought about you all the time. After receiving your letter, I cried and realized I needed to stop being stupid. I needed to be brave and tell you I loved you. I completely love you. I'm so happy you came to see me, and I could finally tell you."

She moved close, and we kissed again for a long time.

"I've got some good news for you also. We don't have to wait till Thanksgiving. I will fly up on Friday in two weeks and spend the weekend there. I booked this same motel chain. Will you pick me up at the airport?" She coyly smiled at me.

I laughed and exclaimed, "Of course! There's a home football game that weekend. You can go to the game with me. I will now show off to the dorm my *serious* girlfriend."

She grinned at my emphasizing *serious*. We lay for a long time, happily chatting. We interrupted our talking by kissing when the mood overwhelmed us, and the distance between us needed to be closed again.

After a while, I remembered something. I sat up and looked at Chloe. "Chloe, I need to tell you something. I haven't been perfect this last month. I didn't know if you returned my feelings, and your first letter said nothing. It left me feeling depressed. I drank heavily at our last party until I was thoroughly drunk. I ended up making out with another girl. I did not intend to do it. It just happened. I'm not trying to make excuses, but I wanted to tell you the truth, so we would not start this new world with a lie between us. I'm sorry I did it, and it won't happen again. Now I know your feelings, and I will do whatever I need. I'm sorry."

She sat quietly for a while as if she struggled with what to say. She appeared on the verge of tears. She said, "It's okay. I could not claim a commitment if I could not say anything. I had not committed. It's okay." She pulled me back, and we kissed again as if she wanted to stop that conversation.

As I kissed her, I realized she had forgiven me.

I don't know what Chloe thought, but I could only guess. We live in our separate worlds with our perceptions and thoughts. When I fell in love, I took a leap of faith over the chasm separating us. She had made that same leap. I believed that once she had made that leap, she needed to keep that trust, our love, and our yes, so she forgave me. I made a silent vow to myself never to need such forgiveness again.

When we finished, I said, "It will never happen again. It's all different now."

She smiled at me and pulled me back into another kiss.

We would have lay there touching, talking, and kissing all night. She ended it by saying, "My parents think I'm just working. I must go. I can't spend the night. I'll be back in the morning, though, and tomorrow we will have all day together."

"Morning?" I asked. "Don't come too early. I want to sleep in until noon, at least. We can find someplace for lunch when you arrive."

She agreed, and we both got up and got dressed. I walked her out to her car in the parking lot. The clear evening was pleasant, with temperatures in the upper sixties.

I undressed and got back into bed after she left. I clutched her answer to me. After all this time with mine out there, waiting for her, she finally gave me her Yes. It still seemed hard to believe. I had been stuck for so long. I wondered how she kept calling me sweetie, honey, sugar, and hon. I had never heard anyone talk like that, but I acknowledged that it made me feel loved. I faded into sleep with that thought warming me.

I awakened to the sound of knocking on the door. I glanced at the clock—noon. *It must be Chloe.* I got up, walked to the door, and cracked it open. She grinned at me, and I opened it. She looked at the dark room and me wiping my sleepy eyes.

She asked, "Did I wake you up? You need to wake up, sleepyhead!" She looked down at me. I had nothing on but my underwear. She stepped to me, pulled my underwear down with her hands, and wrapped her soft hand around me.

She leered at me. "Sometimes, a girl needs to take advantage of her opportunities when they come!"

I grinned, now awake. I leaned into Chloe, and we kissed.

She released me and started to remove her clothes. She said, "I'm going to enjoy my *serious* boyfriend." We tumbled onto the bed and renewed our passion.

We did not linger after sex but got up and dressed. We talked about where to eat and decided on Tropicana in

Ybor City. We went outside, and we took Chloe's car. The temperatures were appreciably warmer than Tallahassee on this late October Saturday. Sunshine washed over everything and made it especially bright. I gave her directions, and she followed them until we found the Tropicana. We parked in their back lot and went inside to eat. We got in line and ordered devil crabs for me and a stuffed potato for Chloe. We sat down in the dining room. With overstuffed chairs, the dining room appeared formal for a sandwich and devil crab place. They even had a table and chairs reserved permanently for the owner in one corner.

We chatted as we ate and decided to watch a movie together at the University Square Mall. Chloe wanted to shop some afterward, and then we could go out to eat.

At the movie, I put my arm around her, and she snuggled against me. We sat close to each other, but we watched the movie. After the movie, we strolled through the mall. Chloe went into several stores and tried on different outfits. She asked my opinion on which ones I liked, and she bought some new outfits with her extra money from work. We acted like a couple out on a Saturday afternoon, holding hands as we walked through the mall. We spent several hours shopping.

I usually hated shopping, but now, if it involved Chloe, it made me happy. I wanted to be with her, doing whatever she wanted to do. As we were exiting, Chloe had specific dinner plans as well. She intended to take me to CDB's pizza. She said they had great pizza and subs, and they were close. I had not been there before, but I always loved pizza.

Once inside the restaurant, I got a beer and ordered a medium pizza. When it arrived, I found it delicious, better than what we made at JB's Pizza. I tried to finish it but ran out of capacity with several beers. She took the last two pieces to go.

"I'm going to feed the leftovers to my dogs," she said.

I asked, "Your dogs eat pizza?"

"My dogs love pizza. I bring them leftovers from JB's all the time. They love it."

I laughed. I had never heard of dogs eating pizza. After we got into her car, we kissed again.

"Back to the motel?" she asked with her eyebrows raised in emphasis.

I smiled and nodded. "Yes, with all haste!"

She laughed and started her car.

We did not arrive at the motel until almost nine. She glanced at the clock and noted she needed to leave by midnight. I nodded at her. We stepped into each other and removed each other's clothing while kissing. She unclasped her bra and pressed her breasts against me. We tumbled onto the bed and soon united again. My desire for her always drove me toward her. She seemed to have the same need for me.

Afterward, we turned to each other. "I love you" came out from both of us.

I said, "It feels different doing it with someone you love. It feels so much better. It has such an intensity to it."

Chloe smiled at me. "It feels much better, so intimate. I like making love to you." She leaned toward me, and we kissed again.

I asked her, "Can I ask you why you told Sonia and Tammie at that party in June that you loved to fuck?"

Chloe made a face at me. "How embarrassing! I didn't like how they all thought I was this inexperienced virgin. You don't know how hard it was being a virgin my freshman year. Everyone knew it. They kept introducing me to guys whom I found gross. I did not want them to see me the same way."

I said, "You shocked them. They thought you were too wild for me."

Chloe laughed, saying, "I had become too drunk, and I did enjoy sex the last couple of times when I did it with Tom. I guess it popped out of me. I'm glad it didn't discourage you." She smiled coyly, "I thought about you when I said it, though."

My eyes opened wide at that statement. "What do you mean?"

"I thought you were like Tom, and I was so attracted to you I had already decided it would be yes from me."

I grinned at that.

Chloe made another face at me. "But now, with you, it's true!"

My mouth flew open.

Chloe laughed, "So you better be ready!"

Speechless, I just nodded my head.

Chloe checked the time and said, "I have to leave soon. I have some bad news about tomorrow. My grandmother is having a birthday party for my sister at lunchtime. I can't escape until two or two thirty, and I must be at work by three thirty."

I sighed, "I need to check out by eleven. I need to be up in Tallahassee by dinnertime to study for some midterms on Monday. I guess tonight is it, then."

She replied, "At least you came down, and we finally got a chance to be in the same place."

I smiled at her. "I am beyond happy I came down. I do love you, Chloe. I love you so much. You don't know how happy I am when you say it."

She responded, "I love you too. It makes me happy to be in love with you. I will be up there in two weeks—at least we don't have to wait so long this time."

I responded, "Thank God, this last month almost killed me. I got very used to spending my time with you. I want to be with you. I need you. I love you."

She said, "I love you too. I love you to the moon and back."

I grinned. "To the moon?"

"Yes!" she exclaimed.

I responded, "I love you from here to Venus, the planet of love that pales compared to my love for you."

Chloe grinned. "I love you to the sun, whose bright light dims compared to my love burning for you."

"I love you to the nearest star whose light fades compared to my love sparkling for you."

"I love you more than the billions of stars in the Milky Way, whose light is nothing compared to my passion for you."

"I love you to the farthest edge of the universe, more than the billions of galaxies whose rotation pales to the orbit of my love around you."

"I love you more than infinity. It can never be calculated how much I love you."

I laughed and replied, "Okay, I can't top that one."

We kissed again to imprint the taste of each other for the long two weeks ahead.

She had to leave. I walked her out to her car, and we said goodbye with a long kiss. She got into her car and said, "I can call you again next Thursday at four. Does that work?"

"Yes, I will be near the phone. I will write to you also."

"I will reply quickly! See you in a few weeks, sweetie."

She pulled out and drove off.

I went back into the room. I had Chloe's love. I thought that I finished it. Everything I had worked for and yearned for had now happened. I had gotten a yes from her, and we had become a couple in love. She loved me!

I got undressed and set the alarm in the room for the following day. I climbed into bed. It had been another great weekend.

Chapter 25

Keeping My Yes

I awakened to the sound of the alarm in the motel room. The clock read ten thirty. I needed to leave. As I drove, I thought about how different my trip north felt. I had come down on Friday evening filled with hope but headed back with certainty.

I had everything I hoped for, everything I wanted. Chloe loved me as I loved her. Still, I realized that I put more distance between us every minute. It would be almost two more weeks before we would be together.

I knew the distance between us presented my most significant problem with keeping her. Of course, the other problem was my tendency to succumb to temptation. The two went hand in hand. The more time I spent away, the greater my hunger grew. Mix in a party with alcohol and lots of available women, and trouble would blow up again. No parties were scheduled for the following weekend, and our team played away, which should help prevent me from being stupid.

I did not tell myself not to drink or party. That's like saying don't be a college student. I lived in a party dorm and had to have some fun. I needed to watch how much I drank and keep myself from being tempted. *Don't be stupid. You have way too much to lose now.*

Then, I thought about Sue. Since Chloe's letter, I'd pushed her and my shame out of my mind. I had been no better than my mother and did the one thing I abhorred. Yes, I had only kissed her, but only luck had prevented me from doing more. Chloe had forgiven me. She had done it without drama or hesitation. I could not ask for that kind of forgiveness again.

I thought about my conversation with my father several months after he reconciled with my mother. He walked me across to that empty lot again one afternoon. I looked at him with apprehension. He said, "I should have never talked to you about my problems with your mother. That was my fault. I know you have felt angry and confused about that, but you need to let it go. I have completely forgiven your mother."

I stared at him in disbelief.

He said, "You need to forgive her also. When you love someone, sometimes you just have to forgive them for their sake and yours. What she did was to me, not you. I have forgiven her, and I need you to do the same. She feels very hurt. Your mother loves you deeply." He waited for a response.

"Okay." The truth was that I had partially let it go. I could not turn around and hate someone I had adored my entire life. When we returned to the house, I hugged my mother. She hugged me tight with tears in her eyes.

I thought again about Chloe. She had done the same thing for me.

I still had a pending date with Sue the following weekend. I needed to cancel that date. Should I go to Reynolds and ask someone to bring her down? I wondered how she would react. What if she cried? I could not handle girls crying, especially if I provoked them. The tears would melt me, and the next thing I know, I'm comforting the girl and looking forward to our date. I needed to show some backbone. I remembered how Rosemary had told me the truth and had the courage to say to me why we couldn't date. I also remembered I took it so badly I had about reduced her to tears.

No, I couldn't handle doing it in person. I envisioned so many ways it could go wrong. I would have to call her. She had told me to call her on certain afternoons to reach her at the sorority house. Sunday and the other day? Tuesday?

Tuesday would be the day I would have to call and cancel our date. I did not look forward to that call. Sue had said she liked me. Why had I gotten involved with her? Now, I had no choice but to hurt her. This subject dragged down the euphoria that had wrapped around me since last night. The distance I kept putting between myself and Chloe and the reality of what I needed to do dissipated it away.

When I arrived in Tallahassee, I had sunk into torpor, tired from driving and a little exhausted by my weekend. I walked into the dorm, planning on heading into my room.

Nelson stood with a girl in the hall outside his room. I thought I had seen him with the same girl at the last party. He saw me and gave me a grin and a thumbs up. I returned it and the grin. Nelson opened the door to his room and escorted the girl inside.

Mike sat on his bed in our room. "Did you have a good weekend?"

I grinned and said, "It was incredible! Everything went exceptionally well. Chloe and I have become very close."

He nodded to indicate he understood. "Emma and I are also very close. It's nice to have that with a girl."

Emma goes to school up here, though, and they get to see each other all the time. I had improved my timeframes for seeing Chloe. Still, a few days out of every two weeks seemed like a minor improvement when another two weeks had started.

I dug through the stuff on my desk, looking for the number Sue gave me. I found it and put it in the top drawer to quickly locate it on Tuesday.

Nelson knocked and entered the room. He had a broad self-satisfied smile on his face.

"Nice girl, man," I said.

He grinned even wider. "Yep, she was *very* nice."

I smiled and asked, "What's the story with your girl? Is this now a girlfriend?"

Nelson replied, "I'm working on it. She is going to the game with me. Her name is Renee."

"Congratulations, dude!"

One thing I had in common with Nelson was that we both loved girls and spent all our spare time thinking about them and wanting them. I knew how much happiness a girl brought. Not sexual pleasure, but real, emotional happiness. Okay, I admit the sexual pleasure was in there as well. A girl who returned your affection did make you happier. My happiest moments all involved Chloe.

When Tuesday afternoon came around, I took Sue's number and headed down the hall to the phone. I decided to call at four thirty, late enough to be out of classes but too early to eat dinner. An unknown girl answered the phone, and I asked to speak to Sue.

She said, "Just a moment."

It took a long time.

Finally, Sue responded on the other line, "Hello?"

I answered, "Hey Sue, it's Chris. I called because I need to talk to you."

She replied, "Hey, Chris. I'm glad you called."

I went on, "Something has come up on your dance weekend. My parents are coming to town, and I can't go. I'm sorry about that."

She paused and did not say anything. Finally, she said, "It's okay, I understand. Maybe next time." She talked so low as to be barely audible and spoke with a slight strain in her voice.

I said my goodbyes and hung up. Ashamed about how I lied to her and ended it, I felt guilty. I never intended to hurt her, but I had.

I found my nights growing restless and disturbed. I awoke late on Tuesday night filled with such an intense desire for Chloe that I could hardly contain myself. I expressed that desire in a poem I wrote the following day for her.

As I worked through my classes on Wednesday, I decided to write Chloe a quick letter and mail it that afternoon. I knew she would call on Thursday, but I wanted her to receive a letter from me on the weekend. I started it with one of those exaggerated claims of love like we traded that last evening. Somehow, some way, those playful declarations had filled me with so much happiness, and I filled my letter with that happiness. I included the poem I had written that morning as well. I told her about the football game and my plans for Saturday. I would bring her to Magnolia and spend Saturday at game parties. I also mentioned we would go to the game and watch it with other guys from the dorm. I included below some of what I wrote in my letter to her.

> *Dear Chloe,*
>
> *I love you more than all the stars in the sky. No amount of light can equal how much I feel about you. I miss you something terrible already. I long to see you again, and I can hardly wait until you are with me again next week.*
>
> *I look forward to your call on Thursday to hear your voice. I've never felt like this, never loved anyone like this. I cannot even express how happy you*

made me last weekend. I can't stop thinking about it and you. I can't wait until we lie together, pressed against each other. I never stop thinking about you. I wrote another poem inspired by you and how you even haunted my dreams.

Days Later
I awoke, startled by the clarity
of my desire.
I stepped out of the dream
across distance
into your waiting arms
and that momentary brilliance of our union.
I will not sleep again tonight.

I ended it with another over-the-top declaration of affection. *Loving you completely, totally, with everything I have, Chris.* I rushed to the union to mail it for the day's post. I found a letter from her in my mailbox that she must have sent on Monday. I opened the envelope and found a funny card.

The cover said, *Cast Wanton Sex from Your Life! Renounce alcohol and tobacco.* She crossed out *tobacco* and wrote *washing dishes. Rid yourself of libertine values, mend your evil ways.* The card cover included a picture of a little guy on a soapbox waving his arms.

I opened the card, and it said, *And it's all over between us! Love, Chloe.*

She had filled the entire inside of the card with lips made by kissing the card with lipstick on. I had a good laugh. She always knew how to make me feel better.

Thursday afternoon, I found myself waiting near the phone as the time for her to call drew near. The RA recognized me and asked if I expected another call from my girlfriend. I nodded yes.

He smiled at me. A few moments later, the phone rang, and he waved me over. "Chloe?" I asked the receiver.

"Hello, sweetie," came the reply.

I responded, "I'm so glad to hear your voice. I can't believe how much I miss you. I can't seem to do anything but think about you and last weekend. I am counting the days until you come to see me next Friday."

She replied, "I miss you too, honey. I think about you all the time. Did you receive my card?"

I laughed and said, "Yeah, many kisses inside. I got it."

She laughed on the other side. "How else can I send you my kisses? I had to include them in something, so I put them on a card. You got the message, too, right?"

"Yep, I'm on board with that message. No repentance from me. You can bet I look forward to giving you a very hard time when you come here next weekend."

Chloe laughed. "I hope so. I miss you terribly. I'm sending you another letter with my flight details. I get in late Friday afternoon. Have you figured out what we are going to do? Other than hanging around in the motel bedroom!"

I laughed and said, "Yeah, we are going to Magnolia early Saturday afternoon so you can meet my friends. I plan on parading you around so everyone can see what a beautiful girlfriend I have. We will do the whole FSU football experience, starting with a pregame party, going to the game with the dorm, and the post-game party. You can count on excessive alcohol consumption and lots of wild partying."

She replied, "I could use some partying. It's so incredibly dull here. All I do is work and go to school. Living at home is driving me mad. My mom said I could live in the dorms, but I tried too late for this school year. The earliest I can move into a dorm is next summer. Yuck!"

The RA signaled my phone time had expired, so I said, "The RA is signaling me. I need to hang up. I sent you a letter too. You should get it on Saturday or Monday. I love you, Chloe."

"Me too, sweetie," she replied, and we hung up.

I did not have any weekend plans and hung around the dorm. Late that afternoon, a group bought a bunch of beer to drink that night. We would make our own small party. Mike and I had decided that we would do it in our room. We would leave the door open to the hall. I did have a stereo system, one of the few in the dorm. After some drinking, we cranked up our air band. Four of us had become a regular air band. We even did a few impromptu concerts in our room. Of course, air band play only starts after excessive quantities of beer. I played lead guitar, and Mike played bass. Nelson sang lead, and our friend Lawrence played the drums. We played to the Doobie Brothers' songs. I had their greatest hits album. They had the right mix of rock and roll for an air band. We acted like a real band, with Nelson up front lip-syncing and jumping around. I furiously strummed my guitar. Mike played with a relaxed cool vibe, and Lawrence frantically pounded the drums in the back. We had gotten quite good at synchronizing ourselves with each other and the music.

Dave hung out with us, drinking and laughing at our crew. Mike's girlfriend, Emma, hung out with us, as did Nelson's new girl, Renee. Renee had black hair and dark brown skin. He liked this girl, and she seemed to like him.

As the evening wore on, other guys and some girls drifted in and out. One was Becky, with another girl I had not met. She gave me a big smile and introduced her friend, another short pale girl with blond hair and blue eyes. Another pretty girl, though not as pretty as Becky. I found myself on my bed, sitting by Becky. She made sure to sit next to me. She showed me nothing but smiles. I had not seen her since I spotted her with Ed a month ago. I did not expect to meet her again, but she sat beside me. I could tell what she wanted, but we hung out in my room. I had nowhere to go, so no temptation would cause me to do something I would regret.

While talking to her, I felt tempted by this beautiful girl. She poured her charm over me. Someone her friend knew came by, and her friend departed.

The others were filtering out of the room. Becky asked me to walk her back to her dorm. I could not refuse that request. The horrific Ted Bundy murders had occurred that fall, one of them only a few blocks from our dorm. With that atmosphere, the administration lectured us that girls should not walk alone on campus at night. I had to walk her back.

We headed out and across the green toward her dorm. I kept my hands away, but she kept talking and flirting with me. She paused halfway across the green, smiling at me, asking me if I had my car keys. I lied and told her someone had borrowed my car. She showed disappointment, and we resumed walking. At her dorm, she stopped and faced me. I knew she wanted me to kiss her, and she did tempt me. I had been drinking, and this girl was beautiful. Instead, I stepped back from her and said goodbye. She gave me an annoyed look and turned and went into her dorm. I did not particularly like Becky and only desired her.

I vowed to avoid her. I had too much to lose and nothing to gain.

The following morning, I was furious that I had put myself in another position to be tempted. How stupid! I loved Chloe. I kept thinking I needed to do something. I realized that staying up here while she lived down in Brandon would lead to heartbreak. I could not trust myself with the beautiful girls at FSU. This place had girls everywhere. Walking across campus, I strolled through an endless stream of stunning young women. Every step took me past another. I could not stop myself from noticing them. Even worse, too many saw me, and I recognized the mutual attraction.

I needed to do something to save what I had gained. I shrank from what came as the obvious answer: I needed to move back to Brandon. I needed to transfer to USF to be with Chloe all the time. I needed to do that to keep her and her yes.

I did not like this answer. I loved FSU and the college atmosphere and living in Magnolia. Magnolia was my home, and I had so many friends who lived there. I did not want to leave. I knew Chloe was miserable back home. A commuter school, USF had no authentic atmosphere. I had spent years in high school striving to attend FSU, saving every dollar and winning a scholarship. Now, I would just leave. I shrank from this choice. It asked too much of me.

I kept thinking about it all week. I knew that, technically, I already had enrolled at USF. I had attended summer classes, so they already had me in their system. I only needed to register for winter classes. I did not think they required any other paperwork. The ease of it made it seem even more terrible. I did not want to transfer. I did not want to leave. I refused and said no, I could make it work up here. I asked my friends for examples of couples who made the distance work. They only mentioned disastrous failures. Surely someone had made it work, but I found not a single example.

By Thursday, I knew I needed to ask Chloe to investigate what I had to do to register for winter classes at USF. I would ask her to bring their catalog and calendar info on her trip up here on Friday. I would ask her to stop at the registrar's office and ask them. I needed to know at least the necessary steps. I knew I would need to talk to her about it when she arrived.

On Thursday, I positioned myself again near the phone in the common area for my four p.m. call with Chloe. But four p.m. came and went without a call from her. Then four thirty, until finally, at forty-five minutes after, the phone rang, and the RA motioned me over.

"Chloe?" I asked.

"Yes, it's me, honey. I'm sorry I'm late, but I could not get my sister off the phone."

"It's okay. I'm just glad to hear you."

"Me too," she responded. "I have my flight info. I'll arrive around four thirty tomorrow. My flight back is one thirty on Sunday."

I replied, "I'll be there. Can you do something for me? Can you bring up the USF calendar and catalog for the winter quarter? Also, can you ask the registrar what a student who attended in summer must do to register for winter?"

She hesitated. "Okay, I should have time to stop at the registrar's office. Why do you need this?"

I said, "I'm thinking about transferring there in the winter so we can be together. I need first to find out if I can do it."

She paused and said nothing for a while. Finally, she said, "I don't want you to transfer to USF and be unhappy. I know how much you love going to FSU. You don't have to do this for me."

I responded, "I appreciate that, but I miss you something terrible. You can't transfer up here, which leaves me coming down there. I'm still thinking about it, but I must figure out if I can do it first."

She said, "Okay, I will bring you the stuff. I would love us to be in the same city so we can be together but not if you're unhappy. I love you. I want you to be happy."

I replied, "I love you too. I'm happiest with you, so I need to consider it. We can talk about it this weekend. My time is up. I'll see you tomorrow. Love you."

She replied, "I love you too. See you tomorrow."

I told my roommate I would spend the night in the motel on Friday with Chloe, so he had the room. I also asked if I could have the room after our post-game party on Saturday evening. He said sure, but he wondered why I needed it. I told him I would like to have her in my bed.

He grinned. "Okay. I get it."

I did my laundry that day, including washing my sheets.

I beamed when Chloe exited the runway. She greeted me with a wave and a smile. When Chloe reached me, we hugged and kissed. She carried a small bag with her clothes so we could exit without going through baggage claim. We walked a short distance from the terminal to the car. Her motel lay on the opposite side of Tallahassee out west on Tennessee Street, so I headed there. Before I started, she leaned in for another kiss.

She said afterward, "I missed you so much. I love you, hon."

"I love you too, Chloe."

She smiled and spoke, pointing toward the road. "To the motel!"

I drove the car to it.

After we got into her motel, she sat on the bed and motioned me to join her. She smiled at me and pulled me in for a kiss. Afterward, she removed her top.

She smiled and said, "I did not ask you to take me to the motel so you could watch. Take off your clothes!"

I laughed and removed mine. When she finished, she lay naked and looked at me. I stopped for a moment, only looking at her. I soon lost control and had to touch and run my hands across her. I marveled at her beautiful glowing skin, full breasts, shape, and her dark bush. I exclaimed, "You are so gorgeous, Chloe. My God! You are so beautiful."

She smiled at me and replied, "Thank you, but you see me through the eyes of love. You love me, my sweetie."

She gestured for me to come to bed. I did, and I climbed on her into her awaiting arms and her passion. I pressed my nose against her as I moved down, kissing her, tasting her, and sinking into her scent.

Chloe said, "I want to be on top."

I grinned and agreed.

After sex, she said, "I want to keep trying different things to learn what works best for us."

I beamed. "Experiment away! You can count me in for anything you want to try. As often as you want to try."

Chloe laughed and said softly, "Let's cuddle and kiss for a while. I want to be against you in your arms, my lips on yours for a while."

We rolled into each other and spent a long time, warm against each other. After a while, I became thirsty. I told Chloe, "I need something to drink." We'd spent almost an hour entangled. I said, "There's a restaurant I want to eat at tonight."

She responded, "We don't have to spend much money. I just want to be with you."

I replied, "It's okay. With my loan money, I have plenty to take my woman on a special date when I see her."

She smiled. "Okay, I guess we need to leave. It's almost seven p.m."

We got up and got dressed.

I took her to a local steakhouse, commenting on some of the Tallahassee landmarks we passed on Tennessee Street en route. I pointed out the all-night McDonalds we would raid late at night and some of the FSU buildings you could see from the road.

We arrived at the steakhouse, and we were soon seated. The location had a quiet, dark atmosphere, making each booth feel private and romantic. We ordered our food and cocktails. We sat quietly, talking to each other. She punctuated each remark and commented with her expressive face. The way she moved her eyes, eyebrows, lips, and hands and tilted her head. She had such a personality that popped out. It enchanted me.

After I spent some time admiring her, she gave me a rueful smile and asked, "Why do you keep looking at me like that?"

"I can't help myself," I replied. "I love being with you and watching you talk. It makes me happy to be with you. I love watching you."

She smiled and responded, "Honey, you are such a honey! You are a silver-tongued devil sometimes. No wonder I love you!"

I laughed at this and asked, "What do you mean by that?"

She said, "You are good at talking, quite charming. No wonder you had all those girlfriends. Of course, I am your latest conquest. I hope I am your last conquest." She gave me a stern look.

"Of course!" I exclaimed.

She went on, "My honey is so hard to resist. You can count me as being all yes now. Just *yes*!"

I laughed and leaned forward, and we kissed across the table. Our food arrived, and we ate our meals while still talking. She provided me with news of home, and I talked about tomorrow and the game and what we would be doing. I promised her a campus tour when we arrived early the next afternoon.

We talked at the motel for a while, chatting happily. Chloe provided me with the info I asked for from USF. She confirmed she had obtained the one form I needed to fill in and provide to attend. I had until the end of November to submit it. I could register for classes the day before the winter quarter started in January.

She said, "I would be thrilled if you did move, but don't do it if it will make you unhappy. I know you love FSU."

"Yes, but I will submit the form to give myself more time. I can withdraw from FSU until the end of the quarter in early December, so I don't have to decide yet. I'm still thinking about it. I need to be with you but don't want to leave. There's no hope of you coming up here?"

She shook her head no. "I've tried. My father will not pay for it if I do. Also, I'm in the middle of my junior year now. I can't transfer with just a year to go. It's too late to transfer again unless I want to put off graduation."

I knew this, and it affected my thinking about USF. If I waited to transfer after this school year in the spring, I would also have to attend longer to graduate. I needed to do it this winter or not do it. I said, "I'm going to decide by Thanksgiving so that I can set up housing in the winter. If I transfer, I'll see if I can rent an apartment with some of my friends who attend USF. I can't handle living at home."

Chloe agreed with that wholeheartedly. "Yes! It's driving me crazy. I'm glad you have a plan for a place to live. We need someplace where we can be together." She gave me a knowing look.

We kissed again, and soon we started to remove our clothing. Once we were naked and excited, Chloe placed her hand on me. She smiled coyly and told me to lay back on the bed. "I'm going to do something special for you."

I lay back down, and she moved down to my groin. She put her hand on me and kissed me. She soon put her mouth on me. She kept her eyes on me. I don't know if watching and seeing her excited me more than the actual act, but I soon throbbed with intense pleasure. I soon exploded. When I finished, she quickly got up, went into the bathroom, and spat what I had released into the sink. She rinsed her mouth out and brushed her teeth. She made a face at me as she returned to bed. "I liked doing it to you but found the ending a little gross."

I replied with a bemused smile, "I'm sorry. It did feel incredible."

She said, "First time I've done that. I've tasted you but only a little. First time I've done it. Another new thing tried."

"Let me do the same to you," I offered.

"Not tonight," she said. "I need to pace her to make it all weekend, including Sunday, with my honey. Not wear her out by Saturday night."

I gave her a rueful grin.

She asked, "Has anyone done that to you before me?"

"No, I've had someone else taste me briefly, but not this."

She asked, "So I did it okay?"

I exclaimed, "Did he not show his enthusiasm? It was amazing!"

She grinned at me. She lay back in bed, rolled over into me, and touched my chest. "I love sleeping with you," she said.

I said, "I love you beyond the moon and the sun."

She lifted her head and smiled at me. "I love you to the nearest star times one million."

I replied, "Gather the stars up and measure the distance. Still nowhere close to how much I love you."

She laughed. "That was a good one. Hmm, let me see. You can multiply the size differential between the smallest atom and the largest star by infinity and still not reach my love for my honey."

I smiled at her. "No fair pulling the infinity out again."

She moved up to me, and we kissed.

I said afterward, "I like kissing my love to you."

"Ditto," she responded.

She lay back down and snuggled close. Bathed in her warmth, I soon drifted to sleep.

She awoke first the following day. Her moving around soon woke me up. I moved to touch her and kiss her. I found myself aroused by her softness and closeness to me. I gently cupped my hand on one of her breasts.

She began to move against me until I was aroused. "Give me a condom," she said.

I handed it to her.

She put it on me and swung up to be on top again. She pushed herself down on me and gave me a coy look. "What I said in Tampa was true. Now, I'm going to enjoy my boyfriend again."

When we finished, she leaned down and passionately kissed me.

When we parted, I said softly, "This evening. I want to have you in my bed in my dorm."

She looked up at me in surprise. "Why?" she asked.

I responded, "I've already arranged to have the room with Mike. I washed my sheets yesterday. I want to spend the rest of the quarter sleeping in your scent."

She smiled. "What a sweetie!"

We kissed again longer and with more hunger. When we parted, we got up and dressed.

After lunch, I gave her a tour of the campus perimeter, pointing out the highlights and landmarks. After I had circled the school, I ended up parking in the clay parking lot across from my dorm. I first walked her around, showing her Landis Green, including the fountain Magnolia residents used to take a dip at. The fountain had been turned on and gurgled with fury. I had never seen the water well up with that much power that it splashed water up into the air. I continued the tour to the student union and other highlights. When we finished back at the dorm, I escorted her inside, holding hands.

The RA, who typically had duties during our calls, manned the front window. He smiled at us and asked me, "Is that the girl who calls you on Thursdays?"

I responded, "Yes." I introduced her to him as my serious girlfriend. He laughed and said, "I knew from your calls that she had to be a *serious* girlfriend."

Chloe gave me a slightly embarrassed look at that and, when we passed out of range, asked, "He can hear our calls?"

I said, "He sits close to the phone. It's hard not to hear what I say. He can't hear you, of course."

She said, "Don't say anything too embarrassing."

I said, "I'm going to say I love you. I don't care who knows that. I hope everyone does!"

She squeezed my hand at that.

I paraded her up and down the dorm halls introducing her to any of my friends who had open doors or stood in the halls talking. I always introduced her as my *serious* girlfriend. I showed her the common room and the shared bathroom area. I ended my tour in my room. I left the door open for anyone wandering past to enter. Mike sat on his bed with his girlfriend. After introductions, we sat on our respective beds talking. Beer time would only occur around four p.m. for the night game. Dave wandered in with a joint, and we lit it up, and all partook.

Todd came in, and soon we had six to eight people in our room. Someone came and told us the keg had arrived. We took turns going to the common room and filling our mugs or glasses.

After a few beers, I suggested our air band give Chloe a quick demonstration. She laughed at that, and we soon swung into full air band action to the Doobie Brothers' song "China Grove." Chloe was delighted with our performance and complimented us as the best air band she had seen. The time soon came for our dorm to depart for the game.

Attending the game with Chloe allowed me to parade around holding hands with her in front of Reynolds girls, who tended to join our Magnolia group at the game. I saw Becky in the distance but did not get close enough to introduce

Chloe. I did introduce her to some of the other Reynolds girls I knew as my girlfriend. At the game, I showed off to Chloe with our usual rowdy chanting, cheers, and excessive beer drinking. I even demonstrated the loud yell I gave when we scored or did something that required extra cheering.

Chloe enjoyed it all. She said, "I missed going to games this fall. They are so much fun."

Our team won, and we joined the rest of the stadium in dispersing back to the campus. We had many people in our common room, drinking and talking. Someone got the music started, and we danced. I had the chance to do several slow dances with Chloe, and I kissed her at the end of each one. After a few dances and a couple more beers each, I took Chloe's hand and walked her to my room.

After we entered my room, I locked the door behind me. We stood for a while, pressed against each other, making out. I removed my clothes, and she pulled off hers. Chloe lay on the bed, and I stood beside her, staring at her.

I said, "I want to imprint the image of you lying naked on my bed. I need that to sustain myself until I see you again."

She smiled and gestured for me to come to bed. I did, and we caressed each other for a long time.

I moved my mouth around her, tasting her, inhaling her scent. After a while, I mounted her, myself on top. I took my time, soaking in her softness beneath me, lounging in her intoxicating scent, basking in that warm glow from her skin. I wanted all of her and needed to remember every sensation. It ended in the mindless ecstasy she always brought me when only she remained, and the world disappeared.

We stayed in bed, entangled afterward. I asked her, "Multiple people have told me you had a hard life because of your father. Is that why you waited so long to tell me your feelings?"

Chloe nodded. "My father has never treated me very well. I didn't want to end up like my mother either. I needed to be sure you would be good to me. I was also afraid even when I trusted you to admit my feelings. It meant putting myself in your hands and letting go of my fear. I knew I loved you over the weekend in Lexington, but I still could not let go. Once we were apart for that long month, I realized that not being with you hurt me more. I had moved past being able to protect myself. I was in love. I needed to be with you, and you deserved my trust."

I held her tight for a moment. "This is because your parents fight a lot?"

Chloe responded, "Part of it. My father cheats all the time too. He never hides it. When my father gets drunk, he takes it out on me. He got my mother pregnant with me and had to marry her. He says I ruined his life by being born." Tears formed in Chloe's eyes.

"What! What kind of monster says that to his child? That's unbelievable."

Chloe said nothing in response.

"My poor Chloe, no wonder you took so long. I will never do anything like that to you. I love you completely. I will always be here for you."

Chloe hugged me. She responded quietly. "I don't know if my father really means it. He usually tries to do something good for me in the next couple of days afterward, but he never says he's sorry. My grandfather will not let my father divorce my mother. My grandfather owns the business and controls all the money. One of my cousins told me he would only let my father get a divorce if my mother initiated it, so he harassed her and tried to provoke her. He knows saying that to me upsets her. I know my mother is seeing a lawyer. I guess it finally worked on her."

I said, "Still, that's no excuse for treating you so cruelly."

She hugged me tight again. She said softly, "I know you love me. I love you too."

"Chloe, you're not the only one who has had a parent disappoint them. I'm going to tell you something I never told anyone. When I was fifteen, I saw my mother with someone else, another man, in our house. About a week after that, my father told me she had said to him she no longer loved him and wanted a divorce."

Chloe responded, "I thought your parents weren't divorced?"

"They're not. After a month of arguing, one day, they were gone until late at night. After that, they went back to the way they were before. Somehow, they reconciled and stayed married. For a long time, I hated my mother. How could she do something like that? Even though it was to my father, I felt betrayed. After about three months of this, my father one day asked me to forgive her. He had forgiven her because he still loved her. I let most of my anger go after that, but part of me will never forgive her. It's been hard for me to trust women since then. I kept thinking will someone do that to me one day."

Chloe hugged me and whispered, "I'm in it with you to the end. You're the only person who has ever truly made me happy. When I said, I love you, I mean it forever."

We tenderly kissed and hugged, staying in each other's arms for a long time, no longer talking but together.

Eventually, we had to let my roommate back in. We got out of bed and dressed, then walked out through the dorm, holding hands and saying our goodbyes. It was brisk outside, and no clouds obscured the full moon's brightness. I looked at Chloe and her light that only I detected glowing in the moonlight. I stopped and pulled her into a hug. I said, "I love you."

She replied, "Me too." We kissed.

When we parted, I said, "You are so incredibly beautiful in the moonlight. No wonder I fell so totally in love."

She raised her hand to my cheek. "I'm so glad you did."

When we parted, I asked her if she wanted something to drink or eat. She said yes, and I suggested we do the late-night McDonald's run to the motel. We stopped at the old one just west of the campus on Tennessee Street. It had no indoor dining. You had to walk up to the window, and all the eating occurred outside on old concrete tables. We ate slowly, enjoying the saltiness of the fries and another great ending to the day.

Chloe woke me up the following morning before eleven. She said, "I want to ensure we have time for one more. I need that to sustain me until Thanksgiving."

I grinned at her and pulled her against me. Exciting me with her soft, sensual body and warm kisses did not take long. Chloe wanted the last one to be her way and got on top. I loved looking at and touching her while she moved on top of me. I said, "This is my favorite position!"

She protested, "You tell me that every time it's your favorite regardless of our position!"

I laughed and admitted, "Every time with you feels so amazing that it seems like my favorite."

She said, "I love you." She kissed me and resumed moving on me, rocking on me. I did not lie. She always thrilled me, always excited me. Every time ended in paradise for me.

When we finished, we did not have time to linger. We needed to eat, and I had to drive her to the airport in time for her flight.

When we sat at the airport, I said, "I always want you. Every time I'm with you, I want you. I miss you something terrible when we separate. I can hardly stand the time and distance between us. Call me and write to me. I need that to help kill time."

She kissed me softly. "I love you. I love you so much. I miss you too. It's not long till Thanksgiving." They soon called her flight, and she was gone.

The next couple of days dragged on. Telling Chloe about my parents had given me a strange kind of release. I had never told anyone about what happened. Sharing our problems allowed us to move more closely together.

I got many compliments from the dorm about Chloe. The guys kept telling me what a pretty girlfriend I had. Only Mike's girlfriend, Emma, asked me how serious we felt about each other. I just looked at her, and she seemed to know.

She said, "Wow." She turned to Mike, and they both smiled at each other.

I had not recognized how intense their relationship had become.

One day when walking back into the dorm, someone behind me called my name. I turned and saw Ed trailing behind me, trying to get my attention. I waited for him to walk up to me. After he reached me, he started talking. "I heard that girl you were with this weekend was a serious girlfriend."

I replied, "Yes."

"Good-looking girl," he replied.

"Thanks."

He continued, "I had a real serious girlfriend my freshman year. I loved that girl. I thought I would even marry her one day." He paused for a moment and gestured out at the green. "You know how it can be—so many girls, so many willing, available girls. My girlfriend lived at home, still going to a local community college. We tried to make it work, but I could not resist the constant temptation. Eventually, she heard about that and broke up with me. She broke my heart. I know I deserved it, but still, I had real feelings for her." He paused again and gestured at the dorm. "Most of these guys think I only care about getting the girls in bed with me, but I never wanted just that. I try to make it work with a couple of the girls every quarter, but they usually break it up. Most of them only wanted the initial experience." He grinned, and I knew what he meant. "I hope you have better luck than I had. She looked like a nice girl." He walked on into the dorm.

Ed's story surprised me. Like the other guys in the dorm, I thought he only wanted sex. I also thought he told me this because he believed I had headed down the same path he had walked. I did not want to go down that path. Yet despite what he told me, I did not believe him. How can you go through so many girls and not fall for some of them? I couldn't be him because I would fall for a girl. I wouldn't keep rotating through them. Still, I knew it had become too easy for me. I had become too good at talking to them, too good at being charming, and too good at identifying which ones wanted me. *No*, I told myself, *I'm not like Ed. I'm not going down that path. I can control myself.*

I kept struggling with the decision to transfer and what I needed to decide. I knew that constituted a decision to stay. I shrank from that as well. I could not bear being apart from Chloe, which staying up in Tallahassee meant. I kept thinking Chloe needed me.

That weekend we had another home football game. I found myself at the after-game party with another freshman girl hanging around me, a short, black-haired girl with dark eyes and dark brown skin named Cindy. After I was drunk, I found myself flirting back with her and feeling tempted. I even danced with her. I wanted to kiss her, and she kept looking up at me, waiting. I managed to gain control before I did it, despite my temptation. I managed to avoid another disaster. The following day I found myself feeling angry. Why did I allow myself to be tempted again? How stupid! I could not risk losing Chloe. She meant everything to me.

I needed to do the right thing. I needed to do the *only* thing. I needed to move so I could be with Chloe. It did not matter that I loved FSU. It did not matter that I did not want to go to USF. The only thing that mattered was that I loved Chloe and intended to keep her. She meant more to me than anything else.

I submitted my paperwork to USF and started making plans to transfer. I had decided. I chose love.

Chapter 26

A Question

I wrote a letter to Chloe, telling her I planned to transfer to USF. I reassured her that I had decided for all the right reasons. She meant more to me than the school I attended. We would be together instead of dealing with this constant separation. I also sent a letter to one of my high school friends who attended USF and asked about his interest in sharing an apartment come January. I filled out the forms to notify FSU about my departure and to let them know I would not be in Magnolia in January. I told my roommate Mike and all my friends. I left no opportunity to change my mind. I had decided, and now I focused on executing my move.

Over the next week and a half, I kept busy with school. I did find myself appreciating FSU and my life there. Knowing it would soon be over caused me to linger in my routine, habits, and dorm life to cherish what remained.

When I talked to Chloe on our last call the week before Thanksgiving, we discussed when we would see each other first on the holiday weekend. I had to drop Larry off, so I couldn't make it home until late Wednesday. On Thanksgiving, she had to attend two Thanksgiving dinners. I protested that waiting till Friday was too much, so we decided she would come to my house on Thanksgiving evening after dinner. I would introduce her to my parents. Chloe expressed a little anxiety over that, but I insisted she needed to meet them.

I told my parents that on Thanksgiving, my girlfriend would come over that evening, and they could meet her.

This news startled my mother. "That's a first," she said.

She looked at me as if wondering what this meant. I realized I had never brought any of the high school girls I had dated over to meet them. It would be the first time I introduced a girlfriend to them.

I kept a watch out of the front window for Chloe's car. When she arrived, I went out to greet her. We hugged and kissed. I had missed her, and she had missed me.

She said, "I'm kind of nervous about meeting your parents."

"Don't worry. They are going to love you."

She managed to smile slightly at that, followed by making a face at me. I laughed.

After we entered and I introduced her, we sat on the sofa in the living room and talked for a while. My mother asked Chloe questions about where she lived and what she studied in school. She intended to get to know Chloe.

My father made a joke at my expense: "I told your mom here the first time we will meet his girlfriend is after he's been married a few years and turns up with a kid in tow. He never tells us anything."

After everyone laughed, I replied, "She's not pregnant, and we are not married yet."

Chloe gave me a sudden look at the "married yet" comment, making me a little embarrassed I had said that. My mother focused on Chloe and moved to the sofa to sit beside her. We talked for an hour when one of my dad's favorite shows came on. We decided to head out. I made an excuse about meeting another friend with my parents.

Outside, Chloe said, "Not a very good excuse. Your mother thinks we're going off to go parking. She knows we're intimate. I could tell by the way she looked at me."

I tried to reassure her. "They don't know that. Besides, we *are* going parking. Aren't we?" I smiled at her, but she rolled her eyes and hit me on the shoulder.

"You are so bad sometimes. Do you think your parents liked me?"

I answered, "Yes, my mother likes you. She's normally quiet, so the amount of time she spent talking to you showed she likes you."

Chloe considered this for a while. "I guess there's no helping this. We are intimate. Everyone can tell now by how comfortable we are with each other." She smiled at me. "Okay, Slick, what's our plan?"

I suggested we drive our cars to the K-Mart on SR 60, leaving her car and taking mine. She agreed, and we headed off. After Chloe joined me in my car, we turned to each other and kissed for a while. After we paused, I said, "I missed you so much. I love you and am so glad to be with you this weekend."

"Me too! I'm glad you're moving down so we can always be together. I have some good news for you. My birth control is set, so we no longer have to use condoms!"

I exclaimed, "Awesome!" I moved to start the car.

She reached her hand up and touched my arm to stop me.

I paused and looked at her.

"I'm feeling full, even a little sick from all the food today. Can we stay here and kiss tonight? Can we do something tomorrow?"

I sighed. "Okay, I understand. I feel full too. I guess I can wait till tomorrow. I also want to read you something. I wrote you another poem. It's called 'Sticky Love.'"

Chloe gave me a bemused look.

I removed it from my glove compartment and read it to her.

<u>Sticky Love</u>
Mine is a sticky love.
Once given, it stays.
It will cloak you with warmth on a cold day,
and splash sunshine onto a darkened one.
It will persist through the dullness of the mundane until
you can wear it like a pair of favorite slippers.
It will reach for your hand when you need it most

and prod you into laughter when you expect it least.
When it finds you exhausted, it will pick up your work,
and when joy lifts you, it will provide you an extra step to soar.
It will give you what you ask
and strive to supply what you need.
I may weaken and falter with age,
but my love will endure,
staying with you until the end.

Chloe sat for a moment, looking at me. She then threw her arms around me and pulled me close. "You say the most incredible things to me. I love you, and I promise you: My love will also stick to the end."

We stopped talking and spent the next thirty minutes passionately embracing. When we broke apart for a rest, I said, "I've got news for you as well. Everyone will be out of the house in the afternoon, so I want you to come over, and we can do it in my bed."

Chloe hesitated and frowned. "Your house? Are you sure? What happens if someone comes home early?"

I reassured her, "I know they'll all be gone. It's okay. It will be the only time we have access to a bed all weekend."

Chloe considered this and responded, "Okay, I will see you right after lunch, around one."

I formulated this plan when I heard about my parents' schedule for Friday. I had spent years as a teenager longing to have a girl in my bed, and now that I could make it happen, I would do anything to make it occur. My experiment with my dorm bed had worked. I smelled Chloe's scent in the evenings afterward. It did help sustain me, and I wanted to duplicate that experience here. I also wanted Chloe. I wanted her all the time.

When she arrived the next day, I led her to my room and bed. Chloe was curious about my room, and I showed her around a little.

She grinned at me. "I can't believe you painted your room orange. It's a little bright." She put her hands up to cover her eyes as if shielding them.

I laughed. "Yeah, it seemed like a good idea at fifteen, but it does come across as a little loud now."

We sat down on my bed, and we kissed. We removed our clothes and entangled ourselves with passion and tenderness. I told her, "I love the way you taste, the feel of your soft skin, your scent, and that warm glow. I love that warm light you emit."

Chloe made a face at me. "Are you saying I glow? I don't think so."

I smiled at her. "You do to me. I can see it on you all the time. I love pressing myself into it and enveloping myself in your warm light."

Chloe replied, "You, honey! You just love me. But I do like pressing my love against you as well. I like us being so close and intimate. It does feel amazing."

I stopped talking after that until we finished. We stayed in bed after sex and cuddled. I felt more satisfied than I had ever been. I had made a longtime teenage fantasy come true and had sex with a woman I loved in my bed. Chloe provided me with everything I needed or wanted.

We got dressed, moved into the living room, and sat next to each other on the sofa. Chloe asked me, "I want to talk about us. Where do you see us going in the future?"

I responded, "I see us being boyfriend/girlfriend."

"No, I mean after graduation and all. A girl needs to know what's going to happen. College is the best time for me to meet guys of my age. I'm already a junior, so I don't have much time left. I want to know what your long-term intentions are."

"Oh," I said, realizing what she had asked me. I told her the truth. "I want to spend my entire life with you, Chloe. I do love you."

She asked, "What does that mean? Marriage? Family? Children? What do you want to happen between us after we graduate? Will you marry me?"

I paused again, surprised by her directness. "Yes. Yes! I will marry you after we graduate. I do want to have a family, to have children with you. I love you, Chloe. I do want to spend my whole life with you. I mean all of it."

She smiled at me. "Good! That's what I want." She gave me a coy smile, tilted her head toward me, and raised her eyebrows. "I have the most intense desire to have your baby. I thought you should know."

My mouth and eyes opened in alarm.

She laughed. "Don't be so scared. I don't mean immediately, but after we're married."

I relaxed. "Whew, you scared me a bit."

She smiled at me and suddenly threw her hands up. "I wanted you to know!"

As I lay in bed that evening, I thought, *Did she ask me to marry her?* I had to smile, for she had indeed asked me that. I said yes and made the ultimate commitment. All this time, I worked on getting her yes when she got my yes to all of it.

Chapter 27

Epilogue

I'll end this story the way I began it: with Chloe. That last yes to her would not be my final yes, but it would be followed by the need for another yes, and then another. Each of life's turns and twists, each change required another one. I would learn I needed to always say yes to my Chloe.

I would keep my commitments to Chloe, and when I look up from my laptop, I can see her sitting on a chair reading a book.

She notices me looking at her and gives me a quizzical smile. "What is it?" she asks.

"Sometimes a man needs to look at the beautiful wife he loves," I reply.

"Thank you, honey," she replies softly, looking back at her book.

We have grown old together through marriage, children, careers, accomplishments, failures, retirement, and grandchildren. I wish it went like a fairy tale ending—and yes, she filled much of it with joy, but it took much work to keep it. I loved, but I had to learn how to love, sustain it, and make it endure.

The first yes would be followed by one yes after another, each a decision made to keep that love, but that forms another story, and the time comes for me to conclude this one.

I wrote this book for Chloe out of love. Her hand guided me through every word from the beginning to the end. I wrote it to remember her, remember how she changed my life. I wrote it to preserve the story of my love for her once and for all. I have lived my life. I have done one thing incredibly well: I have loved Chloe with every ounce of my heart, every pulse of my strength, and every action of my will. I have loved her with everything I have. Time erases everything, and even now, it grips me. I pour my words out to inscribe and preserve the memory of my love for her.

I met Chloe after I turned nineteen, fell in love, and said yes to that love. It changed everything. If you find my words and story, remember how I loved her. She inspired it. She inspired it all. I have given her the greatest gift a man can give a woman. I have given Chloe a lifetime of myself, in love with her.

THE END

About the Author

Tim Hunniecutt's earliest memories include a love of words which he expressed by writing poems and stories for family and friends.
 Tim attended Florida State University, where he studied psychology and English. Home for the summer after his first year, he met a girl and fell in love. The love she gave him inspired this story.
 Tim lives with that same girl, now his wife, in Lithia, Florida. He loves traveling, playing escape games, spending time with his grandchildren, and ballroom dancing with her.

Made in the USA
Monee, IL
01 July 2024